The Station Master's Wife

~ A novel ~

By S.K. DeMarinis

By S.K. DeMarinis

Copyright © 2019 by S.K. DeMarinis

Email: suedem@charter.net

All rights reserved.

ISBN: 978-109909115

This novel is a work of historical fiction drawn from some actual events, people and places as they were archived in newspapers (and quoted with italics in text), family records, and oral stories told to the author. Embellishments and invented additions were woven into the character's lives to create this tale of fanciful fiction.

Colorful dialogue and descriptions of each character's lives and interactions with these actual events is a vision of the author's suspicions and any resemblance to the actual person is purely coincidental and not meant as an insight into or interpretation of their true history.

This story is dedicated to the pioneers

who tamed Oregon and left a little

bit of wild for us to enjoy.

Table of Contents

Chapter 1: Alice, The Station Master's Wife	5
Chapter 2: The Golden Spike, December 1887	18
Chapter 3: The Berry Family, 1850-1884	24
Chapter 4: Romance and Railroads, 1884	34
Chapter 5: Becoming the Station Master's Wife, 1884	42
Chapter 6: Babies and Business, 1885-1888	55
Chapter 7: Family Life, 1888-1890	64
Chapter 8: Marriage and Money, 1891-1892	73
Chapter 9: Ashland Town, 1892-1895	87
Chapter 10: Deceit and Divorce, 1895	100
Chapter 11: New Traditions/New Friends, 1895-1896	117
Chapter 12: Independence and Impropriety, 1896-1901	133
Chapter 13: Advice and Anguish, 1901-1903	142
Chapter 14: Shocking Reveals, 1903	150
Chapter 15: Adventure Abounds, 1904	158
Chapter 16: Times of Transition, 1905-1907	169
Chapter 17: Orphan and Widow, 1908-1909	179
Chapter 18: Weddings and Working, 1910-1913	189
Chapter 19: Sewing Circle Secrets, Early 1913	204
Chapter 20: Wedding Time Again, Springtime 1913	210
Chapter 21: Bay Area Blowout and Back, Autumn 1913	217
Chapter 22: Coast Connections, 1914-1918	228
Chapter 23: Dumb and Dumber, 1920-1923	244
Chapter 24: Downhill Dealings, 1923-1925	253
Chapter 25: Transformations, 1925-1927	261
Chapter 26: Fleeing from Florence, Early 1927	271
Chapter 27: Fugitives Found, Springtime 1927	279
Chapter 28: Convictions, Summer 1927	292
Chapter 29: Moving On, Autumn 1927-1928	300
Chapter 30: The Final Whistle, 1929-1931	310
Epilogue: 1932-1955	321

S.K. DeMarinis

1  Alice, The Station Master's Wife

I feared for their lives and their ears. Our local weekly newspaper showed pictures of them dangling from ropes hanging in woven baskets off the embankment of a mountain in order to tap sticks of dynamite into the holes they drilled in the granite cliff faces they blasted away. One could hear that awful, loud dynamite blasting all the way in town. But the booming had been even worse for the ears of the railroad workers who detonated the charges for the grading and tunneling, especially the Chinese who were given these most dangerous jobs.

I heard even more details of the harrowing stories of these Chinamen from Mr. Wah Chung, who owned the laundry and Chinese grocery in the Railroad District just a block from our house. His yard always had a laundry line of long white shirts billowing in the wind as if a group of his Chinese friends were dancing in the breeze. He was a pleasant man and spoke English so well. I planted the Asian lily bulbs that he gave me, as fragrant as French perfume, in our front yard facing the new depot.

Mr. Wah Chung also worked for Southern Pacific Railroad, as the Chinese labor agent at the depot, translating, helping to resolve conflicts, and coordinating job assignments for the Chinese workers with particular skills. His job often was entwined with my husband Charles', the Station Master in charge of all railroad employees.

In addition to managing train time tables, engineers and conductors, freight schedules, mail deliveries and the telegraph, as the Ashland Station Master, Charles had to see to moving along track construction, which included managing an extra labor force of 2400 Chinese and 1600 white men, mostly Irish. These extra short-term employees, here for the past three years, were called in by the Southern Pacific Railroad to build the long tunnel (over 3000 feet I'm told) and tracks through the rugged Siskiyou Mountain Pass in Southern Oregon.

Progress was so slow, with track being laid at a rate of only twelve feet per day, Charles said. And these Irish men certainly had an effect on our town when they came in for supplies and amusement. Our small town's population was doubled during this time by single, malodorous white men, some of unscrupulous character. Charles insisted that I conduct my errands in town accompanied by at least one of my lady friends. I'm relieved most of these transient workers will be moving on soon.

The Chinese construction workers rarely wandered through town. They remained mostly near Mr. Wah Chung's in the Railroad District, where he provided their provisions and entertainment. Sometimes, I could hear the clicking of the ivory tiles of their Mah Jongg table game, as well as see traces of smoke, like dragon tails, wafting from Mr. Chung's porch window, when I passed by his establishment to occasionally bring Charles his lunch at the depot.

Those men came a long way from their overseas homes and seemed glad to have jobs. I can't imagine how difficult things must be back in their villages for them to leave their families and travel so far for employment. They kept mostly to themselves and retained many of their traditional ways of dress in lengthy untucked shirts, long braided hairstyles and herbal root medicines. Charles appreciated them very much, as they had fewer complaints than the Irish, even though they were paid less than the white men, who made a full $1.00 per day.

Regardless of the impact of these temporary newcomers, I am truly grateful to all these men who built the rails. Today the tracks would be completed and finally our town of Ashland would be connected with the nearest town in Northern California - Yreka. One will be able to arrive quicker, in less than an hour and one half, as well as much less dusty, and in more comfort and style. So, I guess it was worth the past three years of inconvenience for the benefits the railroad will bring, now that the construction was finally done.

Our orchards and mills, both woolen and flour, would now be able to sell their products to markets far and wide, sending and receiving posts and packages before the news was months outdated. Exciting events will have easier passage through our tucked away town. I heard that the Circus will now come by train and bring animals we've only read about in far off lands. *Oh, how I loved the changes!*

Charles has kept the rail building project rolling, but not without it taking a toll on him. Strands of gray are beginning to poke out from his beard. And he's only thirty-three!

I tried to keep things simple at home for him by doing more of his chores like chopping firewood, tending horses, and cleaning out the fireplaces. Of course, I am kept busy enough with our baby and my chores too. But I don't mind.

Sometimes, though, when I'm covered in soot, I do feel like Cinderella waiting for my prince to come home.

However, today, I was excited that the railroad tracks were finally going to be completed. For today's celebration, I had purchased two sets of Chinese paper lanterns from Wah Chung's for only twenty-five cents per set. I hung these globes on our front porch, railings and side yard entrances, ready to be lit as twinkling lights in the winter dusk hours. I wanted it to appear as a pathway of stars guiding the way to our house for the dignitaries who would gather there later in the evening.

Every house in town is supposed to illuminate similar lantern decorations to be like sparkling gems brightening the way for the celebrators and prominent guests who would stroll through town after the Golden Spike was set in the last railway track laid connecting all of the United States in a ring of steel.

The railroad promised to complete the connection with our California neighbors by the summer of 1887, and they were only off by a few months. It looks like they will actually be done today, on December 17th. Most of the delays were reported in the printed newspaper stories, but my Charles, as Station Master, knew more of the behind the scenes details never revealed to the general public.

For example, earlier this year in July, there was a raid on the Chinese worker's camp in the Siskiyous. The Ashland Tidings newspaper reported that:

"This raid was executed by Deputy Sheriff Steadman and his posse for the purpose of breaking up a gambling and opium smoking den that had been chasing the railroad contractors as the construction camp moved more north".

Charles' opinion was, "I bet it's because the deputy sheriff and his friends were upset that these foreigners were making more money than they were."

"How could that be?" I asked.

"The truth of it is," Charles clarified, "even though these Chinese men get paid half that of the Irish, they work more than twice as many hours and volunteer for the more dangerous, well-paid jobs, and that's why they have more pay coming in."

I felt sorry for all of those poor workers, Chinese or white, who had to camp in the cold mountains, especially in the lingering snows of late winter.

Charles continued. He revealed the rest of the untold tale. "There were 50-60 men in that raid who destroyed the property of the Chinese, including robbing several hundred dollars. Some of the Chinese men were even attacked and shot!"

"Oh, my," I said, stunned and fearful of the goings-on.

For my Charles, however, his concern was the definite effect these disturbances had on slowing the progress of laying track. And that was something which Charles had to sort out. After speaking with our beloved Sheriff Dean, Charles convinced him to curtail any further conflicts his assistant deputy officers might have with the railroad crews, so the tracks could be done on time. By the next week, we had a new deputy in town assigned specifically to deal with any disturbances involving the railroad crews.

But troubles continued to delay the advancement of the tracks. Charles was like the conductor of an orchestra of musicians that had never played together before and the only tempo they knew was SLOW. And there always seemed to be a new player that would change or derail the tune.

Just this past August, there was a murder of a white railroad employee in the regular white railroad worker's Siskiyou Mountain camp, nicknamed by locals as, dare I say, "Helltown". In this movable headquarters of vice, which came with a dance hall saloon, the bar keeper became jealous over the attentions this young worker was paying to a certain dance hall girl favorite of his. This poor local working lad was a well-liked, good-hearted fellow, only thirty-two years old when he was shot dead by the bartender.

Charles had to go retrieve his body to be buried at the Ashland Cemetery. A number of men from the railroad, as well as myself and our baby boy Alexander, just about to turn two years the next month, were in attendance for the funeral.

Then troubles hit even closer to home. Not very long ago in October, I heard our alleyway stable door slide open, squeaking on the rusty iron overhead track, while I was gathering our morning eggs from the coop in the backyard. A couple of young men were stealing two of our fine horses! My screams of "Stop Thief!" alerted Sheriff Dean, who lived only a block away.

The Sheriff saw the dastardly fellows riding away on our familiar horses and saddles. They were making towards California and he immediately started up a direct chase. Charles, who was readying for work, rushed to the Depot and telegraphed Sheriff Moxley in Yreka to aid in the pursuit.

"I found the animals dead at the upper crossing of the Klamath River," Sheriff Moxley reported later that day in a reply wire. "As we approached the thieves, in their hurried escape, they shot the poor horses. But don't worry, I have sent word in all directions to capture the rascals."

The culprits were never located, having dispersed into the dense forests around the Siskiyou Pass. I am hopeful that such disturbances will settle down now that the construction is finished and those workers will move on.

But, all in all, life in Ashland has been largely thrilling for a country girl like me. Coming from the nearby old pioneer town of Jacksonville, where my family still lives on the farm, all this city stuff is rather exciting for me.

As a new bride in Ashland since 1884, I've been here for the duration of the three years of construction and the flourishing growth of the town and the depot.

The permanent population of Ashland has doubled from 800 to 1600 in just four years! Jacksonville has only 1200 souls and they were very envious that the railroad chose Ashland, over their town for the southernmost depot on the Oregon line.

Our Kane family, which now included the addition of our son Alexander, born in September 1885, along with Charles and me, has had good fortune benefiting from my husband's prominent position as Ashland Station Master and Telegraph Operator, which comes with a substantial income. He is THE communication link to all the towns in Oregon on the railway line between Ashland and Portland.

With our close connection with Mr. Koehler, the railroad supervisor and my husband's direct superior who seems to know about new business dealings before any announcements are published in our local newspaper, we have invested heavily in the real estate expanding around town.

In 1883, the year before the railroad arrived in town, coming down from the north to its projected southern Ashland terminus, Mr. Koehler bought all of the 156 acres Mr. Lindsay Applegate's original donation land claim, one of the first in Ashland. He subdivided the land on a plat map into multiple lots and named it "The Railroad District". He knew full well the future potential prospects and benefits the upcoming railroad would bring to the town of Ashland, especially the land closest to the depot. I was wary of this man, but respectful nonetheless.

By mid-1885, just a few months after we were married, we bought two of those Railroad District lots, for only $237.50, on which our new home was to be built, a block up from the depot. Tempted by the consistent explosion of real estate prices, and using Charles' considerable income, we bought an extra lot directly from Mr. Applegate, along with the water rights of the East Ashland Water Ditch. We also invested in the north half of Mr. Bennett Million's donation land claim. We intend to piecemeal out these parcels by selling in a couple of years, hopeful to at least double our original investment of $3200.

For now, in 1887, our home is one of the most prominent dwellings in the Railroad District, built in the new Queen Anne Victorian style. It took six months to complete. I picked out a pastel blue color for the clapboard channel siding and a gold hue for the overhanging eaves and stick trim pieces. White painted trim accents the windows, especially around the large front bay window, showing off the tatted lace curtains that Mama's friends made as our wedding gift.

Of course, our house is diminutive in size compared to the outstanding home at the downtown end of our District, that of Mr. and Mrs. McCall, the friends of Papa who moved from Jacksonville to build here in 1883. Their magnificent mansion has two stories with the Italianate architectural detail and millwork, a double parlor, library room and seven bedrooms, just four blocks away from us, overlooking the plaza.

My best friend, Anna Carter, and I drool over that home every time we go to the adjacent flour mill.

"Such a stately manor," Anna had commented one day. "How did Mr. McCall make all his money, I wonder?"

I had to bend to whisper closer to her ears, as she is a good five inches shorter than I, cresting only a little over five foot and three inches. "Oh, I know."

"How would you know that?" Anna had asked, surprised.

"My Papa told us the story before I moved to Ashland. Mr. McCall is just a little younger than my father. He started out in Jacksonville as a gold miner like Papa in the 1850s. But soon after, he realized there was more money to be made as a mining store owner selling supplies to the other miners. I think he was copying Mr. Stanford. Remember him - the former governor of California in the 1860s?" I asked Anna as we had walked along.

"Yes, I think so. Wasn't he also the one who was so involved in building the railroad? We heard of him at our wedding reception in Colorado three years ago. There were people there talking about him then. I thought he was a US

Senator, though. Or, was he the one who established a university in California?" Anna interjected.

"Yes, on both counts," I agreed. "After his governorship, he became and still continues as a senator. And yes, he did open a university two years ago. He named it after his son, poor thing, who died so young of typhoid fever while they were vacationing in Italy."

"Oh, that's so sad," Anna remarked, sniffing. I wasn't sure if she was sniffing the aroma of the fresh bakery we had just passed or expressing her sorrow.

"Mr. Stanford's story however, has a meager beginning. He started out making his money off of miners rather than being one. In his early days, he owned a grocery and mining supply store. It is said that he took a chance on a miner's account and gave him credit with a note against a portion of the miner's claim as collateral. Stanford was to get an undetermined amount, based on the percentage of that note, if and when the miner's claim produced any gold profits," I continued, recapping the tale.

"This bit about Stanford never made it as far in the Colorado news. What finally happened?" Anna asked.

"Well, as it turned out that pay-off on the miner's note landed a half million dollars in Stanford's pocket."

"Oh, my. What a win for a simple grocery man!" Anna exclaimed. "I can now understand how he parlayed his finances into power and political gain."

"Interestingly, Mr. McCall also achieved wealth and fame after running *his* mining store in Jacksonville, although not by a wager. He went into a bigger business when he founded the Ashland Flour and Woolen Mills, and then he also went into politics and became an Oregon State legislator in 1876."

"My goodness. How does your Father know such stories and how do you remember them so well?" Anna inquired.

"Well, the McCalls were the family we stayed with three years ago when we came to see the first train arrive in Ashland in 1884. So, I heard the story repeated then. And, since my Papa was an Oregon State Senator in 1858, he tries to keep in touch with these men who run things in Salem. Plus, he and Mr. McCall also like to trade tales about miners," I added.

But I digress. I must relate the story of this afternoon's festivities. Mr. Koehler, the railroad supervisor, has requested, that since our home is so close to the depot, Charles and I host the officials for the signing of the Golden Spike documents. This is such a historic moment commemorating the completion of the entire US continental railroad loop. We were honored by this request and I've been a nervous Nellie ever since.

Mama came to help with the food and the baby. "Mama, please use the peaches I've canned, in the root cellar to make the pies," I instructed her when I put the baby down for a nap.

She wiped her hands on her apron she brought, which still fit her tiny elegant frame, accentuated by her long neck and full length skirt. She had pulled some curls to frame her face, to gussy up her usual stark braided bun.

"Yes, yes. Your sisters will be here soon too. Mary's bringing her two children and they will watch Alexander, while

Sarah and I get to cooking. I'm glad your friends have room to put up your sisters. Your house is brimming with just the addition of me and Papa," Mama said relieved.

I set Papa to work too. "Papa, would you hang the Chinese paper lanterns around the front and side porches?" I pleaded. "Charles has to be at the Depot all day setting up the chairs, podium and banners. I could really use your help here on the home front."

"Sure, my little darling. I was looking for something to do before your Mama makes me get dressed in that monkey suit," Papa answered. He had a distaste for formal wear, particularly his Sunday suit. He had shrunk with age and poor posture and he was now under six feet. Nearly eye to eye with Mama, and with his waistline expanding from Mama's good home cooking, his 'Sunday best' was just a little tighter than the original perfect fit. His light brown hair remained full, but his beard was now salted with gray.

"And if you don't mind pumping some fresh water for the pitchers on the parlor room table, that would be a big help as well," I included. "And don't forget to light the chandelier and lamps when it gets dark. We'll be coming directly here after the ceremony and I won't have time with the guests in tow."

"Not a problem, my dear. Now you go get ready," Papa said trying to calm me down. I knew all he really came to Ashland for was to shake hands with one of the "Big Four" Railroad tycoons, Mr. Charles Crocker, who is supposed to hammer the actual Golden Spike.

Papa also wanted to meet my brother Isaac's boss, Governor Pennoyer from Salem, who is supposed to come down on the train with Mr. Koehler. Ever since Isaac gave up farming and was appointed by the governor as Assistant Warden of the State Penitentiary this year, my father has been boasting to anyone who will listen.

In the past few days, my Charles has been polishing his pocket watch, brushing clean his bowler hat until it shines, and trimming his full beard and mustache to close-cut perfection.

I rummaged through the sweet smelling cedar chest, taking a deep breath of the memories it held, and unwrapped my wedding dress to wear for this occasion. It took over an hour to iron away the wrinkles that had set-in in the past three years. I knew the deep crimson red silk floral brocade fabric would shimmer in the candlelight of our parlor chandelier.

It is still my favorite gown, but I don it only for very special circumstances. I had to try it on to make sure that the fitted bodice still buttoned around my more maternal matronly figure of the Station Master's wife.

~ ~ ~

2  The Golden Spike, December 1887

The workers at the passenger station and freight depot were brimming with excitement. Innumerable crewmen, conductors, engineers, clerks, and freight handlers were all dressed in their cleaned and spotless official railroad uniforms and caps. Tables with drinks and sweet-smelling snacks were set up outside on the railroad depot platform, in front of the arrival and departure timetable chalkboard. A few young women, who worked as morning maids at the hotels in town, were hired by my husband to add their pretty faces as refreshment servers this afternoon. As the Station Master, my Charles was in charge of making sure everything was perfect at the Depot. The whole town of Ashland was a bustle. Cannons were set to be fired after the final Golden Spike was driven. The cheering crowds expected to gather in the afternoon along the tracks, are estimated to be over 2000 people.

My sisters and I headed down to the depot, leaving the grandparents to watch my little Alexander, age two, and my sister Mary's children Diadama, age eight, Newell, age one, and Isaac's daughter Laura, whom we called Dot, age five.

We bundled up with hand muffs and scarves to ward off the bitter cold that is common here in December. The afternoon fog had settled in, traveling south up the Rogue Valley from Medford, and trapping the wood smoke from all the fireplaces in town, making the air appear an even denser gray. The smell of roasting chestnuts reminded me how close this celebration was to Christmas.

My brother Isaac was already at the depot speaking with Charles. He was easier to spot than most, towering at 6'4", over four inches taller than Charles. The chin curtain beard he sported, without the mustache, gave him an uncanny resemblance to our late President Lincoln. He and his family had arrived earlier in the afternoon on the southbound train from Salem into Ashland, along with the Portland and Salem dignitaries.

The northbound train finally arrived from California, much later than expected due to some weather delays, but the crowd was determined to wait until morning if necessary. I gazed expectantly, along with most of the onlookers, southward along the tracks, which appeared like they converged in the far distance. Just as I saw the barely visible engine smokestack peek out over the trees along the distant track, it belched a puff of steam that looked like a snort from a large metal dragon. Sarah tapped me on the shoulder and mumbled in my ear, "I just saw Charles giving the refreshment girl a pat on her buttocks!"

"What did you say?" I asked for her to repeat her whisper.

Sarah was the tallest of us Berry girls, so she could easily see over most of the crowd. "Over there, by the tea cakes. I was looking for Isaac and I saw Charles groping that young woman's behind!" Sarah said against my muffled ear, which was wrapped in a thick wool scarf tied tightly around my head and neck.

"Oh you must have been mistaken. This fog can shroud things from a clear view. Charles would never do such a thing," I countered defensively. But under her breath, I could hear my sister say, *I know what I saw.*

At 4:30pm, the first railway whistles were heard, just as the pilot engine pulled into closer view. It was trailed by the ten excursion cars, including kitchen cars, dining cars and first-class Pullman sleeper cars, all which rolled slowly towards the cheering masses. The travelers disembarked at the new depot platform, adjacent to where the Ashland Brass and Drum Band was playing under the American flag banners waving in the evening breeze.

Mr. Crocker, a bank sponsor of the railroad, gingerly alighted from his private car at the end of the train. As Station Master, my husband made a point of greeting each of the dignitaries individually, who came from all over, even as far as San Francisco. A gold metal badge with silver spikes crossed on it, was pinned on the lapel of the two most prominent guests - railroad Superintendent Fillmore from San Francisco, and Oregon Governor Pennoyer. The rest of the special guests had a smaller silk version of the badge displayed on their overcoats. I thought Charles should have been given one too! *But who was about to listen to the Station Master's wife?*

Everyone wanted to commemorate the achievement of the railroad completion over the Siskiyou Mountain Pass, the final connection of the circle of railroads around the United States. It was said that one could travel to New York City in seven days now instead of three weeks!

Mr. Richard Koehler, as manager of this final Ashland-Yreka connection project, was the first to give a lengthy speech thanking the workers, both Irish and Chinese, for all their hard labor. Up on the platform, draped with scalloped flags, proudly stood my husband along with many others, including Governor Pennoyer, the mayors from every city along the railroad line in Oregon, as well as some mayors from California, Oregon Supreme Court Judge W.P. Lord from Salem, and Mr. Crocker, the Big Four railroad tycoon of which Papa had spoken.

Mr. Charles Crocker spoke briefly to the audience thanking them for coming as well as all of his workers and employees. He was then ready to hit the final spike to complete and connect the rails. The golden spike and the silver hammer were both set on the black velvet covered table next to the podium, gleaming in the last rays of setting sunlight piercing through the fog.

At 5:00 o'clock, Mr. Crocker, being an older man in his late sixties, gingerly climbed down the platform stairs with the hammer and spike in hand. He spoke loudly, "I hold in my hand the last spike." The crowd cheered with cries of, "Hold it UP!"

Mr. Crocker continued, "With this Golden Spike, I propose now to unite the rails between California and Oregon to cement the friendship between the two states and make them as one people." The applause soared.

Mr. Crocker picked up the shiny hammer and bent down to drive the final connecting spike. With three taps of the silver hammer, separated by intervals of ten seconds, his pounding sent a current through the rails as the metals of the spike and the track met. This current sent an electric signal, to all the chief railroad cities of the West coast, to fire their cannons and ring their bells, similar to what we heard in Ashland at that moment. I was jolted by the depth of the sounds. They were louder than I had anticipated.

The railroad dignitaries were escorted by my husband, me and Isaac to our house. Chinese lanterns, hanging in front of every house, lit our way through the fading light of dusk.

Papa was standing at the top of the stairs waving to our entourage. Mama greeted the gentlemen as they filed in to our parlor, decorated with the finest red velvet and damask silk-covered tufted chairs and fleur-de-lis wallpaper. Mama served some of Mr. Powell's fresh apple cider that she had bought, pressed today from his orchard a block away on 2nd Street. It was used for the toast.

My husband had set up a mahogany table under the front bay window for the signing of the official documents. Governor Pennoyer, Mr. Koehler and Mr. Crocker were the appointed signatories. Papa's special pen, from his time in the State Senate office, was used to sign the papers. Papa was so proud to be present and included in such a momentous occasion. An official O & C Railroad photographer captured the smiles during the signing, blinding all of us for a moment with the bright light from the poof of his flash lamp stick.

My siblings, their families and I lined the sides of the fireplace mantle and watched history unfold before our eyes. As baby Alexander started to fidget, I excused myself from the festivities and bid everyone goodnight.

Charles came in to our bedroom after all the guests had left. He undressed, even removing his union suit undergarment. His choice for a complete lack of nighttime apparel, unusual for a winter, indicated to me his intent, when he slinked under the feather comforter. I warmed him up and we celebrated that night in our own special way that sent bells ringing in my heart and throughout my body. It was the perfect fitting end to quite a memorable day.

Exactly nine months later, our beautiful daughter Ramona was born.

~~~

3  The Berry Family, 1850-1884

I would be remiss if I failed to fill in the details of how I became The Station Master's wife. My tale must necessarily start with my parents and their journeys to the unknown promised land of the "Western Frontier" in the tumultuous 1850's.

Both of my parents were from hardy pioneer families of Indiana. Mama (Mary Ann Wilson) was born in 1824 – the daughter of a prosperous farmer, and Papa (Alexander Monroe Berry) was born in 1815, also to a farming family. Drawn together by their common Presbyterian faith, they eventually courted and were united in marriage in 1850.

My oldest brother, Isaac, born the following year added the first bundle of joy to their family. Papa was always a faithful companion and loving husband, but by the time Isaac turned two, Papa was tempted to follow the path of the western star. He had heard stories of the Oregon Territory, with its fertile valleys and gold-filled hills.

Plus, Congress had recently passed the Donation Land Claim Act the year they were married, and Papa wanted to get in on the free land deal offered to settlers out west. Papa knew that mining could be a gamble, but he felt he could always fall back on his carpentry and farming skills for survival. Mama wasn't very happy to be left behind alone with a toddler.

"We can start a new life out west once I make enough money from mining gold to send for you and Isaac. I will be able to set up a homestead and have a house built before you come with the baby," Papa rationalized to Mama.

"How long do you think that will take?" Mama asked.

"Not sure, darling. I'll work as hard as I can to get things going. Don't you worry none. We can send letters and parcels by the mail wagons. They are setting up routes all up and down the western coast," he continued trying to appease her concerns.

"I don't want to stay here alone. But, if you think it's best for me to wait, and we can't really afford to go together, I think I'll move in with my folks. That way, I can be helpful to them and they can be the extra helping hands I'll so need with raising Isaac," she said declaring her own plan. "You just be safe and hurry along our plans the best you can. I don't want to miss out on too much of our young lives together."

"The next wagon train leaves in April. To get to the departure point in Missouri on time, I will have to leave here in March," Papa said holding her face in his hands, planting kisses on both cheeks.

"Then, I suppose I should tell you now. I was going to wait until I was absolutely sure," Mama hesitated. Her eyes were demurely downcast as she coyly smiled.

"What is it, my love?" Papa stepped back to look at all of her, apprehensive and a bit confused.

"Oh, no. Nothing to be worried about, dear," Mama quickly replied to allay his fears. "I think we're going to have another baby, that's all," she said, as her smile widened.

"A baby? Are you sure? That's wonderful!" Papa squealed. "Maybe I shouldn't go then. How far along is this one?"

"I think just about six weeks. I'll be fine. Mother and the midwife can take care of me. You go along and get our new life set up. I'm sure I'll be on my way there next spring, my love," Mama reassured him as well as herself.

So, Papa set off by wagon train over the plains, enduring six months of dust and hardship on the Oregon Trail northern route, through mountainous Idaho and down the treacherous Columbia River into the bustling port of Portland, Oregon. He didn't stay there long, as his eyes were focused on the southern part of the Oregon Territory.

News of Jacksonville gold had struck front page of the Portland papers. In October 1852, just about a month after my sister Sarah was born in Indiana, Papa rolled into this Southern Oregon gold mining town of Jacksonville, Oregon after many connecting stagecoach rides. He sent a letter to Mama immediately upon arriving in Southern Oregon telling her the name of the town in which he had settled. He didn't know he had a daughter until Mama's return mail arrived around Christmastime. Papa always said that news was the best present he could have received that year.

Well, as it turned out, Papa didn't strike it rich but he did manage to survive. His meager fractions of gold ore had to be supplemented by the carpentry services he provided to the budding town of Jacksonville, five miles from his 160 acre donation land claim farmstead. Year after year, he sent letters to Mama explaining they would have to wait just a little bit longer to be reunited.

Other events also drew Papa's time away from making money to send for his family. The Rogue Indian War was started by a mob of angry miners from Jacksonville who attacked the Table Rock Indian Reservation in 1855, killing twenty-eight natives. Relations weren't great before that, but after that was when things really started to heat up.

After a while, when the retaliatory battles moved closer to Jacksonville, Papa volunteered with Mr. William Bybee and about fifty other menfolk to fight the Indians, who were also raiding outposts and merchant wagons traveling through the Rogue Valley. He told the story of one fight from which he barely escaped.

"We were attacked around 2:00 am that June morning. On account of the location of our camp – the Indians occupying a bluff several feet higher – we were placed under a severe and galling fire for about seven hours, being compelled to abandon our camp and baggage for the purpose of saving ourselves and take refuge at a house some three hundred yards distant. It was where we corralled the remaining animals that had not been killed. This gave the red men an opportunity to possess themselves of all our camp equipage, baggage and cargo. Six of our men were mortally wounded. The rest of us escaped the following afternoon when other volunteer help arrived to replace us," Papa had written. After that letter, Mama asked him to not send such news.

It took another two years for things to settle down in the Rogue Valley. Mr. Bybee became the sheriff and Papa had joined the community as a well-known contractor and carpenter. By that time in 1857, Papa was finally ready to send for Mama and the two children, now ages six and five. He advised and insisted that Mama take the Panama route to get to the West Coast, instead of the Oregon Trail with the children. He saw too many young ones not make it on his overland crossing.

Therefore, it was decided, at age 33, that Mama would say goodbye to her family in Indiana and start her adventure west by initially going east to New York by train. There she and the children boarded a steamer headed south to Panama, where they eventually disembarked weeks later, wobbly-legged and queasy.

The weary family immediately caught the next overland train across the Isthmus of Panama. The Panama Railroad had just been completed two years prior, in 1855, and was a welcomed and long awaited option for travelers. The trip was much safer and shorter, although still plagued by swarms of mosquitos. The trip was reduced from four days to four hours for the Isthmus land crossing.

Once they arrived on the Pacific side, Mama then headed the family north on another ship to San Francisco. After two and a half months of dusty travel, mixed with sea sickness and cramped quarters, Mama and the children reluctantly climbed aboard their last boat, shipping out of San Francisco, bound for Crescent City, the last California settlement before the Oregon Territory border.

Finally, when all their trunks and bedraggled bodies set ashore, they joined a mule pack train for the ten day ride overland to Jacksonville, where Papa was waitin with unending hugs.

"Is that you Mary Ann?" Papa had asked of the weary, unkempt and filthy traveler who slightly resembled his beautiful young wife from five years prior.

"Oh, Alexander!" Mama replied, dropping the luggage and running to him. The children stood there clutching their teddy bears, whose stuffing was pouring out from the worn seams, looking as if they, too, had suffered from seasickness.

"And who might these little ones be?" Papa asked as he and Mama walked back over to the exhausted looking children standing wide-eyed next to the leather suitcases, apprehensive of this man handling their mother. Mama introduced Isaac and Sarah to Papa since neither had any memory of this tall bearded man with bright blue eyes. Only when Papa produced candy sticks for each of them, did they smile.

Shortly after they reunited as husband and wife, nine months later in fact, Mama gave birth to my sister Mary in 1858. While Mama tended to her growing family, Papa, a well-respected man in town by then, decided to run for the Oregon Territorial Senate, as a representative for the interests of Southern Oregon. He was elected and held that position as the Territory gained its statehood in 1859. He was gone often for weeks, traveling by stagecoach to the State Capitol and Legislature in Salem.

Mama had a break in childbearing as a result of Papa's commitment to politics, until I came along in 1860. Alexander, or Aleck as he was nicknamed, my younger brother and the last of the Berry clan, was born in 1867.

Often, Papa would serenade us after dinner with his violin. Mama had taken extra special care to line his instrument case with red velvet fabric to cushion his violin and bow with the abalone inlays. I would drift off to sleep, lulled by his sweet tunes. On those musical nights, I would also get a special piggy-back ride afterwards, when Papa carried me upstairs to bed. My childhood was perfect and filled with love.

The friends we made in Jacksonville included some of the wealthiest families in town. Papa was usually the one they called on to build for them. I had the most fun playing with the Beekman children, especially Benjamin, who was close to my age, because his father owned the Beekman Bank.

"May I help sweep up, Mr. Beekman?" I would ask when he was ready to close the bank. Millions of dollars in gold passed through the bank he started in 1863. The miner's brought in their ore samples to be weighed, sold or safely stored and often upon opening their bags, fine powdery particles would spill out and cover the floor boards like sparkling fairy dust, settling on top of and into the cracks between the planks.

"How much did you collect today, Alice?" Mr. Beekman would ask peering over his wire-rimmed glasses. "Ready to weigh in?" I'm sure there wasn't enough gold dust to tip the scale, but he always gave me a few pennies for my effort. Then Benjamin and I would rush directly to the mercantile for a sugary treat of some striped candy sticks.

Papa also made fast friends with Mr. McCall, a Masonic Order brother and a fellow miner turned mining store owner. When he and his family would join us for picnics, I would hear them discuss the tall tales of mining mishaps, adventures and who struck it rich. His farm was along Wagner Creek but he was looking to invest in the nearby town of Ashland.

Even though Jacksonville was three hours away from Ashland by horse and buggy, Mr. McCall could tell from his frequent trips there, that all the mill businesses there were going to make something of that town. He had purchased an interest in the Ashland Flour Mill in 1859 and watched it grow. By 1868, he had become the leader of the company running the Ashland Woolen Mill, which by then was shipping its textiles far and wide.

"I'm going to help set up that town for great things," Mr. McCall would tell Papa.

"Well, the way to get things going is to have a say up in Salem. You ought'a run for the State Legislature like I did in '58. You could do more now that we got Statehood," Papa said encouragingly.

"I think I'll do just that," Mr. McCall retorted. In 1876, he was elected on the People's Ticket as a representative in the Oregon State Congress. By 1879, Mr. McCall had moved to Ashland and helped organize the Ashland Library. In 1883, he built his mansion downtown, right next to the creek and flour mill. Of course he was one of the incorporators of the first Ashland Bank in 1884, as well. No matter how our families grew apart, by money matters or miles, we always remained friends.

My older sister Mary and my older brother Isaac both got married in 1878. Mama's quilting circle and Papa's carpentry shop were very busy that year making wedding presents. They continued to pump out presents when my siblings each had a daughter the next year. By the year after that, Papa was appointed as one of the head carpenters to build the First Presbyterian Church in Jacksonville. Our Reverend Moses Williams, who started preaching in Jacksonville in 1857 was the first pastor in the new pulpit in 1880.

Unfortunately, we needed the services of Rev. Williams sooner than expected, but it was not for a wedding or another christening. It was early in December 1881 after my brother Aleck, only 14 years old, went out hunting with a lad of the same age, near Bear Creek.

"Let's cross the creek here. We can use this foot-log as a bridge," the other boy said. The log they used for crossing was the trunk of a small fallen tree, still with limbs on it, which laid across the narrowest part of the icy cold creek.

"I'll go first," Aleck said. He straddled the fallen tree and started going across in that manner. With his friend still on the riverbank holding both their guns, he handed Aleck his gun before he was out of his reach.

"Hand it here," Aleck demanded. He pulled the gun towards himself by the muzzle. However, the butt end of the gun was heavier at the handle and the weight of the rifle fell onto the log with the hammer down, which caught on a limb of the log, and caused the barrel to go off. The gun was heavily loaded with duck-shot and the whole charge struck poor Aleck just above the stomach.

"I feel stiff," were the last words he said as he fell off the log into the freezing river water. His friend dragged Aleck out onto the bank, frightened by the red ribbon of blood trailing downstream, and immediately ran for help. But it was too late. My little brother's spirit had fled, and Aleck, who had been so full of animation, lay mute in death.

Rev. Moses Williams officiated Aleck's funeral, with family and friends attending at the new Presbyterian Church. Customarily, school was adjourned so that classmates could join a funeral and say their last goodbyes to a well-liked friend.

However, the current professor of the school was new and unclear on the rules for such a school closure. He refused the dismissal of the class to attend the funeral event since he had no such directive from the principal and was reluctant to do so without permission.

It was only after Papa's stern demand of the School Board to close the school on the day of the memorial for Aleck that the students were allowed to initiate a procession to the church and subsequently to the cemetery to pay their last respects. The well-publicized letter Papa wrote to the paper about the incident must have made teaching public school, as a permanent career, seem a lot less rewarding for that professor.

A cloak of darkness and bad fortune seemed to hang over our family at that time. Just about a month later, my little niece Cassie, a bright little girl, contracted scarlet fever. The poor petite two and a half year old departed this life in the early hours of Sunday morning, January 22nd, 1882.

My brother Isaac and his wife Dora were inconsolable. Sorrow-stricken, my brother, kept to his own farm for a while, with only Dora by his side. They consoled each other for months and then came over for Easter Sunday dinner and announced they were pregnant again. Baby Laura, or "Dot" as she came to be called, was born to them later that year on Christmas Eve.

~ ~ ~

4  Romance and Railroads, 1884

Big news in our southernmost county spread like a wildfire. In the spring of 1884, the railroad was finally coming as far south as Ashland. Financial troubles had halted the rails in Roseburg for the past three years, but the tracks were finally to be finished all the way to the Rogue Valley. Papa said we were going to see the first train ever to come into the new Ashland Depot. That was May 1884.

Back then, only two of us five Berry children were still at home. Sarah and I, plus Mama and Papa, made the long bumpy three hour ride from Jacksonville into Ashland in our covered buggy on a beautiful spring morning.

The site of the valley, was beautifully dotted with pear, apple and almond tree blossoms, pink and white like drifts of snow blanketing the hills of Jacksonville. They left behind tree branches with fresh shiny vibrant green leaves bursting forth, reflecting and dancing in the spring sunlight. Mr. John McCall invited us to stay at his new Ashland mansion for the weekend to join the festivities commemorating the arrival of the train.

"Remember when John and I used to boast about who got the biggest nugget out of the Applegate River?" Papa would tease and nudge Mama's arm as we trotted along.

"I guess John did, because his house is much bigger. Glad he is going to let us all stay for this grand railroad event," Mama retorted.

When we pulled in alongside the house, towards the rear yard stables of the McCall mansion, all I could do was look up. Their home was a building which seemed to touch the sky.

It was two stories tall with bay windows on each side of the entry and another set stacked above those, on the second floor. A tall woman was coming out of the glass door leading onto the balcony between the upper bay windows that sat above the front entry door. She waved as we drove up.

Sarah and I were shown to our own room with a bed for each of us. I picked up the Ashland Tidings, the local newspaper which the servant had left on the dressing table, to see what this town was all about. I promptly plopped into the softest feather bed on which I had ever laid, feeling like I was floating on a cloud.

That day, Ashland became the southernmost depot of the Southern Pacific Railroad in Oregon. The railroad company was prevented from continuing any further south than Ashland on to California by the steep grade of the Siskiyou Mountains that divided Oregon from California. They realized it would take a LOT more money and time to conquer and traverse that mountainous engineering challenge. I was ecstatic to have any train connections this close to home, even if just going north.

Mostly, I remember that warm day in May because I met the handsome new Depot Station Master of Ashland. He rode his horse five miles north from his residence in Ashland to be part of the group to ride the first train south into town, cheered on by the Ashland Brass Band. As he stepped off the train, he checked his pocket watch. The sun glinted off the back watch cover and hit me square in the eye. I gasped as he looked into the crowd following the reflected beam.

I thought I blended into the hollering crowd, but his eyes were definitely pinpointed on me. "Is that Station Master looking at me or you?" I asked my older sister Sarah, tilting my head away from the ray of light. I was only twenty-three and Sarah was almost ten years older. We shared the same hair color, but her hair was loosely piled under her dark velvet blue hat, with only the curls of her bangs framing her face.

"He's definitely eyeing YOU!" Sarah said. "It must be your beautiful dangling, golden brown curled ringlets blowing in the wind that caught his attention. Look at his gold watch-chain and three piece suit! I bet he's not from around here. Oh, shhh. Quiet now. He's coming over here. Let's stand behind Papa."

Mr. Kane, the Depot Manager and Station Master, made a point of introducing himself to all the spectators. He especially made a point of shaking hands with the elders of the town whom he knew probably arrived out west by various means other than a train.

"Thank you for coming to our celebration," Mr. Kane said to Papa with a vigorous double-clasped hand shake. "I am in charge here and would be pleased to give you a tour of our locomotive anytime. My name is E. C. Kane, but my friends call me Charles. I prefer it to my first name of Ellsworth."

"Thank you, sir. I would certainly enjoy that sometime. My family and I are from Jacksonville but we will be here all weekend. Possibly tomorrow after church around 11:00 am?" Papa replied.

"That would be just fine," Mr. Kane answered. "Perhaps your whole family would like to join us as well?" he asked craning his neck to point his chin behind Papa.

"That would be lovely," I answered a bit too quickly. "I've always wanted to see the inside of one of these steel dragons." Mr. Kane laughed with a chuckle.

Papa turned around and glared at me for being so forward. I could see it in his narrowed eyes. I didn't care. I, in fact, continued my conversation with Mr. Kane, much to the chagrin of my whole family.

"Actually, we are all going to the Masquerade Ball at the Masonic Lodge Hall tonight. Both maskers and spectators are invited, especially new neighbors and neighbors from out of town. I'm sure you'd be welcome as one of the newer folks in town. We've come from Jacksonville, ourselves," I uttered the words so fast I didn't realize I repeated what Papa had already said. I knew I must have sounded nervous.

Sarah looked at me with her raised eyebrows as if to say, "Really, what ball?" I guessed then that she had not perused the local newspaper as thoroughly as I.

"I would be honored to join your family there," the Station Master replied with a touch of his hand tipping the rim of his brown bowler hat that matched his finely tailored, broad chalk-striped brown suit. "I look forward to it. I assume it is easy enough to locate downtown. See you around seven, then?"

Papa cleared his throat with a slight "ahem" noise. "Yes. That sounds about right. Good day then, Mr. Kane." Papa turned and ushered us away from the depot, his arm scooping Mama's back and corralling us between them. "I wasn't aware of us attending any masquerade party this evening? When was that plan enacted?"

I gave a begging look to Mama who caught my drift. She covered for my forwardness and smoothed things in the right direction. "Oh, dear. We talked about it over tea at the McCall's. I guess you weren't there. You and John had so much to catch up on," she said with a sly smile. "It's okay, isn't it? The girls will have so much fun. And the McCalls have plenty of masks to go around, if you choose to join in. Otherwise you can just sit and converse with your Grand Mason brothers."

I grabbed Mama's arm and mouthed a silent "thank-you Mama" as we strolled through the wide streets of the new Railroad District of Ashland.

That evening when the dance was over, we returned to the McCall mansion. Papa and Mr. McCall had lots to talk about. "How's things going up in Salem?" Papa inquired, lighting his cigar, as we raced up to our bedrooms.

I'm sure they could hear us girls giggling about the new Station Master and all the dances he requested with me, a masked stranger. I told Sarah how the depot manager also explained to me why his dancing came with a slight limp.

"I'm sorry if my feet don't keep up with the tempo, Miss Berry," he whispered in my ear over the loud band music. "I am still recovering from an injury I sustained at work a few months back."

"Oh, I hadn't really noticed," I said demurely. I didn't want to let go of his dancing embrace to look at his feet, so I steered the conversation to find out more about him. "But I thought you worked at the station, not on the rails or construction line, Mr. Kane."

"That's mostly correct, Miss Berry," he said. Then he added, "Please, do call me Charles. Is it alright if I call you Alice?"

"That would be fine," I replied, blushing a bit. "So what happened, if I might ask?" I asked, hoping to keep him talking.

"Well, as general timekeeper, I sometimes must travel to other depots or construction sites along the rail line to manage issues. I was disembarking from a construction train, which was still in motion somewhat, and I lost my balance and struck my head as I landed on the slanted gravel rail bed.

"I was knocked senseless for a time and it seemed that I twisted my ankle in the fall as well. I'm sure I'll recover with a little more time, however, tonight I still display a slight awkwardness in my step. I do apologize, Miss Berry. Or rather, Alice," he said smiling shyly.

Charles asked if he could come calling sometime when he traveled to Jacksonville by train or buggy. I said I would be delighted and I reassured him that it would be fine with Papa as well, as he enjoyed entertaining important people and showing off our town of Jacksonville. Besides, I told him since we were to meet the next day for our Train Tour, he could ask Papa himself.

The next morning before church, Papa and Mr. McCall continued their political chatter over the huge long breakfast table crafted from one large piece of dark mahogany. The fresh baked bread, made from the flour ground at the mill next door, smelled sweet and nutty as I cut a slice for everyone. Mrs. McCall opened a jar of peach preserves she had made from her backyard trees and passed the delectable sweetness around. Papa reached for the bacon and sausage as he commented on the movers and shakers involved in the railroad.

"They call 'em the "Big Four", Papa announced. "They are villains and heroes together in the same dapper suits and top hats."

"Now then, Alexander, they also do get things done. Why, I heard that Mr. Stanford not only is involved in the construction of the railroad through those government grants, but he also owns a steamship company that travels to the Orient and brings back eager Chinese men to help as railroad workers," Mr. McCall said.

"Yes, yes. And it's that other railroad big-wig, Mr. Crocker, who hires all those Chinese at a much lower pay than any local fellow would work for. I guess that's good business, but it just doesn't seem right," Papa said, sounding genuinely concerned.

"Well, I guess it won't be a problem for any new Chinese workers since Congress passed that Chinese Exclusion Act two years ago and they won't be coming into our country anymore."

"True enough, John. I guess the ones already here, should count themselves lucky being in America and having a job at all. I just wish the white workers didn't treat them so harshly. It's not like there aren't enough jobs to go around, especially the dangerous ones that the Irish won't do," Papa declared.

"And what about this Mr. Henry Villard? The rail construction inactivity ended when he became the new president of the O & C Railroad. And, didn't he bail out the University of Oregon when it went into debt last year? I heard he is German and brought lots of money from bank investors over there in Europe. Do you think they are trying to get ahold of power in our country?" Mr. McCall queried.

"Not sure. All I know is THAT money, which came through Villard, bailed out the O & C Railroad's declining finances. The end of the line had remained in Roseburg up until then. I think it's because of him we have a train in Ashland today," Papa concluded.

"Well I heard that five years after he got to the United States, he became a newspaper man in Illinois covering the Lincoln-Douglas debates in '58. As an anti-slavery campaigner, he kept close ties with Mr. Lincoln's administration. So, I liked the man based on his principles back then. I'm sure he's still got our country's best interest at heart, even if he is making money for his friends back in the old country," was the final say about the railroad by Mr. McCall. Papa, ready to argue further about foreign money, was interrupted by Mrs. McCall who stood up.

"Ok, then. Let's get to church."

At church, I prayed for a miracle of more romantic interludes with Mr. E.C.Kane.

~ ~ ~

5  Becoming the Station Master's Wife, <u>1884</u>

I ndeed, our romance did continue throughout the summer. Mr. E. C. Kane, or rather Charles as everyone now referred to him, visited Jacksonville quite often. He would join my whole family, even when Mary and Isaac's families were present, for church picnics and parlor games. Charles took advantage of his free rail travel to come calling.

Sometimes, during "courtship calls", Mama and Papa would allow Charles and me to sit together, alone in the parlor. Occasionally, he would read aloud to me from the latest newspapers that came in on the mail train from Portland. That would always spark a lively discussion. Or, he would tell me of his travels from when he headed out west, leaving his home town in New York.

But we both knew that just behind the beveled wooden pocket doors that led into the dining room, which were always left slightly ajar, my parents sat listening to our every word. Papa made sure we knew of his presence by lighting up his pipe and blowing his cherry flavored smoke through the gap between the door panels.

We expressed our passion at my parent's home with glances and holding hands. We would only be able to steal a kiss or two during a stroll through town, sometimes behind the old oak tree near the brick two-story U.S. Hotel or in the shadows behind the Masonic Hall building.

Many years later, I found a pocket sized book of "Sweet Phrases to Whisper to Your Girl" in the back of his chest of drawers. I remember the ones he used when he got down on one knee. Charles had arrived early in Jacksonville that Sunday by buggy rather than train, so as to not miss my Fall Equinox piano recital, which was scheduled before the first train arrived later that morning. I was giving a performance at the Presbyterian Church and he wanted to be there to hear me play and cheer my accomplishment.

"That was wonderful, Alice!" Charles declared as the throng of recital attendees filtered out of the church. "These are for you," Charles said as he handed me a bouquet of resplendent burgundy roses that smelled divine.

He was dressed in his best suit, the three-piece one I first saw him wearing at the Ashland Depot in May when we met. He was nervously twirling his hat between his thumbs when he asked if he could drive me home in his piano-box two-seater covered buggy. Charles walked over to Papa at the bottom of the church stairs, to ask permission for this request and I eventually saw Papa happily nod in approval.

After my debonair suitor helped me up into the carriage, I noticed a small wooden box on the red leather seat cushion. I assumed it was another gracious gift he often brought for Mama in thanks for the lunches she prepared for him. As we rode over Griffin Creek Bridge, he pulled off the main road onto a side lane towards of one of the orchards.

"What's wrong?" I asked concerned that we had stopped short of my family's farmstead. The afternoon sunlight was dappled through the branches of the orchard trees. It danced across his face like little fairies as he helped me down. My black and white striped dress had a hem of black satin bows that snagged on the carriage step. I blushed when Charles reached down, eyeing my stockinged legs, to unhook my hem. A curved, carved bench, something I had never noticed before, was right next to the entrance of the lane. I averted my eyes from his gaze, as he led me toward the bench.

"Nothing is ever wrong when I'm with you," Charles said taking a hold of my gloved hands. "I just wanted to speak with you alone before we are surrounded by everyone at your house."

He motioned for me to sit while he whisked out his handkerchief and spread it on the ground. Fumbling in his jacket pocket, he withdrew the small wooden box he had scooped off the buggy seat, as he bent down on one knee over the square of white cloth.

Taking a deep breath, Charles began his monologue of sweet phrases. Following his proposal, he opened the lid of the box and proffered a beautiful engagement ring to me, made of swirling gold filigree with a large central raspberry ruby surrounded by small diamonds. My eyes were streaming happy tears as I accepted his proposal of marriage. Removing my gloves, taking my left hand in his, he slipped the ring on my fourth finger. It was a perfect fit.

I snuggled up closer on the remainder of the ride home to my family's farm house. When we arrived, I jumped into Charles' arms as he assisted me out of the carriage. The farmhouse door burst open and my parents rushed to our sides, ready to congratulate.

"But, how did you know?" I asked perplexed by their excitement.

"Oh, Mr. Kane here asked me for your hand already, directly after your recital. He didn't just ask if he could take you in his surrey," Papa laughed. He knew I had no idea at the time. We all had a good laugh and started to plan for the ceremony that would launch us into married life in just two months. Both Charles and I were so anxious to be wed.

The next few weeks were a flurry of anticipation and preparation. Mama searched for the most beautiful fabric from which to make my dress. I told her I wanted it to match the color of the roses that Charles gave to me the day he proposed. We took a weekend jaunt to Ashland to peruse Mr. Hargadine's mercantile. It was said that he imported some silk brocades from France for special occasions.

"Mama, I would like the dress to be fancy but practical. As a new wife, I will have to watch our money. Having a dress that can be worn for occasions other than my wedding day will be most efficient for our finances. The rest of my trousseau will have dresses made of more simple and functional fabrics," I relayed to her as we entered the store.

"Oh, dear Alice, I will make the most stunning wedding outfit. Perhaps a fitted bodice and separate skirt?" Mama said.

"That would be lovely. Then I can mix and match the parts with other coordinating pieces that I already have. Would it be alright to add a pleated ruffle at the hem for a little extra style?" I requested.

"Not a problem, darling. I would also like to include crossing drapes on the front and back of the skirt with a bustle in the rear. And don't forget to pick out a nice taffeta for the petticoat, with extra material for the serpentine flounces. It is so important for the fit of the gown to hang correctly," Mama advised.

"Let's make sure to visit Mrs. Boynton's millinery store," I added. "I absolutely must have a hat that matches the fabric we get for my dress. I would like a bonnet that tilts to one side and is adorned by a few feathers tucked into a matching red silk band of trim around the top, with some pink or white tulle netting wrapped around the crown of the hat and cascading down the back. And maybe they could make a pair of white gloves with matching tulle trim. I'm sure Charles wouldn't mind bringing the hat and glove boxes the next time he comes to Jacksonville."

"Tell him not to peek!" Mama warned. I giggled at her belief in Victorian superstitions.

Our buggy was full to the brim with packages on our return ride to the farm. Papa had been busy fixing the porch railings, making a wedding arch and building a cedar hope chest for all my clothes and collectibles. In November, our farm would be having its third wedding. Rev. Moses Williams was kind enough to agree to ride out from Jacksonville to officiate.

Mr. E. C. Kane did some sprucing up himself. His boarding house room and he himself went through some transformations. He had a calf-length coat tailored to match his suit and waistcoat, and purchased a silk ascot to match. He made arrangements with his landlord to include his future wife in his rental agreement. The proprietor was so kind, he moved Charles into his largest suite.

Work duties still demanded the Station Master's attention. The train schedule was busy now with multiple arrivals and departures daily. With the dispatching offices open day and night, Charles, or the associates he had trained, had to record and dispense orders to every conductor and engineer who stopped at the Ashland Depot. They had to include the number of cars comprising each train, delineate whether the trains were passenger - recording the number and destination of each patron, or freight - noting what kind and amount of product was in each car.

Additionally, tracking was required of the construction trains, special trains, or any other type of train arriving or departing from Ashland. All this information proved essential in preventing accidents and getting trains through in better time. The Station Master had to keep a chart to know at which station every train would be at a certain time, their arrival and departure times, and the type of train. Constant telegraph communication was mandatory. Receiving and sending telegrams over the railroad wire between all the other stations on the rail line, was essential for safety and efficiency.

Ashland was going through some changes of its own. Since the railroad arrived in May, the town and local manufacturing boomed. The town newspaper boasted of five hotels already, and the railroad was in the planning stages for its own hotel right at the depot station. It has been purported that the hotel construction alone would bring in thousands of dollars in revenue and jobs, and that the hotel will continue to support the town with traveler's dollars after its opening.

The name of the town itself changed from Ashland Mills to just plain Ashland. I suppose that they wanted an image other than only being known for mill manufacturing. Our air was now filled with a mixture of smoke from the mills and the locomotives, filtered through the surrounding fir and madrone trees by the regular afternoon winds. Even though they changed the name of the town, the mills were still a major portion of town employment. In fact, earlier this year the town council levied a mill tax in order to build a more permanent school building for all the children of these mill workers and railroad families.

The three mills - a lumber sawmill, a woolen mill and a flour grinding mill - were now considered to have competition for employee attention. I heard that a Chautauqua, an outdoor educational and performance center, was in the works for summer programs in the park on the hill above the Ashland Woolen Mill. Mr. George Billings had been spearheading this idea for a place to hear sermons, political debates, lectures, poetry readings, and music. He's even proposed to offer classes for music too, hinting that he might secure that band master of marches, Mr. John Philip Sousa as an instructor.

Livestock and fruit sales saw an increase in their production thanks to the distribution of their goods along the rail lines. These companies were now able to sell to more distant markets with a fresher product due to the freight trains that Charles keeps on time and moving along efficiently. The produce from the orchards of Oregon have been examined with a critical eye. One northern newspaper had an interesting comparison for our miners to consider. It read:

"Raise enough fruit from this temperate zone in Southern Oregon, enough for one train a day, of at least twelve cars in the train, and your orchards will be as lucrative as a gold mine and a good deal more permanent."

With all this increased production, more employment opened up. Settlers arrived these days and were able to find jobs easier than when Papa came thirty years prior. They were able to build houses quicker with the extra available help and more consistent wages. More and more families were arriving along the rail line, and they were snapping up homesteading parcels like cowboys grabbing for ribs at a barbeque.

"I picked up a copy of the Oregonian newspaper at the Jacksonville Mercantile yesterday," Papa said after dinner while Mama was doing another fitting with me for my wedding dress. "It came on last week's train, and it had an interesting article about the shady goings-on in Portland just last month."

I sat motionless on the swivel piano stool while Mama pin-tucked the bodice pleats of my wedding blouse. I drifted in and out of listening to their conversation.

"Now Alexander," Mama said. "Don't you go stirring the pot with those tall tales from up north."

"No, truly, MaryAnn," Papa replied with his senatorial voice. "They've exposed this scandal concerning the railroad and the Oregon Land Grants. I'm sure you remember that Congress gave the railroad federal forest land to sell to bona-fide settlers so towns could develop along the rail lines? Congress wanted to help the railroad recoup some of the monies laid out for building the tracks, thereby encouraging them to continue to build their 'snake of steel'."

"Of course I do, Alexander," Mama answered with a slightly defensive attitude. I kept twirling on the fitting stool, my arms crossed above my head, keeping out of their discussion.

"Well, those railroad officials decided they could make more money selling off the timber on those lands than selling to pioneering folks like us. I heard a family could buy a parcel of 160 acres for $400. However, those lumber barons are snagging the land and paying more than twice that!" Papa bellowed.

"How on earth are they getting away with such shenanigans?" Mama asked. "Won't the government find out that those company names on the deeds are not actual settlers?"

"Oh, but those sly Portland railroad officials have figured out a way to work around such rules," Papa retorted. "Mr. Ned Harriman, the main railroad official in charge of the land sales, kept these transactions at arm's length. He recruited a Mr. Puter, not a railroad employee, to round up needy souls from Portland's saloons and skid row. Then this Mr. Puter escorted these 'settlers' to the land office, and had them register for an Oregon and California Railroad Land Grant 'homestead parcel' as a bona-fide settler. And get this," Papa added, "Those poor souls did all this in exchange for a bottle of liquor."

"Still, that doesn't help the railroad any," Mama queried.

"Precisely. So after the 'settler' recorded his land deed, he would be able to legally transfer the land into the railroad's name, and happily walk away with his bottle in hand," Papa summarized.

"That's just despicable. Wait till I tell the ladies at my monthly Eastern Star meeting. Did they finally put a stop to such land fraud?" Mama asked.

"Not right away. Says here this underhandedness has been transpiring for over a decade. The railroad was able to gather up large blocks of parcels and sell to the highest bidders for timber harvest. Of course, being such smart and scheming fellows, the railroad men made sure to have middlemen between themselves and the sales. Now big patches in the checkerboard pattern along the rail line are owned by companies who are cutting down more timber than would ever be needed by a settler. Some of the mountains are starting to look darn near naked!" Papa finished in a loud enough tone to snap me out of my honeymoon dreams.

Mama worked feverishly to get my wedding dress finished in time. It was four weeks from when she started that I had my second fitting. I stood on the stool as she bent over, pin cushion strapped around her wrist, to perfectly level up the pleated hem. The hardest part was when she needed to fit the bodice to the linen twill lining.

"Ouch!" I protested. "That whalebone stiffening is jabbing me in the ribs, Mama."

"Oh, stop your complaining. At least I haven't stabbed you with my pinning," she countered. "I just hope I have enough time to finish. The bow on the back of the tapered bodice has to hang just right over the tailored points. Now hold still!" she commanded.

I continued to turn on the stool like a ballerina in a music box. I knew the rhythm and pace of Mama's handiwork by now. "Has Sarah finished making the covered buttons? The woven cord wrapping each one will certainly set off the front pleats of the bodice top. You ARE making pleats in the back of the bodice to match, aren't you?" I asked Mama, probably for the tenth time. "Will the long sleeves be tapered? Remember, I don't want the poufy bell style sleeve, alright, Mama?"

"Yes, yes. And the draping overskirt pieces will continue around to the back of the skirt and cross just as they do in the front, except over the bustle. Now stop your worrying and tell me who you are going to invite to this blessed event," Mama said. I began to rattle off names of invitees from school, church and my choir group for whom I played piano.

Three weeks later, the baking and cooking began. Mama, Sarah and I worked on twisting bread dough into braids, baking apple pies, cooking cranberry sauce and plucking turkey feathers off of what would be the center attraction of the dinner table. Since the wedding was to take place on the Sunday Sabbath after Thanksgiving, we would still have a fair bit of leftover ham available for the reception guests. The fall salmon run had been a good one, and now the smell of the smoked fish was wafting over the farm from the smokehouse.

I pressed the rose petals from the bouquet that Charles had given to me the day he proposed, and divided most of the dried maroon colored petals amongst my nieces, ages five and two. I kept a few for my cedar hope chest. The youngsters were excited about their job as flower girls walking in front of the bride, throwing fragrant petals on the grassy aisle, to the outdoor wedding arch. My sister Mary had made their dresses of a lighter rose pink satin to blend with my crimson dress. My sister-in-law Dora wound the willow branches into a heart on the arch to match the heart handles of the flower girls' baskets. Everything was coming together.

On the big day, though somewhat chilly at the end of November, I dressed in my outfit, thankful that it was lined with thick, but soft, light brown linen twill. The violin and flute musicians were the first to show up and practiced the melody to which I would walk away from maidenhood. Reverend Moses Williams rode up on his horse, Prince, with a heavy cloak over his preacher suit. Finally, I heard Charles' carriage pull into the stable.

My brother Isaac went out to get the boxes that my fiancé brought from the millinery in Ashland. I already had my suitcase packed for our two week honeymoon getaway to Salt Lake City, Utah. Charles was eager to show me the railroad that he knew so well. Our train trip would take about two or three days to get to Promontory Point, Utah, a special spot he wanted me to see.

"This point is the location that the east-west transcontinental railroad was finally joined together in 1869. Mr. Stanford drove the Golden Spike which connected the rails at that celebration," Charles said, remembering I knew the story of Mr. Stanford's illustrious life.

"That will be amazing to see. I am so looking forward to riding in a Pullman sleeping car of our own," I said with a slight blush. "And I will certainly relish being introduced to all your colleagues as Mrs. E.C. Kane," I said proudly.

"Well, hopefully we will have a Golden Spike celebration of our own in Ashland soon. The Oregon and Pacific Lines have just started building again. This time they say they are going to conquer the Siskiyous and take the tracks all the way into California. Won't that be something to celebrate as Mrs. Kane?" Charles said setting his eyes on our future. "And maybe we'll celebrate in our own way too," he added with a chuckle and an "ahem".

The wedding, on November 30th, was beautiful and perfect in every way. We ate and danced in my parent's revamped hay barn, heated by the cast iron stove they moved in for the celebration for that afternoon. Charles danced and twirled me effortlessly, as his leg had thankfully healed.

By the time we cut the wedding cake, I was so full that I could feel the whalebone stays start to constrict my breathing. I took the traditional bite of cake from Charles' hand, and he from mine, even though it was more food than I thought I could handle. But, my partaking in the symbolic commitment of providing for each other, showing our love, and caring for each other, was something I would have to swallow to express our togetherness.

Very soon after, I happily changed into my traveling dress and we said goodbye to all the well-wishers. Papa dropped us off at the U.S. Hotel in Jacksonville for our wedding night, so we could start fresh the next day on our honeymoon train. I never realized how much warmer a winter night could be sleeping with a man. I really didn't need the long white lace nightgown for very long.

~ ~ ~

6  Babies and Business, 1885-1888

It was a good thing that we started building our own home within six months of my arrival in Ashland. It was to be completed by early 1886 and not a moment too soon. Our first born arrived, exactly nine months after our honeymoon, in September 1885. Space was getting tighter in our little apartment with the addition of the carved wooden cradle Papa made for baby Alex and the clothesline of diapers crisscrossing the room.

After transitioning to our stately new home, on the corner of Third and Spring Streets, we became visible as one of the prestigious families in Ashland. I would stroll through town, pushing Alex in the navy blue silk canopied baby carriage, to visit his favorite new site, the Ashland Fire Department which opened in 1887.

"May he sit in your wagon again?" I would ask the volunteer on duty. "My son absolutely loves the Fire Laddie's bright red wagon with the hoses, ladders and shiny brass bell. Do you mind if he rings the bell?"

"Only once, Mrs. Kane. If the town hears more than a single ringing, it will call the whole brigade into action," he said with a pinched smile.

Most of the Railroad District homes were owned by employees of the railroad. Within a few blocks of our home, in either direction, there were homes of engineers, freight workers, conductors, and locomotive operators. Along with them came wives, children and stories from their old countries. I seemed to be one of the few who had actually been born in Oregon.

We had Irish, German, Hungarian, and Dutch immigrants bringing variety to shared recipes, clothing styles, and even cooking methods. Charles had to contend with all the complications that came from such a mixture of workers. He kept things running smoothly at the depot, but was frequently called away for business meetings and trainings as the railroad developed more.

In the winter, particular transportation problems presented themselves concerning the rails, once the railroad connected over the mountains into California in 1887. Our winters often get bitterly cold and an occasional snow storm can dump inches over the valley floor. More frequently, fog rolls in over Ashland like a blanket, tucking us snuggly in between the Cascade and Siskiyou Mountain ranges. The Siskiyou Mountains are over 7000 feet and snow regularly accumulates on them to seven feet on the tracks, and up to fourteen feet in the drifts.

The frisky brakemen, affectionately known as "Brakies", were to be given a raise upon the completion of the rails to Yreka, increasing their salary from $65 to $80/month. The conductor's salaries were also to be increased from $85 to $100/month. Even with such incentives, neither of these regular employees offered or made themselves available for extra duty shoveling during snow storms.

Charles had to hire additional crew to shovel and clear the tracks over the Siskiyou Pass. "I'm going to have to call in some extra boys from Medford. We had over eight inches last night," Charles would report. Lucky they don't have much farming to do this time of year."

"I guess they'll be glad for the work, then," I added.

"Yes, and with no complaints. I'll remind them the work will keep them in shape for spring tilling and timber harvesting," he said, in his most managerial voice.

"Even so, it is hard to find help willing to work in such harsh conditions," he continued. "The wages are slight, at 18 cents per hour, but after 6:00 pm they go up to 27 cents per hour. That sounds like a good incentive until they get out there with shovels. The men already working along the line are suffering and getting sick from exposure and not having enough to eat. Deliveries are dwindling due to the snow and Ashland storehouses are hardly keeping up with enough to feed the city. Now food supplies are being even more depleted from trying to feed all this extra help."

"Oh my, is there anything we town ladies can do? Would a collection of our canned green beans and peaches help?" I offered.

"Why, yes. That would be very nice of the Ashland ladies. Next time your Masonic O.E.S. Ladies Meeting gathers, you go on and stir them up Alice. Canned jars or fresh bread even, would be a great help. The railroad company would sure appreciate the aid, and I'm sure the men would as well."

"I'll send word to Mama in Jacksonville to ask her Eastern Star ladies as well. Mrs. McCall is headed that way tomorrow. She's off to tell Mama the news about her husband John becoming the new mayor of Ashland," I concluded.

"I heard at my last company meeting in Stockton that they're trying to develop a plow to attach to the front of the lead engine for pushing the snow off the tracks. Wouldn't that be a hoot?"

"And it will hopefully get the trains going again more quickly," I piped in while spooning mashed potatoes into the gaping maw of our two year old Alexander, his bright blue eyes wide open, anticipating the next bite.

Our investments in real estate were starting to pay off. I had become clever at managing money, and I suggested further investments around town. Charles and I would buy undeveloped lots and smaller portions of old donation land claims.

Our original purchase of half of Mr. Bennett Million's land claim brought us over a $6800 return on our original $3200 investment. Home sites the size of ours, were now selling for almost double than what we had paid.

Aside from enlarging our surrounding yard to include landscaped gardens and an elegant stable along the alleyway behind our home, we decorated the interior of our house with the latest wall coverings imported from San Francisco. I was known around town to be one of the most gracious hostesses of my time. I am sure that, in addition to Charles' position, was why we were picked to host the signing of the Golden Spike documents.

Well, after the hullabaloo of the Golden Spike Celebration, and nine months after our own celebration that very same night, Charles and I welcomed our second born in September 1888 - beautiful Ramona.

Ramona's grey eyes were striking, but most folks noticed her length first. "She's gonna be a tall one, just like her

Mama," people would say. At 5'8", I nearly met Charles eye to eye, only off by a couple of inches.

In our family portrait, Ramona's extra-long christening gown draped across the full width of my lap and Alex stood over three feet tall between me and Charles. We were lucky to have Mr. Peter Britt, a friend of Papa's from Jacksonville, offer to take photographs of our family. He was in Ashland to photograph the grand opening of the Ashland Depot Hotel, right after Ramona was born.

The Depot Hotel and Dining Station were built of wood, with a Victorian flare. At about 300 feet long, splendidly furnished throughout, the hotel had a gabled roof and dormer ends which sported elaborate spires. The two and a half stories were filled with long windows to overlook the mountains on both sides of the tracks. A single story kitchen wing was built on the south end of the Depot Hotel, to service the dining hall which accommodated the many guests just passing through with their thirty minute layover, or staying overnight at the hotel for their visit in Ashland.

It was reported that the Depot Hotel was *"the largest and finest depot station in Oregon on the Oregon & California line to Portland."* Outfitting and maintaining forty sleeping rooms, plus hiring dining room and kitchen staff, consistently provided employment to more than a dozen individuals and over twenty-one new families in town.

Brick, however, was used for the Roundhouse. Masonry was a sign of stability and permanency about which Ashland boasted proudly. The railway used this ten port semi-circular building for servicing and storing the SP locomotives. It was adjacent to an in-ground turntable which allowed trains to maneuver onto their proper tracks when needed. The outlay of monies for the land and construction brought over $65,000 worth of improvements to Ashland.

"Oh, Charles, do you think we could celebrate our fourth anniversary at the new Depot Hotel Dining Station this November?" I pleaded, after the dining hall was completed.

"Of course, my love," Charles replied. "I'll tell the chef a week ahead that we're coming. They will save the window seating next to the fireplace for us."

"That will be exquisite! I will ask Anna and EV Carter if they wouldn't mind watching the children during our evening out. Anna so loves reading to them from her books she brought from Colorado. She has quite a collection of children's stories," I proclaimed.

Anna and her husband, Earnest V. Carter, were a new couple like Charles and I, also married in 1884. They were slightly younger and closer to my age of 27, than Charles', who was just a little more than five years older than I.

The Carters built their house the same time as we did, however up the hill a bit more, by the main road heading south out of town. They chose the Queen Anne style as well, but with a more whimsical facade with sunbursts carved into the overhead window trim. Anna didn't have any children yet, so we both overindulged mine. Anna loved to read to them when I had other engagements. The Adventures of Huckleberry Finn had become Alexander's favorite. I'm hopeful his antics may not be as daring when he is a teen.

EV, as he liked to be called, often teased my Charles, whom he called EC. They constantly tried to outdo each other financially and in their real estate dealings. However, I think

Earnest had us beat, as he had just set up the Ashland Bank with his father and brother. We wives had more money than we needed for things, so we didn't see the point in their silly competition.

For our special fourth anniversary 'night out' in November, I once again unfolded my wedding suit from my hope chest, breathing in the smell of the remaining dried rose petals from my engagement bouquet and cedar wood of the chest Papa had carved. I now had more accessories to add to my original wedding ensemble, like my fox fur-lined gloves and a navy cashmere cape, for my fourth wedding anniversary outfit. Charles wore his wool brown tweed **cloak** over his three piece suit.

We walked arm in arm, down the two blocks to the depot, and entered from the crisp evening air into the golden glow of the coal oil lamps which hung in rows above the lines of tables set with white tablecloths and interestingly folded napkins.

As we passed the tables to be seated at our special spot, I noticed the napkin shapes varied from lilies to pleated fans. The silver was sparkling and reflected in the mirrors hung along the walls. We were seated in between the fifth and sixth pillars. Each pillar had floral baskets suspended from its crown molding, filled with fragrant flowers and dangling tendrils of long blossoms. Quite an unusual sight, especially in early winter.

"Charles, this is incredible! Where did they get these flowers this time of year?" I whispered, leaning across the table as we were seated.

"Remember, darling, this station is part of the railroad that now extends all the way to Southern California. We include these adornments as a necessary expense of running our depots all along the line. These particular bouquets are sent from San Diego. And, I hear the fried chicken is shipped here by the barrel-load from Roseburg," Charles recited proudly.

Even the chairs were unique. Not only were they attractively covered in tufted green velvet, but they had an added feature under the seat. A second level platform below the seat, for placing men's hats or women's purses, was incorporated into all eighty seats of the dining hall.

We arrived for the 8:00 pm dining service, available after the last train left the depot for the evening. This later seating, which catered more to locals and overnight guests, served meals at private individual tables. The earlier dining services were set up more as family-style meals. The servers for those meals would pass the food down the tables, set up in long rows, and everyone would help themselves from huge platters of food. The Depot Dining Hall served three family meals per day, with each meal costing 50 cents for all you could eat, with seatings based on the arrival times of trains.

The dining staff would take their breaks in the upper floor hotel lobby where they could spot the approaching trains through the tall bank of view windows and dash to have the tables set by the time passengers unloaded.

After our splendid three course anniversary dinner, Charles and I blissfully dawdled through town. Boughs of sweet smelling pine were already draped over shop entrance doors. The Masonic Lodge Hall was preparing a gala for the feast of John the Evangelist, to be held the weekend after Christmas. I was overjoyed that my parents would be coming to Ashland to join us for that celebration.

Papa always brought carved wooden toys for Alex. This year he was bringing a toy train and rocking horse for him to share with his new little sister. She was getting a wooden-handled rattle with tin bells inside.

However, the holidays were not the only changes in town. As more and more railroad workers and tradespeople moved into Ashland, the boon not only brought one story vernacular frame affordable houses for the worker's families in the Railroad District, but also lodging houses, saloons, stores, warehouses and restaurants forming a separate commercial area on the street adjacent to the tracks.

I cuddled closer to Charles, wrapping both of my arms around his elbow, as we passed the rowdier establishments on our way back home. Feeling protected by Charles' presence, I felt brave enough to take a peek in the saloon windows. I was dazzled by the dancing women I saw through the large plate glass panes of these pubs, with their twirling skirts and sparkly bodices revealing more undergarments and anatomy than should have been seen outside of a private boudoir. The gold painted name of the establishment barely occluded the view of any passer-by.

~ ~ ~

7  Family Life, 1888-1890

In the next couple of years, my attentions were drawn in many new directions. I was involved in primary school preparations for Alex and joined in gathering books and donations for the new library with Anna Carter. Together, we organized book socials, benefit concerts, and a business carnival. I became confident in other roles outside that of the Station Master's wife.

The Ganiard Opera House had a library benefit performance, "Mistic Midgets" which netted $56.45. The 'Business Men in Baseball' club contributed $100.00 from their coffers to buy library books. We even hosted an ice-cream social on the Plaza, which made $13.00 for our literary cause.

Because of these efforts, we were able to purchase books for the community library and for Alex's school. I even approached Mrs. Mabel Million to collect a donation directly from her, because I knew she had money after Charles and I bought half of her original donation land claim.

On alternating Saturdays, Anna and I would rotate manning the library room, a donated space from Mr. Anderson. We made sure to have either iced tea or hot tea for our patrons, filling the room with the scent of cinnamon or lemons, depending on the season. The sitting area was always filled with patrons reading at the tables, or mothers and youngsters resting on floor pillows, reviewing the latest donated or purchased books.

I would leave Alex and Ramona with Charles between 2:00 and 5:00pm., assured by him that my work day coincided with his weekend time off.

My Masonic ladies group, the Order of the Eastern Star, or O.E.S. for short, added an embroidery club to their meeting rotations. We scheduled meetings on my weekends off from the library, making my beautiful parlor available for the needlepoint gatherings so I could keep an eye on the children and still entertain and connect with the ladies of Ashland. We were assigned the making of curtains for the town hall and the library windows.

Charles, of course, didn't want to be anywhere near our home during these events filled with gaggles of garrulous women, so he busied himself at work. There was always an endless supply of paperwork for him to do and he would jump at the chance for out of town trainings on the weekends of my O.E.S. social affairs.

Once a month, on "picnic Sunday", our family was assured to all be together after church for a blanket-style lunch on the grass behind the Ashland Woolen Mill. Along the babbling creek, the children would splash and play while we shared stories of events in our lives that seemed to pass each other like trains in the night. The demands of the children, community and the ever expanding railroad seemed to distance Charles and me from our intimate beginnings. I had expected our romantic interludes to become somewhat less frequent as time chugged along, but was surprised by the unaffectionate gap growing between us.

I remembered how Mama had spent five years alone when Papa took to the Oregon Trail in search of gold to bring his family to a frontier paradise. *At least Charles and I were in the same town!* I decided to make plans for some time alone with my husband, in hopes of converging our life paths back on the same track.

"Oh, Cha-rles?" I tweeted in a sweet trill one night after settling the children into their beds. I walked into the parlor where he was reading the most current Ashland Tidings.

"Um-hmm," Charles responded without lifting his head from the folds of the newspaper.

"How would it be if we went on a vacation this upcoming summer? Just the two of us," I suggested. "I could arrange for my parents to take the children for a week or so. Ramona will be weaned by then and Mama would love to spoil her with delicious mashed concoctions she loves to create for baby food."

"That sounds nice," he numbly replied.

"I was thinking we could visit the San Francisco Bay Area. I've never been..." I was interrupted before I could finish my sentence.

"The Bay Area! No! Absolutely not!!!" Charles blurted out in an abrupt and louder than called for tone one would expect in a simple private discussion.

"What was THAT about?" I said as I sat down on the overstuffed couch next to his wing-backed chair. "It was just a suggestion, sweetheart. No need for such a reaction. What do you have against the San Francisco area anyway?"

Charles folded the paper into his lap and reached for my hands, surrounding them in his, as he looked into my eyes. "Oh nothing, dear. It's simply such a big town filled with unseemly characters and so congested. I spend so much of my training time there. I ....I would like to see more of our home state, if you wouldn't mind," he explained in a quick, albeit stuttering, calmer voice.

"Well, alright. You know best. I wouldn't mind going to the Oregon State Fair in Salem next August. They say the 1891 displays will highlight some of Southern Oregon's finest produce, especially our Rogue Valley peaches," I declared with growing enthusiasm.

"I hear they have a grove of White Oaks across from the fairgrounds for tent campers. But perhaps we could stay with your brother and his wife while we are there?" Charles proposed as an alternative. "Maybe Isaac could plan some time away from his work at the State Penitentiary and join us for some of the horse races at the State Fair's new track, with Dora and baby Laura as well, perhaps?"

"That sounds fun, but she's not such a baby anymore. We haven't seen our niece since that Christmas after Ramona was born, two years ago. She must be about eight by now," I proclaimed.

"Well, it's settled then. I'll start making arrangements and requests for our travel plans after the New Year when the work rotation schedules come through. I'll be the first to sign off for that week of the State Fair," Charles declared with a huge sigh, sounding relieved.

I was happy we made plans, but somewhat perplexed by the abrupt re-direction of our conversation away from San Francisco. *Was there something else going on?* No matter now, Charles and I were going on a vacation next summer, and I was determined to make it like a second honeymoon.

Winter hit hard in January. Snow knocked down telegraph wires and closed the train tracks both north and south. We had no mail, packages, deliveries, nor any shipments in or out, much less any travelers showing up for nearly a month. Even though the first "power-driven" snow plow, a pointed steel grate that attached to the lead train engine, finally arrived in Ashland that winter, Charles still had to coordinate extra help for clearing the track. The metal foot managed to push the snow ahead on the tracks, but the drifts would just fall back onto the tracks if the shovelers didn't level them away from the rails.

Finally, winter lost its grip to the warmer hand of spring, but the snow melt presented even more problems. Draining waters collected and overflowed in the creeks. Mixed with spring rains, flood waters caused great damage in town. Segments of the railroad bridge across Ashland Creek were taken completely out by high water. The rails were bent beyond use. The mills had to disconnect their water wheels when the creek currents started rising. The water would get too high and forceful for turning the wheels, especially when the current carried huge boulders in the river during such weather.

I kept the hearth fires going and filled our home with sweet piano serenades. I started teaching the children how to play little tunes for their Papa when he came home from a long day at the depot. I was glad we had screened in the back porch and added folding winter shutters over the walls of screens. I could hang our washing out of sight, yet still somewhat indoors. The heat from the kitchen filtered into this area as an extra indoor play space for the children and their friends.

Alexander now had a complete train set with wooden tracks and tunnels that Papa had carved. Charles occasionally spent time playing 'train master' with Alex, but more often than not, he choose to relax reading the newspaper rather than doing more of the same thing he did at work.

The new mayor in town, Mr. Grainger and his wife Kate, had just finished their grand house on Granite Street with double wrap around porches on each of the two levels of their Victorian home. They however, chose not to enclose either of their porches. I envied their double decker bay windows that mirrored the porches on the opposite side of the flower-bordered entry stairway. I told Charles that someday I would like to add a larger parlor room with a full floor-to-ceiling bay window facing the depot.

"Not now, dear. Our finances are spread amongst four mouths now and we must plan in our budget for such extravagances. A project such as that will require a withdrawal greater than our savings will allow presently," he explained rather dismissively.

The Railroad District kept growing, even if our house did not. The owners of the lodging houses and saloons were respectful of the residential community and set reasonable closing hours on the weeknights.

Occasionally though, on the weekends, stray disturbances often could be heard coming from the direction of the tracks. One Sunday, in the dark of night, around two o'clock a.m., a woman's scream startled us awake, "Murder!"

I gathered the blankets up around my throat and whispered nervously into Charles' ear, "What was THAT?"

"I don't know, dear. You stay here and I'll go investigate," Charles advised, as he pulled on his pants and overcoat over his knee-length nightshirt and grabbed his silver capped walking stick.

I was too worried by the hour and the screams coming from in front of our house to stay in bed, so I decided to don my robe and peek out from a slit between the front curtains. I curled up in in a ball on the padded bench under the center window of our front parlor bay window.

There on the street was a young woman, hatless and shoeless, roaming alone and not walking in a direct manner or toward any particular destination. I saw Charles approach the woman and she wrapped her arms around his neck, as if she was glad to see him. He pulled her hands down and took her by the elbow and started walking her towards the tracks.

When my husband returned after what felt like a long time, I was frantic. "What happened out there? Who *was* that woman?" I asked trying to keep my voice subdued so as not to wake the children.

"Just a crazy woman. She was disoriented and I could smell the liquor on her breath. She thought to scream for help, but all she could manage to yell was 'murder'. She was obviously lost, but did remember her room was at the Oregon Hotel. So I took her there."

"Why did she greet you so familiarly, like she knew you, throwing her arms around you? DO you know her?"

"No....not really. I....I've seen her around the depot and I know some of the lads that have spent time with her occasionally. Maybe she thought I was one of them," Charles explained a little reluctantly.

"Well then, what took you so long to return?"

Charles started to doff his coat and pants, managing to avoid my eyes as he continued. "I had to speak with the lobby manager and get a key to bring her to her room. When I took her upstairs, it took a quite a while to settle her down and make sure she stayed put," Charles added to avoid me casting aspersions.

"Well, this all sounds so absurd. Let's be off to bed, now," I shrugged with a "hmmph" and a flip of my hair towards my husband trailing behind me.

"Yes, let's," Charles readily agreed.

According to the Tidings report the next day, *"This woman wasn't ready to subside for the night. More disturbances were discovered the next morning. Church goers passing by the corner of Oak and Main Streets noticed the glass on one side of the entry door to Bolton's Drug and Jewelry Store was broken out. Concerned citizens called on Mr. Bolton to come down from his store's upstairs apartment and peruse his inventory for any missing items. Indeed, a bottle of morphine and a lot of cigars were taken."*

"Some of my jewelry merchandise left in the showcases has been mussed over, and a brooch pin, in for repair, has been taken," Mr. Bolton reported to the Tidings. "I assume the morphine was what they were really after."

A little later that day, the wandering woman was found and questioned. She admitted that the drug bottle had been taken for her. "That nice young man said he obtained it from a physician at my request. I had no idea he had stolen it from the drug store!"

The questioning continued, but the woman refused to relinquish the young man's identity. The investigators determined that she was a woman of the night, one of the 'fallen women' who come and go through town. She was told to gather her things and, "report to the sheriff post haste".

This woman knew that exposing her clientele would have hindered her future business. So, while her arrest warrant was being drawn up and about to be served, she left town on the next outgoing southbound train towards Yreka. It was said her family lived in Siskiyou County, California.

Not much further effort was put forth to bring this case to court, and it seemed several men in town, many of them acquaintances of Charles through the railroad, were much relieved she had gotten out of town without arrest or further interrogation.

~~~

8  Marriage and Money, 1891-1892

Our finances seemed to hit a plateau by the beginning of summer. I couldn't quite understand why, as Charles was still working and traveling just as much. For whatever reason, Charles took on some extra work to supplement his wages. He joined our friend EV Carter as an estate appraiser for the real estate in town that was being bought and sold and going through probate. Charles said it was a great financial backup plan.

"This is a good thing, darling," Charles told me after establishing his position with EV. "This will allow me to become aware of land parcels in transition before they are put on the market. We can make a tidy profit without much risk," he explained.

"That sounds all well and good. But dear, you don't know how to measure or record legal descriptions or the official terminology required for representing such parcels on formal documents," I warned gingerly.

"Don't worry. I'll have EV review things before they're presented to the judge." However, this was not always the case. EV had his own business to run and Charles had assured him he could handle the extra work unsupervised.

Regardless of Charles' due diligence, it was his EC Kane signature on deeds that eventually landed him in a lawsuit that went back to court three times. By the end of the second appeal, a final judgement was issued that the property title Charles tried to convey did not exhibit "an abstract, free from encumbrances and defects, from which the validity and marketable quality of the title may be ascertained or determined." A judgement was affirmed by trial against Mr. EC Kane for court costs and all disbursements already received. That was a big blow to our new financial 'back-up plan'.

Charles retreated into the woods for solace and occasionally for supper supplies. He and Clint Coleman would regularly go fishing on Wagner Creek, near Mr. Coleman's land parcel. I was grateful for the fresh catch to add to our dinner menu, until the day the story was bigger than the fish.

"You would not believe it Alice," Charles reported. "I didn't even hear it coming until Clint cautiously and calmly advised me to step back from the creek." I was just about to reel in my biggest salmon of the day when Clint said, "Drop your line and walk backwards towards me NOW, Charles. If you want to know why, slowly look up at what's coming down the hill across the creek."

"The next thing I heard was the crack of the shot from Clint's rifle that hit the animal square between the eyes. I'll be forever indebted to him for that. I tell you Alice, it was the biggest black bear I have ever seen around here. If I had to guess, it must have weighed a ton, more or less," Charles roared.

"Thank goodness he was ready and able to save you both, and, our dinner, I might add," I exclaimed, trying to make light of the danger. "Maybe you should stick to the railroad from now on, dear. I can put in extra beans in the garden this summer to supplement our meals."

Right before Charles and I left for our 'marital alone time' excursion north, at the end of summer 1891, another exciting event came to the Rogue Valley. The traveling circus came to town, and this time bigger and better because it came by train.

The Sells Brothers' Circus was set up to perform in Medford on some ten acres under red and white striped big topped tents. Posters were plastered all around the Valley for two weeks prior to their arrival. The regular entrance fee was 50 cents per adult and children under nine - 25 cents each.

The railroad company worked with the circus to draw more visitors for the event by offering "excursion rates" or discounts to rail passengers - one and one half fare for the round trip, with extra trains running between Ashland, Jacksonville, and Medford. There was even one running in the dark after the evening performance.

No one knew what to expect from the curiosities of the acrobatic troupes soaring dangerously through the air or walking on a wire higher up than a house roof, or from the strongman, clowns and other oddities that came with the circus entourage.

Everyone in town was also intrigued to see the unusual wildlife from faraway lands that accompanied the circus. It was hard to imagine the drawings of story book animals coming alive in our very own valley. The children, especially, were anxious to see a five continent menagerie with an elephant they could ride, plus see a roaring tiger jump through a ring of fire and zebras prance around the three ringed stages while ballerinas danced on their backs.

The circus had their own special train cars for the animals and equipment, which included a huge tropical aquarium, a train car sized aviary with exotic birds, and a hippodrome for the hippopotami. They parked their transport train a ways down from the exhibition site on a side track, so that the performers and animals could make a splendid entrance with a free street parade, whilst gathering more attendees.

Several thousand people attended the day performance, including Mama, Papa and Sarah from Jacksonville. Charles and I joined them with our children, in Medford, having arranged for the children to return with them to the Berry Family Farm after the show. We had more fun than we bargained for as we watched the parade of preparations precede the performers to their places.

The large tank, which held the big pair of hippopotami, got mired down in the mud in front of Doc Jones' place, about a half mile from the big-top tents. The animals had to be liberated before the vehicle transporting the tank could be extricated from the muck. With a slight semblance of freedom, the huge animals took complete advantage of the nearby water ditch for several moments to show off their natural talents. A pair of elephants was required to lift the tank from the mire after which the mud-coated hippos could return to their confine and continue rolling forward, finally finding their proper place at the exhibit grounds. Quite an unbargained for sight for free!

The Jacksonville paper summarized the whole event as follows: *"Those in charge of the circus affair were courteous and honorable, which is too frequently the exception to the rule. Another noticeable feature was the absence of the sure-*

thing gamblers and sneak thieves, who have often been the adjunct of the modern circus. The only serious complaint we heard since Sells Bros. left is that they took away a few thousand dollars of the cash so badly needed in the valley."

However, the Ashland Tidings had a different view on the circus extravaganza: *"The circus had a big crowd at Medford last Monday, and the people were roasted, boiled or broiled, according to their position in the big tent. The lemonade boys became millionaires, and the vendors of palm-leaf fans did a business that made them as autocratic as an unrivaled railroad corporation. The departing circus train went over the Siskiyous in three sections, and there were fourteen engines in the Ashland yard Monday evening, ready and waiting to haul the circus over the mountains."*

Charles and I continued directly from Medford, north to Salem for the Oregon State Fair that next weekend. Papa and Mama gave us a special handmade doll to give to their granddaughter Laura, Isaac's child now eight years old. Papa had carved the doll from white pine, sanded it smooth, and painted the legs, arms and head with delicate details. Mama attached a stuffed fabric body to fit. The doll's wardrobe of outfits could compete with my wedding trousseau.

Anna Carter had secured another dedicated soul to take care of my library duties while Charles and I had our romantic getaway. Miss Blanche Hicks was very enthusiastic in reviewing potential book donations and was also very well read. Her advice to new readers always seemed to hit the mark and peak their interest in returning for more good reads.

I took materials to read about the Oregon State Fair we were about to attend, while Charles chatted frequently with the conductor and others, who knew him as a familiar face on 'his' O & C line. I was content to occupy my time reading, although, I was truly looking forward to our night time in our private Pullman car, reminiscent of and hopeful that we could recreate our first train travel honeymoon experience.

I thoroughly read about the State Fair in Salem. It had been going for over twenty years, and recently expanded to its current size of 175 acres. The fair annually showcased new and inventive agricultural practices and held competitions for fruit growers statewide who entered their prize produce. Through the years, the fair has awarded ribbons for the best breeding livestock, hosted many food booths and offered a venue for statewide vendors to display their arts and crafts.

Charles and I wanted to be there specifically to watch and cheer at the horse racing events on the mile-long race track. There was a special concert with popular entertainers from back east on Saturday's docket. That also caught my eye.

When we arrived the next morning in Salem, Isaac was waiting for us at the train station with his carriage. We were given a tour of his town, with him showing us the new Salem Canning Company and Woolen Mill, located right next to the railroad tracks for ease of loading freight shipments. Isaac also showed off the domed State Capitol building, the Ladd and Bush two-story bank building with its carved granite Greek columns framing twelve foot glass double entry doors, and finally he drove us up to 'his' Oregon State Penitentiary.

My brother had just been promoted to the position of warden, after four years of serving in his prior capacity as assistant warden, where he gained invaluable experiences in the details of prison management. We were saluted and waved in by the guards as we passed under the arched entryway gate framed by the iron fence with tightly spaced vertical bars that surrounded the front of the prison.

"Wils," I said, using his familiar nickname which came from his middle name Wilson which was really Mama's maiden name, "are you sure it's alright for us to stay here with you and Dora and Dot? The sign over the arch says there are certain visiting hours and that visitors are not admitted on Sundays or holidays."

"Don't you worry little sis, I am the Warden now. I call the shots," Isaac answered. "We have set you and Charles up on the second floor of the front wing of the administration building where we live. Only employees occupy that area. We even have our own kitchen and dining room in the basement of this wing. So, you won't have to eat with the convicts," he said with a chuckle.

"I'm glad of that!" Charles spurted out, watching the fifteen foot tall iron gates latch together behind us, as our carriage headed towards the administration building's front stairs to drop us off.

I had the overall feeling that we were guests in a medieval castle or fortress. From the front view you could see the peak of the octagonal clock tower peering over the crenellations of the roof edges on all the buildings, their scalloped tops reminding me of the crown of a castle chess piece.

As the servants gathered our bags, Isaac took us on a short tour of the employee area. From the side of the front lawn we could see the iron fence, with gold tipped points atop every bar looking like a warrior's spear, connected to a similar height brick wall which enclosed the entire prison yard behind the front administration wing.

"You cannot really see from here, and I am definitely not taking you on an inside tour, so I'll tell you about the layout of the rest of the grounds. I'm sure you'll feel totally at ease once you understand how we're set up here," Isaac reassured us. "We have seven sentinel watch towers in the corners of our compound, connected together by an elevated guard promenade surrounding the entire stockade. The inmates are housed in the side wings, off of the central tower. Those buildings have tiers of cells, with tall arched windows covered by iron grates running floor to ceiling."

"My, that sounds quite secure and organized," I agreed, trying to compliment his complex.

"How do you keep those fellows occupied during the day?" Charles inquired. "Do they ever give you any trouble?"

"Oh, they try. But they don't get very far," Isaac bragged. "We have a creek that runs through the center of the prison yard and that powers a large water wheel keeping a turbine going in our engine room. That turbine generates electricity to the prison for our security locks. With the push of a button, iron bars are lowered across the doors of each cell until I can get around to padlocking all latches shut at night. It's like having a second set of hands at every station whenever I need to lock things down quickly, for whatever reason."

"Oh my. I don't think I want to hear about those reasons," I declared.

"It's never that bad, Alice," Isaac pointed out. "I always have lots of help around. I don't worry about the really bad inmates. They usually rotate in and out of the dungeon once. After a couple of days down there, they seem to become model prisoners," he winked.

"And, to answer your question Charles," Isaac continued, "we keep our inmates busy by using the prisoners for labor in our commercial activities. They are the ones who made the bricks which helped build our new laundry facility. We also have workshops in which the inmates can learn new skills in either our iron stove foundry, harness factory or the farm and gardens. We grow the food for the prison and even some excess to send to other state institutions."

"So Wils, your seventeen years of working the land, before you got appointed by the governor, are coming in handy I assume?" I teased my brother endlessly about his never wanting to follow in Papa's farming footsteps.

"Very funny, Alice, but quite true," Isaac retorted. Just at that moment, we heard our names being called in a squeaky scream, and turned back towards the entryway to see little Dot running in our direction.

"Auntie Alice! Uncle Charles!" A voice carried across the breeze, as we saw our niece floating with it, her arms waving like a windmill.

"My, my, look at how you've grown! Is that really my little Dot?" I chided my niece.

"Yes it is, Auntie Alice. It is really me," Laura asserted.

"Well, hello there big girl," Charles said to Dot.

Curtsying and pulling the sides of her skirt as wide as the fabric would allow, Laura said, "Good morning to you too, Uncle Charles."

"We have brought a special gift from Grandmother and Grandfather Berry, all the way from Jacksonville," I told her. "But first, would you kindly show us to our room, Miss Berry?"

"Right this way, if you please," Laura instructed, as if she were the matron of the house.

After a few days of reminiscing, playing cards, and catching up on family news, Charles and I accompanied the 'ladies' of the house for sightseeing in downtown Salem. Along the way, my sister-in-law Dora explained some of the local political happenings in town as we rode past some of the tallest buildings I'd ever seen.

"The Salem-ites lost interest in securing an Indian School in town a few years ago. But, I've recently heard that one has just been built in nearby Forest Grove. Our US Senator from Oregon has finally agreed to let Pacific University build one, on 60 acres of donated land, as an Indian Training School overseen by the Commissioner of Indian Affairs. Finally, those poor folks can get a proper education," Dora huffed.

"At least they have an option for education around here. Most of the Indians from our region have been deported to reservations without that kind of academic option. In fact, you probably don't know that my brother fought in the Rogue Indian War many years ago. He hates to speak of it," I murmured to Dora.

"Oh, he did mention a little something about that. I believe he said it was five years before we were married when he served. All he would say was that the conflict had to be settled and the only way to be assured of peace was to relocate the natives," Dora admitted with mild contentment in Isaac's summary. I didn't want to stir up any uncomfortable feelings or further discussion on the point, so we carried on with our ride through town, just enjoying the mild summer breeze in the beautiful landscaped neighborhood gardens.

Charles asked Dora if she wouldn't mind heading our carriage toward the Salem Train Depot. Charles wanted to show us around and introduce us to the folks he knew at this big city station. Our route took us past the Marion County Courthouse on the way to the railyard. The courthouse had four tiers which were accentuated with ornately carved marble trim and columns, so as to make the building look like a wedding cake. The clock tower topped the structure, looking like a decorative bride and groom adornment. I took in the sights with awe and wonder. For a small town farm girl like me, it expanded my world and stimulated my yearning for more travel. I would have to remember to ask Charles to take me with him on occasion, when he went for his out of town trainings.

Finally, on Saturday, when Isaac had his assistant warden take over the reins, we were able to all be together for the whole day at the State Fair.

"This is even more enormous in person!" I commented. "I have never seen such a gathering of people. Look at all the animals, and woodworking, and quilts blowing in the sunshine. This is better than the circus!"

"I am looking at all the food booths," Charles replied, licking his lips.

"May I go on the pony rides, Mama?" Laura begged, while tugging on her mother's skirt.

"Let's get some fruit at the stands over there," I suggested. "Then we can all go over to the horse racetrack while you have your own pony ride, Dot."

Dora nodded, giving Dot the okay. We walked and gawked at the different displays of produce. There was a pagoda-style building, with curled up roof ends, made entirely of fruit. It appeared to utilize different types of fruit for its roof 'shakes' and other elongated fruits for its architectural wall features. It was surrounded by a short white picket fence and had a sign proclaiming "Progress" on it. "Progress?" I asked my brother, perplexed.

"You should see the new tools and techniques that are being used in farming these days. The yields of produce are astronomical compared to when Papa started," Isaac explained. "That's progress!'

"Well, let's take that progress to the track. I'm betting I can double my purse just as easily," Charles said, nudging Isaac in the ribs. I worried about Charles' carefree money attitude so soon after our recent 'back-up plan' debacle.

On Sunday morning, we all went to the prison chapel in the administration building. A cabinet in the rear of the chapel contained many curious specimens of handiwork by the convicts - picture frames, miniature bedroom sets, wood carvings, etc. Some pieces must have taken weeks of hard work to make. Isaac said these talented inmates could bring in money from the sale of their creations, ranging from one to three dollars per item. I bought a carved cross for our home.

When services were over, I asked my brother if the prisoners used this chapel or if there was a separate one particularly assigned to them.

"Oh, this is our only chapel. It is used by the entire compound," Isaac clarified. "We do, however, have to set different schedules for each of the Faith's incarcerated here."

"What types do you have?" Charles piped in. "I have to deal with a mixture of Chinese and Irish in my position. Everyone seems to have a different way of doing the same thing."

"Well here, divided amongst our 243 convicts in the Pen, we have 206 whites who vary between Christian faiths of Protestant, Methodist, and Catholic. They pretty much get just thrown together for a generalized Christian service. But we also have twenty-seven Chinese who require special bowls for burning holy leaves and herbs in their service. Then there's the eight Indians, who have their own rituals and burning sage plants for their spiritual cleansing. We just figure the remaining two Negros do their own praying in their cells," Isaac rattled off his management statistics as if he was reading a menu.

"That's awfully kind of you to accommodate everyone here for their own prayer times," I said, complimenting his prison management before we left. I loved seeing my brother's compassion come through in this difficult line of work.

"Is it possible to get a good cup of coffee before we head out to the train station this morning?" Charles asked.

"Sure thing," Isaac replied. "I can offer you the strong stuff I drink made from real coffee beans, or you can have the lightweight stuff we give the prisoners made from toasted crusts of bread and roasted chicory root."

"How about one of each? That way Charles and I can try a little of both," I answered diplomatically. We thanked everyone for our stay in the prison, happy to have been on the right side of the pointed-bar fence.

I was also glad to have had alone time with Charles. We renewed our physical connection as husband and wife, although Charles had a faraway look in his eyes as he stared out of the train car window. I tried to reel him into my world as we rocked along the rails on our way home, trying to spark tidbits of conversation. However, his head repeatedly returned to lean towards the window after responding to the subjects I broached.

I eventually settled into the rhythm of the train and our lives on this ride home, nuzzling into the crook of my Station Master's arms. I entwined our bodies as much as was properly acceptable in public, hoping his distraction was just from being tired.

~ ~ ~

9  Ashland Town, 1892-1895

As 1892 rolled in, Charles and I were often found together in our parlor discussing, which sometimes elevated to debating, how to bring more commerce into Ashland. The railroad superintendent always looked favorably upon managers that marketed and boosted usage of their transportation lines. Our town was becoming more beautifully sculpted with the addition of a new park downtown, and Ashland garnered the nickname of the "hometown" of Southern Oregon.

One of the original pioneers, Abel Helman, had his Chinese cook plant a new tree, called the Tree of Heaven, at the entrance to the new park behind the Ashland Woolen Mill. The name Lithia Park was chosen because of the lithium water bubbling up in the mineral springs around Ashland. Lithia Park occupied eight acres, in a combination of an open grassy meadow leading up to treed canyon slopes wild with native plantings like ponderosa pine, California black and Oregon white oaks, manzanitas and madrones.

The Southern Oregon Chautauqua Association finally created their performance venue on the hill above Ashland Creek. They built a beehive dome building as a place where traveling entertainment and culture could come perform in Southern Oregon. Ashland's easy train access, established hotels and restaurants provided the city with a major advantage over its competitors in securing these mobile productions. Tents could be rented near Chautauqua Park, and horses could be boarded at neighboring livery stables. People attended classes in the morning and watched various forms of entertainment in the evenings, such as theatre productions, music performances, and discussions on topics ranging from American foreign policy to the benefits of temperance of alcohol usage.

"The Women's Christian Temperance Union, or WCTU as they prefer, is at it again," Charles would announce at dinner, exasperated by their growing national plight.

"Oh dear, you should not be so hard on them. It would not be particularly unpleasant to limit the flow of alcohol in our community," I disputed. "Such reform could be connected with solving other social problems in our society. Just think how much more money families would have for food or education."

"Oh, please, Alice," Charles whined. "Men need a little escape from family life every now and then. A drink is not going to break the family budget."

"Well it certainly could if you only have seasonal or inconsistent employment!" I countered. "And, if the saloons and pubs - which, might I remind you don't allow women - shut down, then an alternate more public location would be required for our local political meetings which are currently held in those establishments. Maybe the female opinion should be considered in some matters in town," I huffed.

"Now don't tell me you're starting to agree with women's suffrage!" Charles replied, a little too loudly.

"Surely it wouldn't be such a bad thing. I will be attending the Chautauqua presentation of the WCTU when they come through Ashland. I'll let you know my opinion about women voters after that," I said as I picked up my knitting. Charles was inflexible when it came to hearing my side, especially if he had already made up his mind on the topic. Continuing such conversations tended to split us further apart, so I often left the room.

Regardless of the events held in Lithia Park, the increased success of this Chautauqua organization led to more beautification of the park grounds. Flower beds were tended by the local women's groups like my OES Ashland Alpha Chapter. I would even pull Anna Carter away from her library duties on occasion to partake in 'digging in the dirt', with me and the children, at Lithia Park.

I made new friends as our town and our children grew. Anna introduced me to Mrs. Sarah Ganiard, who worked with her at the library, and to Sarah's niece, Charlotte Pelton. I was especially happy to meet Charlotte, another mother with children. Charlotte's husband John, was just elected as the new sheriff in town in 1892, a big step up from running his meat business. He and Charles were already acquaintances, having met through interactions of the Station Master coordinating with the meat freight shipments the railroad provided for John.

Charlotte's parents, Mr. and Mrs. Oscar Ganiard, were already well known in town. In 1889, they built their own Opera House. It was said to be the finest opera house between San Francisco and Portland. Charles and I had attended a few events there ourselves. The Ganiard Opera House was home to a variety of entertainment, not only operas, but plays and certain community events like graduations, as well.

At dinner, I tried to keep Charles updated on the news around town. His work kept him focused on business from out of town mostly, and how it would help or impact Ashland. In addition, with his frequent traveling for business, he often missed the subtle changes in our neighborhood.

"Oh, Charles? Did you hear Charlotte and John Pelton are building their new house just a couple of blocks down from us on Spring Street?" I asked.

"That's great, dear," Charles answered inattentively, picking up his next forkful of meatloaf.

"I would think so. They have children of similar ages to ours, so being closer will make for easier gatherings and playtimes. Ramona and their daughter Mabel are becoming fast friends. The boys are even thinking about using one of the empty lots between our houses as a baseball field. Perhaps you and John could join them in a game sometime?" I said, trying to engage Charles with the family more.

"Oh, maybe. I have to go down to San Francisco again for another meeting next week. I'll be gone for almost five days. But, possibly upon my return I'll be able to make some time for a game. I'll talk to Alex about it before I leave," Charles responded as he got up from the table.

He left the dining room to retire to the parlor. I joined him after cleaning up the kitchen, to continue our conversation. Charles was reading the paper when I entered, but stopped to light his pipe when I walked in. He took a deep draw on his pipe and filled the parlor air between us with vanilla scented smoke.

"Why do you have to leave so often? Doesn't the railroad realize you are a family man? Your mind seems so far away sometimes, even when you are home. How important are these trainings to distract you so? Maybe I could go with you this time. I like traveling," I implored him.

"Oh no, Alice! That would be highly improper," Charles reacted, somewhat irritated. "These are important railroad matters involving the new developments with the telegraph. I have to be top notch and focused when it comes to communication. It is a matter of safety and security for everyone. Why don't you take the children and visit your family in Jacksonville while I'm away for these extended trips?" Charles suggested.

"Maybe I will. It gets rather lonely here without someone to talk with at night," I agreed. "Good idea. When are the dates you are out of town next?"

"I'll write them down for you. Would you like me to arrange the train connections for you from my office?" Charles asked helpfully.

"Thank you dear. That would be most helpful," I concluded. However, I still was miffed that the railroad was using the very tracks that employed him to distance my husband from me, time and time again.

Some of my solitude was gladly interrupted when my sister-in-law Dora and niece Dot came down to visit in the summer of 1893 for a while. Dora confided in me that her husband was often distracted by his work and dealings at the State level for Penitentiary business. I understood, but it didn't make me feel better about Charles being absent so much.

I was relieved when Dora left, not for her visit being in any way difficult, but rather I was glad she missed the outbreak of scarlet fever. I crossed paths with Anna at the Ashland Flour Mill, which was about the only place, besides the dairy, that I ventured during the epidemic.

"Keep the children home, Alice," Anna warned. "I have had to destroy some books that were exposed to the dangers of infection when they were returned from certain contaminated households."

"Goodness! Have you heard when things might clear up?" I asked.

"Doc Jones says if the sick stay home, the danger of transmission should subside within the week. I've been catching up on a lot of my reading, staying inside my house," Anna said with a sullen pout.

"My children are bored stiff and I'm trying to keep them busy by utilizing their help baking pies and canning peaches. Alex says he'd rather play solitaire, but to call for him when the pies are ready to eat," I sighed, with a smirk.

"Earnest has had to close the bank," Anna added. "He cannot take a chance on knowing if contaminated hands touched the paper notes and metal coins. Who knows which currency was exposed?"

"Yes, I agree. The Mill is taking credit during this sick time. They don't want to handle money either. Charles said the trains are just for freight this week. No passenger trains are coming or going anywhere. I guess that's for the best to help contain this outbreak," I responded.

"You stay well now. See you on the bright side soon!" Anna waved as she hurried home.

During the fall of that year, in 1893, Ashland faced another town trouble, the burgeoning coyote population. Backyard chickens, clutches of eggs and small pet dogs were disappearing quite often. Sheriff Pelton put up a reward for coyote pelts brought to his jail house. Then, he gave the pelts to my OES Alpha Chapter to make into hats and gloves. We, in turn, sold them to replace the library books that had been burned during the summer's scarlet fever epidemic.

"Otto Williams just brought in four coyote skins this week," Sheriff John told me when I brought Ramona to his house to play with Mabel. "I've been saving them for your group, Alice. He also snared several squirrel scalps that he threw in for free, for you ladies to use. The city coffers paid him $20 dollars and we're all very happy for his services."

"Thank you so very much, John," I replied overjoyed. "Those skins will go a long way toward replenishing our library shelves. I believe we will turn a tidy profit with our handiwork and your donation. That twenty dollars will become closer to fifty, I'm sure!"

Other events of 1893 were more nationwide. Our very own Mr. Max Pracht's orchard was producing the "Ashland Peach", which won a premium at the 1893 Chicago World's Fair. Fruit was shipped in thousands of boxes by the railroad. Charles declared one late summer day, "Yesterday noon, we had to use six engines to haul a load of peaches over the Siskiyous."

However, Charles faced more pressing matters when the national Pullman Strike started in May of 1894. It was a direct result of the National Panic of 1893, which continued into 1894, and spread from the east coast to the west. Folks were pulling their money out of the banks, attempting to redeem their silver certificates for gold. When the actual gold reserves ran out, their paper money was devalued and became almost worthless. Many banks failed, thankfully not EV Carter's. All this panic was followed by an economic depression in business, and a rise in unemployment and prices. The nationwide Railcar Worker Strike, basically put the nail in the coffin of the US economy for months.

"With those workers on the Pullman cars joining their national union members in the strike, we can't move any passenger trains through Ashland. Their boycott has effectively tied up 50,000 miles of rails across this great nation," Charles said, as he described his work scene with annoyance.

"Maybe a compromise will be reached soon. This won't affect your job, will it Charles?" I prayed.

"Not too much. Thank goodness we've such a strong freight business in Ashland," he answered confidently.

When things started to smooth out the next year, the railroad had to implement changes to perk up business. They began offering round trip fares at reduced rates in 1895.

"Well, you'll finally get to hear those Temperance Women, Alice," Charles announced one evening after dinner, when the children were in bed. "The railroad is giving reduced rates to all their county delegates for their first WCTU convention held here in Southern Oregon."

"That's swell. When is this set to happen?" I asked enthusiastically.

"Sometime mid-May, I've heard. Town should be bustling with loads of ladies extolling the virtues of abstinence by then," Charles said, rather sarcastically and disappointed.

"I can't wait," I countered.

"I can't either," he said in a cynical tone. "Maybe I'll be out of town around then," Charles replied, hopeful to be able to schedule an escape.

Another change the railroad decided to make to boost business, was to get into the real estate business to offer accommodations to those travelers that preferred a more homey-type atmosphere than the grand Ashland Depot Hotel. So, in Ashland, Southern Pacific Railroad purchased two lots and built a lodging house directly across the street from our home.

I wasn't usually opposed to such structures, however, this one cut my view of the eastward mountains by being smack dab in front of my parlor window. I could see straight across to the second floor hallway and all the comings and goings from each of the eight narrow rooms for rent, each of which peeled off the main hallway like little spider legs. I especially didn't like the resident manager who preferred to smoke his stinky cigar out in front, just as the occasional winds would pick up and sweep the fumes across Spring Street to be trapped on my entry porch.

One day in early May, I decided to avoid these lingering vapors and bring Charles his lunch as a surprise. Upon arriving at the Depot, I found out that my husband had been called to a meeting in Medford and wouldn't be returning until his shift ended that evening.

"Oh, but Mrs. Kane, the mail train just pulled in. I usually give Mr. Kane your mail, but since you're here, would you mind taking it home? I'd hate for anything to get lost this evening in the piles of paperwork on the Station Master's desk," the postal freight worker explained.

"Certainly, Angus. Not a problem," I said, as I placed the stack of letters and the Oregonian newspaper from Portland in my basket.

Barely making it through the depot swinging doors before the tricky wind once again swept across my path, one of the letters flew out of my basket. Retrieving it, I noticed the return address. It was a stiffer envelope from San Francisco and the sender's name and cursive writing was definitely female. It wasn't on company letterhead stationary, nor was it a name I recognized from the numerous acquaintances Charles had mentioned from his many trips to the San Francisco Bay area.

Intrigued, I sat on the depot platform bench, and opened the letter addressed to Mr. Ellsworth Kane, thinking it could be important family news from a long-lost distant relative who used his proper first name, since he has never used it as an adult, especially in Ashland. The closest he got was E.C., or E. Charles, but never Ellsworth.

Inside, was a handwritten letter, as well as a cardboard framed oval photograph. The sepia-toned picture was definitely taken at a professional studio, with their silver insignia imprinted on a slant across the bottom right corner. I was glad I was seated, as I thought I would faint when I focused on the subjects in the photograph.

There, seated in the center, was a woman much younger than I, perhaps about twenty-five or twenty-six years old, with a boy about five years old, standing by her side. Behind her chair, and slightly to the right, stood my Charles with his one hand resting on her shoulder and the other cupping the upper arm of the little boy. I gasped for air as I realized the features of the young boy identically matched those of Charles'. They both had the same dark wavy hair, with a slight dimple in their cheeks when they smiled. That child's dark eyes stared defiantly at me, betraying my husband's secret.

At that point, I forced myself to read the letter, hoping for a simple explanation of who these relatives were. There was none. It cut through me like a knife as I read:

Dear Ellsworth,

I was so happy to see you last month, and for five whole days! I know the railroad keeps you so busy that you are away from home more than you are here. Young Clarence misses his father so much. I tell him how important you are to the railroad, so he doesn't complain too much when you are gone. Thank you for the lovely red roses for my birthday - they arrived fresh on the train and were delivered directly by your colleague to the house here.

I know you keep saying we can't get married until your promotion brings you permanently to San Francisco, but I am getting more uncomfortable pretending we are married, especially as Clarence gets bigger, and with his different last name than mine. He'll be starting school this fall and I would like to be back closer to my parents in Stockton. There, no one will know the particulars of my family life since I will be arriving with a child, rather than single and pregnant. I will change my name to Kane, matching Clarence's, when I register him with the schools, and we can start fresh. Please try for a promotion or transfer to the San Joaquin Railway, as its main hub is in Stockton. Maybe it would be easier to secure a post there, rather than the highly sought after positions in San Francisco.

You often say we can't marry until we live in the same town. What a silly regulation your company has! I've never demanded your time as they say a long distance marriage would require. Why haven't you moved us up to Oregon? Please darling, consider our lives as much as your career. We need you. We will be at my parent's house in Stockton in the fall. But, I am sure I'll see you here before then! 'Till next time, my love.

Always affectionately yours,

Amy

PS. I am enclosing a copy of our family portrait that we had taken the last time you were here. I'm glad we finally have one.

Oh, MY GOD!!! I can't believe this! I was shouting inside. *This isn't happening. This can't be real. How could I not see this? I should've believed my sister Sarah when she said years ago that she saw Charles womanizing. He's probably had other women here, like that one running through the streets screaming "Murder!" She seemed to know Charles too well for being the stranger he described. That rascal!* I thought, as I reviewed every suspicious moment in our marriage that I had brushed off as inconceivable.

No wonder he seemed somewhere far off when we were together. I bet he couldn't keep his tales straight between the two families. Silence was easier. When we did have conversations, especially of late, he tended to contrast and dispute my opinion. I bet his "other wife" is much more complacent, I speculated as I recounted and rationalized recent events.

My mind kept spinning to connect the inconsistencies over the past few years that now were starting to make sense. *Of course that is why he had to take on the extra work as an appraiser with Earnest Carter. He had two households to support!*

"No wonder we couldn't afford to build that grand parlor I always wanted. This made no sense at all. How could he do this to me, to Alex, to Ramona? He is even lying to this other woman, too!" I screamed, brokenhearted and unaware my ruminations were now verbalized. Angus, the postal clerk, came running outside when he heard me yelling.

"Is...is everything alright, Mrs. Kane?" he asked hesitantly.

"No, nothing is alright, Angus," I blubbered. I tried to catch my breath and composure long enough to excuse myself. Anger was boiling under my self-control.

"I will be fine, in a while. I just need to go home now. Please tell Mr. Kane to come directly home when he arrives. I have a surprise for him," I finished, cackling like a wicked witch about to eat her prey.

~~~

10  Deceit and Divorce, 1895

Charles walked in with a big smile, not only expecting dinner but also the big surprise Angus must have mentioned. The children greeted him as usual with hugs, albeit Ramona's arms just reached up to the bottom of his waistcoat since she was only six. I had gathered my wits and plowed through the rest of the afternoon, even devastated as I was by uncovering the grandest lie of my married life. I had arranged for the children to spend the night at the Pelton's, so that Charles and I could discuss this issue unfettered.

"Mother is letting us sleep at Mabel's house," Ramona joyously announced. "Mabel has her own room. I will get to share a room with someone else other than my brother!"

"That sounds exciting, Ramona. I'm sure everyone will have a special night," Charles said with a wink in my direction. I am sure he assumed the reason for our change of routine had something to do with love making. I could see the anticipation in his smile.

After dinner, Charles walked the children down the street to their friend's house, while I cleared up the dinner dishes and lit the parlor fireplace. Once I had the flames roaring, I set the photograph of Amy, Clarence and "Ellsworth" on the marble mantle. Earlier, I had packed all of Charles' clothes, except for his three piece suit, in his valise. I set it down next to his favorite parlor chair. I settled into the tufted couch with a warm cup of mint tea. The escaping steam gave a freshness to the parlor that was calming. I needed the scene to be as relaxed as possible for me to speak my piece.

"I'm ba-aack," Charles trilled with optimism.

"In here, dear," I responded. Charles was peeling off his overcoat as he entered the parlor. He hung up his hat and coat on the brass coat rack in the corner, then turned to the whiskey cart and poured himself a drink. As he passed by the fireplace, tiptoeing towards his chair, his eyes caught sight of the photograph on the mantle. His shot glass dropped from his hand onto the marble hearth, shattering into sharp pieces and splashing the golden brown liquid all over his polished work shoes.

"That's about the same reaction I would have had when I saw that photograph, if I had had a drink in my hands," I sneered. "But alas, I just collapsed on the bench in front of the Depot entry doors when it fell from my hands, after picking up the mail.

"Where did you get that?" Charles demanded.

"Oh, that's right. You haven't seen this in print yet. Your ..."other... wife"... was so excited for you to have it!" I spit my words out one at a time.

"What? Who? What are you talking about Alice?" he asked with a furrowed brow, trying to act all confused and innocent.

"Really? That is how you want to play this?" I laughed. "Well let me tell you how this is actually going to go. I want to remain civil about this, although I would really like to go get the shotgun right now and show you how I really feel. But, since I was raised to be a polite lady, I have courteously packed your things and expect you to leave this house tonight and never come back," I hissed, pointing to the valise by the winged back chair.

"I will be filing for divorce tomorrow with an attorney, Mr. Wm. Colvig. You remember him, don't you? He was your attorney in that land title case we had to pay off because you jumped into a job with no business knowledge and made such inexperienced decisions. I guess your need to maintain two households was what really necessitated our financial 'back-up plan'.

"I'm sure Mr. Colvig will understand our irreconcilable differences as I explain them, and knowing us will make it easier. I have left your three piece suit here, so that you appear properly attired when you return for our divorce court hearing," I concluded, with more resolve than I ever had.

"But, Alice," Charles began to beg. "Can't we talk about this first?"

"I'm not sure how you think you can sweet talk your way out of this one, Mr. E.C. Kane," I replied, disgusted. "These are the facts, as I see them:

1) You've been with another woman for years.

2) She has had your child.

3) You maintain another life in another city and frequently return there to keep that facade of a family continuing.

4) You leave me and the children here alone with no regard for our hardship while you are repeatedly gone, gallivanting around with your other family.

5) You are lying to everyone you know.

There, did I leave anything else out that you wanted to "talk about"?

"Yes... I love you, Alice," Charles pathetically added.

"Well, I'll remember to use that tidbit when I tell the children you had to leave. I suggest you wire Mr. Koehler tomorrow with your request for reassignment, and find a room for tonight at the Depot Hotel," I said with finality.

I couldn't resist spitting out my opinion, so I continued. "Oh, and by the way, I think you are the lowest of scoundrels and should live the rest of your life in agony. I mostly feel sorry for our children. I will tell them, as well as our friends, that you have been transferred to a position in San Francisco. You can embellish that story with any supplementary details you choose to conjure. You have proved to be good at that."

"I'm so sorry this happened, Alice. I wish I was never sent to those meetings in Oakland and San Francisco. I didn't intend to meet anyone or for anything like this to occur. It just did. Please accept my apologies, Alice," Charles said, looking forlorn and regretful.

"If it wasn't in the Bay Area, it would have happened somewhere else along the railway line. It is YOU, Charles, that made the choice. It didn't happen TO you because you were the Station Master," I clearly said. "I'm just upset that I didn't realize what kind a man you were before we married and brought children into this world. It is they who will suffer the most when they finally understand how weak, dishonest and disloyal their father really was."

Charles opened his mouth to say something else and I put my hand up in front of his face to stop any more lies from spewing. "No. No more. There is nothing more to say. Please do me the final courtesy of respecting my wishes and leave tonight. However, I am requesting one last thing. Please leave a forwarding address with Mr. Colvig, if it is different than the one on the letter that arrived today, if you don't want your "other wife" to find out about me the way I found out about her. My lawyer will be in contact with you. Now GO! Get out of here before I lose my dinner from the churning disgust of being around such **vermin** as yourself."

Charles removed his pocket handkerchief to wipe off his shoes, and then picked up his bag to leave. His long face made him look pitiful and meager. I **closed** the door behind him, with a louder than necessary slam, to make my final point clearly understood and irrevocable. I flipped the metal door latch with a **clink**, sounding like a jail cell, sealing out riffraff.

The following day, with the children off at school, I took the train to Medford to enlist the services of Mr. Colvig. I scheduled my trip around Charles' freight schedule, knowing when he would not be at the Depot. My train traveled through a lead-colored veil of chilling spring mist, which shrouded the upper valley. The weather seemed to match my mood.

When I arrived in Medford, the sky opened up and a soft light peeked through a patch of blue, as I stepped off the train. I took this as a sign that I was making the right decision, walking into a brighter life. Mr. Colvig, a well-respected attorney, was sincerely interested in my circumstances.

"I'm sorry to hear about your troubles, Mrs. Kane," Mr. Colvig said. "However, if you have truly made your final decision in this matter, there are some things we will need to sort out."

"I told Charles, um, Mr. Kane that he had to leave our house and the Ashland Depot. There is no way I can continue with him around, knowing what I now know," I said mortified.

"That's all well and good, Mrs. Kane, and I'm sure Mr. Kane will respect your wishes, considering how this situation developed. But there is the matter of your welfare, as well as the custody and welfare of your children. Do you have any means of support other than your husband?" he inquired.

"Well, not a regular income, per se. We do have some savings from investments. I suppose I could get some sort of job now that both the children are in school. But won't Charles have to pay alimony and money for the children's lives?"

"Well, yes and no. If he loses his job, then no. If you get remarried, then no. Other than that, the court should mandate that he pay something. That of course, will be decided in a couple of months by the judge. Will you be alright financially until the court hearing? I often suggest the transfer of some assets and a shift of a substantial portion of savings into the wife's name, solely, if it is obvious that the children will remain with her. I advise that Mr. Kane and you do this before he leaves town.

"Thank you for the recommendation. Once the paperwork is done, the harder part will be explaining this situation to my six and nine year olds, especially without falling to pieces or painting a big lie."

"I find that keeping it simple is best. Perhaps, stretching the truth a bit would be easier. Does Mr. Kane travel often?" he asked.

"Oh, yes. That's what got him into this mess." I grunted.

"Does Mr. Kane have any medical issues or conditions that would do better in a milder climate?"

Mr. Colvig continued to guide the story that I would use to soften the upcoming announcement about the changes that were happening in my life.

"Well, he has asthma which gets worse in the winter with all the fireplace smoke trapped in the valley. Plus in the fall, with all the freight cars transporting ripe produce, there is an increased number of engines spewing thick exhaust to get the heavy loads over the Siskiyous," I described the complaints I so often heard Charles relay.

"Perfect. Now the last piece. Are your parents still alive? Are they in good health?" the attorney asked, as if he had written this story before.

"Yes. They are both alive, but Papa is 79, and has slowed down quite a bit. I think his heart gives him pains quite frequently."

"So there you have it. Mr. Kane needs a transfer for his health, to a location he has frequented for work. You need to remain here, not wanting to uproot your children or leave your failing father. It is a rather respectable version of the truth, without spilling any sordid details," this experienced attorney summarized. "I'll do the rest of the paperwork for the filing of the petition, as well as make the necessary court date arrangements. We'll be in touch. Good day, Mrs. Kane."

Charles left within the week. Mr. Koehler wasn't happy about the divorce filing or the request for a transfer. I guess he believed there was a chance we would reconcile. Charles was given a mandatory sixty day unpaid vacation by Mr. Koehler with the hope things would resolve, rather than being fired, in deference to all the time Charles had invested in the railroad.

There was an announcement in the Medford Mail newspaper that Mr. D.L. Rice was promoted to Southern Pacific Agent at Ashland Depot, in charge of the station and yard until further notice. The paper reported that:

"It is not known as yet whether Mr. Kane's leave of absence is permanent or not. But, it is said due to health reasons, that he has been working diligently of late to secure a position on the new California railroad, and is now in San Francisco for the purpose of looking after the new situation. Mr. Kane has held the position of Agent Station Master in Ashland ever since the road was first completed and has a host of friends in Jackson County who will regret to see him move away."

The children understood that their father would be gone for a very long time, this time. They were used to his absence and didn't seem to ask anything further than what I explained using the story Mr. Colvig and I concocted.

I kept a low profile through town. People were starting to talk about our suspicious arrangement of Charles' move. Most of my close friends were privy to the truth that we were divorcing, but only Charlotte and Anna knew all the despicable details.

"Oh, Alice. I am so disgusted with this whole mess," Anna said infuriated. "Please let me know how I can help. You know I love your children and my house is so big and still empty of little pattering feet. Let me take them often, so you can have a break from the overwhelming job that should be shared by two parents."

"You're a dear, Anna," I graciously accepted her offer.

"I'll let you know when I need some time. In fact, I thought I'd apply at Mrs. Boynton's Millinery Shop for some work. Would you be available to retrieve the children from school tomorrow, so I could interview with the proprietor?"

"Not a problem," Anna answered. "We'll have some tea at the library and read *The Adventures of Tom Sawyer*. I know Alex loves that one."

"Great. Thanks a million," I breathed a huge sigh of relief, knowing I had some outside help.

However, the job hunting was harder than I imagined. I was told there were no openings at the moment, especially for a woman in my 'predicament'. Divorcées were shunned. For some reason, people assumed it was the woman's fault in not keeping their husbands satisfied. I never realized how cruel our society was until I was thrown to the wolves.

I seemed to find out what was happening with my husband at the same time the rest of town did. The *Medford Mail*, and now the *Jacksonville Times*, seemed to be very interested in reporting about our lives. Mrs. McCall sent news from Ashland faster than the telegraph, utilizing her delivery wagon driver to hand-carry letters on the way to their old Jacksonville store. Mama arranged a trip by herself to Ashland as soon as she heard that Charles had left. She brought the paper from Jacksonville, with similar news and a very repugnant look on her face. But there was even more detail in what she read from her newspaper:

"D.L. Rice, of Albany, has been promoted to the S.P. Agency at Ashland, and it is believed that the change is permanent. Mr. E.C.Kane, has gone to San Francisco and has been given an unpaid sixty day vacation from his Ashland duties. He has been dissatisfied with the reduction of salary

during this period, and is endeavoring to secure a better place on the proposed San Joaquin and San Francisco Railroad line, headquartered in Stockton."

"So, I guess Charles is rather disappointed that he doesn't have the money coming in to which he has grown accustomed. I bet his "Amy" is very confused as well. I wonder how he has explained all these changes to her," I commented to Mama.

"Not your worry, dear," Mama asserted. "It's just a good thing that your lawyer advised you to put money into your name before Charles realized he wasn't going to get paid for two months. He better not ask YOU for help. Papa would shoot him directly!"

"Do you know where the new San Joaquin Railroad goes to? I wonder if he can get another Station Master job on that line. I certainly hope he sends money to the children here, in the coming years. I'm not sure I can make it without his money," I confided in Mama.

"Don't you worry darling, the courts will serve justice where it's due," she said confidently.

I knew justice was said to be blind, but I had no idea how slow it was. It was practically two months from the day I signed on with my attorney before he sent word of the circuit court hearing date. I hadn't heard from Charles, and I didn't expect to. I just hoped that he received our assigned date to show up in court, which was set for the following week.

"Where is Mr. Kane?" I demanded of Mr. Colvig when we met on the courthouse steps on the day of the hearing.

"He has not replied to my notices I sent to the address he gave me. I assume he will be here soon. Don't worry, the judge will rule on your petition regardless of who is present. All that is really needed are the lawyers. Relax, Mrs. Kane," my attorney spoke calmly and with composure.

The sun was shining through the tall glass windows of the courthouse. I had removed my cape and hat, and sat in the lobby waiting for our name to be called. My throat was tightening up and my mouth was dry. Beads of sweat formed on my forehead just under my curls. My body was nervous and the thought of seeing Charles made me quiver even more.

"Next up, Kane. Petition for divorce," the court clerk announced as he held the heavy wooden door open for us. I was mortified all over again, hearing this pronouncement.

The courtroom was empty, save for the judge at his bench and the clerk at a table to his side. No Charles! The judge asked Mr. Colvig if he represented the plaintiff or defendant. Mr. Colvig **clarified** his position and proceeded to lay out all the reasons why I was pursuing this divorce. Hearing the words made me cry inside. Mr. Colvig's list included infidelity, repetitive emotional and physical abandonment, reckless financial management and distress, absent interaction with his children and lack of support.

When the judge called for the defendant and found no reply in his courtroom, my divorce decree was granted by default. I was awarded "full care and custody of the minor children produced from the marriage, with the costs of the suit to be taxed to the defendant", if they could find him.

Since Charles didn't show up, there was not going to be any alimony or child support coming in until he was located. The last inkling anyone had of his whereabouts was that he was headed towards Stockton to that new railroad, in hopes of a job, which at this point, I assumed he had not obtained. I could not believe any other reason for his not appearing for this court date. I didn't want to believe Charles could be that manipulative to avoid alimony or purposely hurtful toward his children's welfare.

Nevertheless, I walked out of the courtroom door a free woman again, although I had much more about which to be concerned, than just reliving the fun flirtations of freedom I had in my younger years of single womanhood. My money was only going to last another few months before I would have to sell the house. My goal was to keep my family from returning to the Berry Farmstead, hat in my hands, begging for help.

Later that month, Mr. Richard Koehler, my ex-husband's former supervisor, came down from Portland, stopping in Ashland, on his way to a funeral in San Francisco. The overall general manager of the Southern Pacific railroad, Mr. Towne, had died suddenly and *"his death was a great surprise to all persons who knew him through the railroad. A proper service was to be held at his San Francisco home with Mr. Koehler and other railroad officers attending,"* the *Medford Mail* reported, in addition to the announcement notice tacked up on the depot bulletin board, under the train timetable chalkboard.

Despite his limited time in Ashland, Mr. Koehler made a point of visiting me at my home on Spring Street while he was in town. I was rather taken aback by his face at my door.

"Mr. Koehler!" I choked a little in my greeting.

"Good day, Mrs. Kane," he said in his deep, resonant voice. "I hope I'm not interrupting anything at the moment. May I come in?" he asked as he removed his hat.

"Yes, of course. Please, come in. I believe you remember the way to my parlor?" I said, with an extended arm pointing the way.

"How could I forget such a momentous occasion hosted by such a lovely railroad wife? I still have that photograph on my office wall showing all of us present at the Golden Spike signing and this beautiful wallpaper behind us," he said, outspreading his arm to indicate the fireplace wall. "But, if I may get directly to the point of my visit, that would help to keep my schedule on time," he bluntly said, sitting down in Charles' overstuffed winged-back chair.

"Yes, please do explain. I hope it is good news regarding my family's welfare," I said, trying not to sound desperate.

"I have been advised of your situation as a result of your husband's indiscretions. The railroad doesn't stand for such shenanigans and usually the results are financially severe for the employee, as in the case of your former husband's dismissal from our company line. However, since Mr. Kane was married, we - the railroad company that is - insist on helping the employee family, as if they were our own."

"Excuse me, Mr. Koehler," I interrupted. "I am not sure what you are saying, exactly. What do you mean by helping the families of dismissed employees?"

"Well, this is certainly not an offer we extend to the general pool of employees. This is specifically for your family because Mr. Kane held such a visible and prominent position as the Station Master of Ashland for a very long time with our company. It would be an embarrassment to us if your family were to suffer any mal-effects from his dismissal. And this proposition would help us both. Please allow me to spell it out."

He continued on. "The railroad has always put me in charge of real estate dealings in and around our depots in Oregon. You may recall the development of this Railroad District in 1884?" he asked.

"Oh, yes. Charles and I bought this property right after the subdivision was platted," I nodded.

"Exactly. And just recently, I took the piece of property across the street from you, which was still owned by the railroad, and developed it into a lodging house. Are you familiar with it?" he asked raising his eyebrow and tipping his head in the direction of my front parlor bay window, which faced the new house to the north and towards the Depot.

"Actually, I am mostly familiar with your resident manager who likes to smoke his cigars out front. The air gets rather distasteful on my front porch if the wind is blowing south when he takes his breaks," I said waving my hand in front of my nose.

"Oh, I do apologize about that. I had no idea. But what I am about to propose might offer a solution to that issue, too. I was wondering if you would be available to become the boarding house keeper who manages the lodging house business. You would be able to work from right here in your parlor. You wouldn't have to move at all, and it would free up another room for rent in the lodging house by not having a resident supervisor on site. This would provide more income for the railroad and a steady income for you. You would still be able to remain at home with your children while having a job. What do you say, Mrs. Kane?" the supervisor inquired so politely.

"Oh, my! That sounds absolutely perfect. When may I start?" I anxiously asked, aware my finances were dwindling.

"Hold on there, Mrs. Kane," he said, picking up a large envelope, which he had placed on the circular wooden end table between Charles' chair and the fireplace. Mr. Koehler sounded like there was a "but" coming to burst this bubble of fortune.

"I need to explain how things will work before you jump on board. This lodging establishment is mainly offered to men traveling through on railroad business or related issues. They sometimes stay the entire night and then catch the early morning train, but some of them only chose to occupy the rooms by the hour. Those lodging guests usually spend the rest of the night at our more prestigious lodging accommodations in the Ashland Depot Hotel. Do you understand my meaning of this type of room reservation, Mrs. Kane?" he murmured softly so the children wouldn't overhear this part of his conversation with me.

"Umm...Oh!" I gasped. Then I thought better than to judge from my precarious financial position. "I do believe I follow you. Will these patrons be bringing lady friends with them or is that part of the services the boarding house keeper must provide herself?" I asked with blushing cheeks.

"Oh, Mrs. Kane. Absolutely not! I would never expect or assume that you would participate in such services. No, these

The Station Master's Wife

guests might ask you where to FIND such female company, and that would be the extent of these "extra services" in which you would be involved. Never would it BE YOU! Have you seen the saloons along the tracks which have the dancing girls? Only your help in sending these guests in that direction would be needed.

"Your position would only require you to take the boarder's money for the rooms in the lodging house, and keep records of the reservations, names, and dates for the rentals. Some of the prior reservation information may be brought to you by a telegraph messenger, ahead of the client's arrival. The railroad would pay you a salary plus bonuses for garnering repeat customers. How does $85 dollars per month sound to start? I have all the necessary paperwork and forms to begin the first of next month," he said, patting the thick envelope in his lap.

"Would that be acceptable to you, Mrs. Kane?" Mr. Koehler asked respectfully, raising his eyebrows.

"It sounds like a life saver ring tossed to a sinking ship. I would be happy to help the railroad men on their stopovers in Ashland. I may have to keep an arm's distance from the internal affairs of the lodging house to protect my reputation, but I certainly can manage the details from here in my home. Do I need to oversee the maintenance and cleaning staff as well?" I said, assuming nothing.

"Good question, Mrs. Kane. Why don't you go over and introduce yourself to the staff the next time you see them around. Tell them you will be organizing their schedules and payments after the first of next month. There's an extra ledger book in here that you may use for tracking that piece of the puzzle," he said handing me the beige manila packet.

"I think this will work just fine. Just send these reports through the mail clerk, I believe his name is Angus at this Depot, to my office in Portland. Your salary will be sent to you through the same channels. Thanks again for hearing me out, and...... your enthusiasm and discretion in this endeavor. Good night, Mrs. Kane," my new supervisor said with a tip of his hat as he walked out my front door.

And just like that I became a Madame. Madame Kane, brothel manager. Now I had a reason to be shunned. If reputable society doors were to be slammed in my face, at least with this door of impropriety, which has opened a new chapter in my life, I'll be able to collect a paycheck.

Now, how was I going to explain this to Mama?

~~~

11  New Traditions/New Friends, 1895-1896

That Christmas in 1895, my home was noticeably lacking a parent figure, and I decided to change our tradition of celebrating the holidays in Ashland. I packed up the children, now seven and ten, and we rode the train to Jacksonville for a Berry Homestead holiday. I felt chilled to my bones that winter, as if the warm feelings that love used to fire up in me, were snuffed out. A deep empty pit inside sat where marital love used to be. Slowly, it filled with mistrust and despair, and occasionally nausea.

Giving up, however, was not an option as a single mother. I was very glad to still have had my parents nearby and that they had been so understanding of my plight. Like me, neither of them saw any signs or had suspicions of the betrayal concealed in my marriage. My sister Sarah was sick about it. Fortunately, she didn't bring up her reservations and spit out any "I told you so's". Gracious as usual, Sarah had internalized any uncomfortable feelings and always presented herself with a smile. She still lived at home, destined to remain unmarried we all presumed, since she just turned forty-three in September.

My darling sister willingly dove into extra activities over the holidays with my children, mostly with Ramona. She and Ramona played house with Sarah's own treasured dolls from the attic.

With real hair on the dolls, cut a long time ago from someone's long hair trim, they created styles in the new Gibson Girl fashion with the hair piled high upon the doll's head in a bouffant and chignon bun, trailed by a waterfall of curls down the neck. They also made cookies for everyone to decorate. Alex was ready to participate when it came to that activity and the sweet sugary smells floated outside to the backyard to alert him that things were ready.

The other amusement Alex was interested in was besting his Aunt Sarah in a card game. What he didn't know, was that my sister had a lot of practice with Papa over the years and she could easily win over a ten year old, if she was so inclined. They played for over an hour, with hoots and hollers, as the winning hand shifted back and forth between them.

Mama and I did most of the cooking. The pleasant scents of roasted turkey and cinnamon apple pie filled the house and my heart with joy, at least for a little while. We spoke of my new job as a boarding house keeper, albeit, I left out the details regarding the intermittent accessory clientele. I mentioned my duties and connection with the railroad, now that I was an employee of the company.

I proudly announced, "I get the inside news of the latest events and business meetings related to the railroad. It is part of my job to have rooms available and/or reserved prior to the businessmen's arrivals."

While hovering over the stove and stirring the bubbling cranberry sauce, I quietly mentioned a little aside tidbit, only for Mama's ears. "One newsletter reported something about Charles, in a sidebar of Interstate Rail News:

"*Mr. E.C.Kane was recently appointed as the Station Master for the San Joaquin Railway Line in Stockton*".

I wonder if Mr. Koehler made the recommendation for Charles. He must know all the other railway line superintendents. All I do know, is that other woman is originally from Stockton."

"That good-for-nothing cad! It figures he'd go running to her as soon as he was untangled from here. I am glad you are free of his wretched lies," Mama's words exploded as she bent down and opened the oven, infusing the air with the smell of the golden turkey, and basted it with drippings marinated with lemon juice, basil, and thyme.

"Me too," I agreed. "Although, now that the court can find him and he is employed, maybe the children and I will have benefits from his garnished wages. How ironic that I will be getting paychecks from two different railway companies."

Upon hearing Ramona's fast-paced footsteps headed for the kitchen, I changed the discussion subject before she came in for more taste tests. "Another railroad employment bonus is that we have free train travel, so we can visit much more often, Mama," I hinted for future visits.

"That would be lovely, Alice. Your father is getting on in years and having Alex around to pitch in would be very helpful," Mama suggested. "Have you seen those two out by the barn?"

"Not recently, no. Why, what are they up to?" I asked trepidatiously, while sautéing the almonds for the bean dish.

I handed a bowl with a spoonful of sweetened cranberries to Ramona, who tugged at my skirt for a snack.

"Oh, I think they are alright. I saw your father setting up a sheet painted with a black circle around a central red dot, and hanging it over some stacked bales of hay. Right now they are just whittling some sticks to have pointed ends. It's when he brings out the bow, I think we should be there," Mama said, implying caution.

"He's not going to teach Alex how to hunt like an Indian, is he?" I squeaked.

"Probably so. It is a skill that has come in handy for your father over the years, and he is very proud of his ability. Let them be boys, Alice," Mama sighed, resigning her control.

"How about the three of us sit on the back porch to shell our peas, so we can keep an eye on them?" I bargained.

"Yes, alright, dear. I'll get some lap blankets to ward off that chill," Mama remarked, reminding me of the insidious fingers of winter's grasp that could take hold within minutes.

Sarah was setting the presents under the tree when we all came back inside. Dinner was set on the table and the house had tantalizing smells that made my stomach growl. Mama piled the plates high with the slices of turkey Papa had carved and we ate until our clothes felt too tight.

"May we open our presents now?" Ramona piped in between our conversations.

"I guess so," I conceded. "We will need to settle our food before we do anything else. Okay, get to it young lady. You are the 'present-servant'. That means you pick the person who opens their present first, then you go hand it to them. Sound like a job you would want?" I asked Ramona.

"Oh yes, please," she energetically replied, running into the parlor. Everyone followed Ramona in, finding a place around the tree.

"This one is for you, Mama," my little girl said as she handed me a big package wrapped with a yellow ribbon.

"What is in here, I wonder?" I murmured as I untied the ribbon wrapped around the newspaper. "Oh, Mother! It is exquisite! This dress will be perfect for my new work," I said as I held up the full length gown. "The slate blue wool even matches my eyes. And the grey velvet ribbon trimmed around the leg of mutton sleeve cuffs, collar and hemline give it such a professional accent. Where did you get these delicately crafted, intricate wooden buttons on the front of the bodice?"

"Those would be from me, my darling. Just something I whipped up while whittling," Papa said.

"Oh, you two are so thoughtful. Thank you, thank you," I cried a bit. "Now who is next, little present-servant?"

"Me!" my daughter answered, unable to maintain her composure. Ramona opened the package with her name on the tag, and held it up for everyone to see. "Look Mama, it's a new coat! This must be from Grandmother. I love the little cape on the shoulders. Are these white buttons also made by you, Grandfather? They go so well with this dark navy blue wool."

"Certainly are, little lady. And you know your Grandmother made it so the cape part can be detached, if you want a different style. She is so clever, my MaryAnn. Now who is next?" Papa tried to keep things moving as the hour was getting late.

"Alex is next. Here you go, big brother," Ramona said as she handed him his package wrapped in newspaper and red satin ribbon. "Careful, it's heavy!"

My son untied his package and I watched his mouth drop open with no words forthcoming. He removed a tan canvas pouch and set it on his lap, pulled open the red twill tie surrounding it, and unfurled the bundle to expose four neatly sewn pockets inside, each containing woodcarving materials.

"It's a whittling kit!" Alex exclaimed with joy. "Grandfather just showed me how to use these tools this afternoon. And look, Mama, in addition to the two curved knives and the sharpening stone, there are two canvas thumb guards. I bet Grandmother made them, and the pouch too!"

"I insisted on including them," Mama declared. I mouthed a silent 'thank you' to her across the room. "Your Grandfather said he would show you how to carve a wooden spoon, or a boat or even a pipe for him for his next birthday, if you get good enough by then."

"I will surely try!" Alex sounded encouraged.

The next set of presents were from me to my all my relatives. I had spent the whole time since my divorce just sitting and knitting at night, after the children were tucked in. Everyone loved their scarves from me, each made in a different color and pattern.

Lastly, my sister Sarah handed a silk purse to each of us, tied with different colored ribbons. In the golden light of the oil lamps and parlor candles, her skin looked as if it had a yellow hue. I couldn't decide if she looked tired, sick or simply relaxed. I reminded myself that I would have to check in with her later regarding her health.

"I have collected these flowers from all over Jacksonville this year. The dried petals are for relaxation and calming. And there is a silver dollar in the bottom of each purse. It is only for spending on yourself when it is your birthday. That way my present will be a gift given twice," Sarah teased us all.

Alex nudged his little sister and they both jumped up together. "We will be right back," he said. They ran into the kitchen and came back with two big burlap sacks, handing one to each grandparent.

Pulling out the treats inside they declared, "We made these for the Christmas tree."

"I only stabbed myself once," Ramona added.

My parents opened the bags, which smelled like roasted corn, to find huge strings of popcorn garlands. "Would you help us hang them, Grandfather?"

"I surely will. This is exactly what we needed to complete our tree," he said as he grunted getting up out of his cushioned chair. I worried about his heart and how just the slightest exertion seemed to break him into a cold sweat.

"Let me help, Papa," I suggested. "You take your seat and just tell us on which bough to place each scalloping loop." He smiled and gladly plopped back into his favorite well-worn spot.

When we returned to Ashland, I felt rejuvenated by all the love that had been showered over us. The winter had been slow for my new business and I was glad of the time to spend with my friends and volunteering at the library. By April, almost a year since my divorce, I was starting to feel more resilient and not so wounded, like I initially had, when I felt as if I was hit by a train. But now, another great shock in my life completely derailed me.

"Mrs. Kane!" the voice yelled through the pounding on my front door. "Mrs. Kane? Are you in there?" The visitor started twirling the handle of the circular bell I had inserted into the door frame for use by my new clientele. It was so loud, I could even hear it in the rear of the house. I set my stirring spoon down on the kitchen stove and walked to the front door, wiping my hands.

"I'm coming. I'm coming. What is so urgent?" I asked as I turned the rosette-shaped brass door knob and opened the door to a frantic messenger dressed in the uniform of the Depot telegraph office.

"Oh, Mrs. Kane," the boy said, with his final knock in mid-air as I pulled the door open. "I'm glad to have caught you at home. An emergency has occurred at your family farmstead in Jacksonville. We just received this telegram from their depot office and Mr. Angus said I should deliver it directly to you," the office boy huffed in one long breath.

"Oh, no! Is it my father?" I breathlessly shrieked.

"Please, Mrs. Kane, read it yourself," he handed the mustard-yellow slip of paper to me with the typewritten message in all capital letters:

"APRIL 29, 1896. STOP. DEAR ALICE. STOP. PLEASE COME HOME IMMEDIATELY. STOP. YOUR SISTER IS VERY ILL AND THE DOCTOR SAYS SHE COULD BE GONE ANY DAY. STOP. DO NOT BRING THE CHILDREN. STOP. SARAH DOES NOT WANT THEM TO SEE HER LIKE THIS. STOP. COME SOON. STOP. LOVE - YOUR FATHER."

The paper floated down, out of my grasp, just as the messenger boy caught my arm to steady my wavering body. He helped me into the parlor and poured some water for me from the sideboard. "Can I do anything else for you, Mrs. Kane?"

I thought of all the arrangements that had to be set before my imminent departure. "Yes. Yes, please. Would you run up to Mrs. EV Carter's house, just a few blocks up on the main road? Do you know the one I mean? The one with the sunbursts carved into the trim above the windows?"

"Surely. That's the banker's house, isn't it?"

"Yes, that's the one. Please ask Anna, I mean Mrs. Carter, to come here immediately. She should be home now, it is before her shift starts at the library. Go, please hurry!" In the meanwhile, I scribbled a note for the children explaining my pending absence and ran into my room to pack a bag.

When Anna arrived, I showed her the telegram. I pleaded with her to take over my parental duties for a few days. Whatever was needed, the children would help her do.

"I'll send word through the telegraph office of my plans once I know what's happening with Sarah. Thank you a million times over! I'll let the railroad know to send a substitute for manning the boarding house. Sorry, Anna, I really must go," I cried and ran out the door to the Depot, my coat flapping in the wind, half buttoned.

"Don't you worry about a thing at this end. We'll all be fine here! Send Sarah our love," Anna instructed, waving goodbye from my front porch.

My sister died the day after I got to the farm. The doctor said she had been increasing ill for several weeks with stomach trouble, of which she had complained on and off over the past few months. When she admitted this symptom to me at Christmastime, I did not realize how serious things could get. Numerous friends had come to visit during her sickness, but it was just the family by her side when she departed this life on Thursday, April 30th, 1896, at the age of 43. I was devastated and felt more lost without my oldest sister, than I did when I lost Charles. Sarah had always been the more perceptive one and always readily shared her wisdom. She had been my guiding light.

My brother Isaac, still so far away in Salem although now retired from the State Penitentiary, had moved on to the position of proprietor of a grand Salem hotel. My only other remaining sibling, my older sister Mary, was living in Kerby, a good four hours away by buggy, with her three children. She manned the mercantile with her husband Isaac, whom we called by his middle name, Newell, to avoid confusion with my brother. I was the only one close enough, only an hour away with train connections, to watch over Mama and Papa.

I made arrangements for a summer replacement to take over my sensitive position as "boarding house keeper", being sure she would understand the subtleties of the job that required being diplomatic, as well as the having the skills required for record keeping and money handling.

"Thank you so much for offering to step in to this position, Mrs. Brundige," I said while pouring some tea for her at our parlor interview. She was a friend from my divorcée group, aware of my employment status.

"Please, call me Josephine," she insisted.

"Alright, then, Josephine," I nodded. "My children and I will be leaving as soon as they are dismissed from school for the summer. That should be around June 1st. Your sons and you are welcome to move in the day we leave. I am happy your ex-husband is willing to help you move into our home temporarily. It must be a God-send to have a divorced husband living in the same town and still remain pleasant with you."

"Oh, dear Alice," she said consolingly. "I am so sorry to hear the troubles you have had since Mr. Kane decided to leave. I completely understand the need for this railroad lodging house position you took on. I believe everyone knows these "lodging arrangements" go on in town, and it is just a bonus to have a respectable woman keep an eye on these type of scenarios. I don't think it will upset me, or my reputation one bit, to take over for you while you care for your parents in their time of need, and at their advanced ages."

"Thanks again," I said graciously. "Especially for understanding my situation and this 'business agenda'. If you would return for a training this coming weekend, I will show you how to keep the books and send the records and monies through the telegraph office at the depot. I'll make sure to have my children home to entertain yours while we chat. My Alex is almost eleven and would love to show your boys the baseball game he has been perfecting. Then, I can show you around the lodging house and you can meet the staff. I'll also introduce you to Mr. Angus at the Depot."

The summer of 1896 was like a breath of fresh air. The children loved spending time on the Berry Farmstead. Mama taught Ramona the intricacies of her expert sewing techniques and pie baking, while Papa kept Alex captive with his whittling instructions. I had tried to make our presence less of a burden by taking over the house cleaning, clothes washing and kindling chopping. Although, Mama still had insisted on doing all the cooking.

"Well, I think it's time we took these young ones out for some fun," Papa said. "The Masonic Hall in Jacksonville is having their annual Fourth of July picnic next weekend. How would you two like to do some go-kart racing or try to beat me and your Grandmother in a three-legged race?" he asked the children.

"Oh, yes. Please, can we go Mama?" they sang in unison, looking at me with pleading eyes.

"That sounds like a challenge to me. I think we should take Grandfather up on it," I answered. "How are those sewing projects coming Mama?"

"Almost done. By the middle of next week everyone should have something new to wear to the picnic," she said.

"Our new white cotton blouses are almost matching, Mama," Ramona piped in. "Mine has a ruffle on a scooped lace neckline and Grandmother says yours has a sweetheart neckline, 'cause your her sweetheart. Grandmother made hers with a high collar so she looks like a queen. All the ribbon trim on each of our blouses will match our skirts."

"What about us men?" Papa queried the assistant seamstress.

"Oh, Grandfather. You and Alex won't be left out. We made matching vests for each of you," Ramona proudly announced.

"Then it's settled," Papa concluded. "I'll make my special roasted chicken to bring to the picnic, if you wouldn't mind making some fresh potato salad, Alice?"

"Not a problem," I replied. "I know just the perfect peeler who's been practicing his knife whittling skills. I gave a sideways glance to Alex, who nodded in agreement.

The weather was perfect for a summer outing. Sunshine beamed on the rolling hills making them look like golden velvet, crowned with a dark green fringe of pine and fir. The grass in front of the Masonic Hall was trimmed short so the contestants wouldn't trip or get stuck when racing. There were hand-built boxes, big enough to fit up to a twelve year old, attached to four dinner plate sized solid wooden wheels, the front two of which were connected to a steering mechanism. Each go-kart was painted with a number. The numbers referred to the Mason who built the cart.

"May I enter the go-kart race, Mama?" Alex begged.

"I don't know. That hill looks pretty steep and the finish line is a long way down," I said nervously. "Do you think you know how to drive one of those things?"

"It's just like a sled, Mama," Alex fearlessly answered. "I'll be fine and I want to win the award for you. The prize kite will be the perfect addition to our backyard games."

"Well, alright," I acquiesced. "Now go pick your number and find the builder of that cart. He may have some special instructions for operating his particular vehicle."

Alex was so excited that he looked like he flew from our picnic table to the entry table. I could barely see his feet touch the ground, he ran so fast. Within minutes, he was holding, or rather tugging, the hand of the cart craftsman toward our table. I stood up and turned to greet our guest.

"This is Mr. Cameron, Mama," Alex announced. "He built cart number five, the one I am going to race."

This clean shaven man, perhaps my age or a slight bit younger, walked up to me. When he removed his hat to politely shake my hand, I noticed his golden brown wavy hair toss around in the breeze. "Pleased to meet you, Mr. Cameron," I curtseyed with an extended hand. "I assume your cart is sturdy and safe?"

"Quite so," the builder replied. "And you must be this boy's mother? Um, Mrs.......?"

"Kane. But you can call me Alice. I'm no longer a Mrs.," I clarified. I felt more independent with my honesty.

"Oh, hello, Daniel," Papa interjected as he twisted around on the picnic bench, hearing a familiar voice. "Didn't know you would be here."

"You two know each other?" I asked.

"Oh, yes. We have done some carpentry together on Masonic projects around town. He's in the Jacksonville chapter with me. How's that mining claim been treating you these days, Daniel?" Papa questioned.

"Well enough to put food on the table. Now I just have to learn how to cook it for myself," he giggled nervously. "But, now's not the time for chatting, I've got to reveal the secret to winning this race for your boy Alex, here. Come on lad, I'll show you a few tricks to make things go faster and smoother."

Daniel winked at me and Papa, and then as he took Alex's hand, he looked back at me and smiled. It was a refreshing pleasure to see a man interested in my son. That was something I rarely saw his father even do. And, his second glance in my direction made me blush slightly.

The go-kart race was an exhilarating success. Alex could not stop jabbering about the secret swivel technique that helped him win the race. Mr. Cameron stood by his cart, proudly holding the winning ribbon, behind Alex. My son wanted to fly his new prize kite immediately, but I told him we would have to wait to return to the farm where there was a bigger field and not so many people to bump into.

"The three-legged race is next, Grandfather," Ramona reminded her elder. "I will team up with Alex, and you have to get tied to Grandmother. That's what you said, remember?"

"You are right, young lady," Papa admitted. "But your Mama has to be in the race too! How about it, Daniel? Would you mind rounding out our family race and teaming up with my daughter, Alice? She's not too far off from your height, so it should make for an easy stride."

"Papa!" I admonished him. "Mr. Cameron does not need to do that."

"On the contrary, Alice. I would be honored to join in the fun, especially with you as my partner. And please, call me Daniel," he corrected.

I could feel my skin getting flushed again. I had not felt that pang of flirtation in so long, I didn't know what to do, so I threw my hands into the air and said, "Alright, then. Let's sign up for the challenge!"

By some miracle of coordination, Daniel and I appeared to have won the three-legged race. I say appeared because as we broke through the ribbon at the end of the course, we both fell onto our knees laughing so hard, with our two ankles still strapped together. I wasn't sure if that final strategy eliminated one from the competition.

Papa and Mama invited Mr. Cameron to join us at the farm for another picnic, later on in the summer. "When the peaches come in, you'll have to try Alice's pie. It's better than her mother's, but don't tell her that," Papa lowered his voice as he elbowed Daniel in the ribs.

We loaded up in the buggy, Mama and Papa in the front with the picnic basket at their feet, and the children and I in the back seat, with our new kite across our laps.

"See you at the next meeting in August, Daniel!" Papa called out as we rode away. Mama turned around from the front seat and gave me a knowing smile, suggesting that nothing, not even a glance between me and Daniel, got past her.

~ ~ ~

12  Independence and Impropriety, 1896-1901

Mr. Daniel Cameron did indeed pay a visit to the Berry homestead later that August. Papa made sure to extend an invitation to Daniel at his early August Masonic meeting. On the appointed August picnic afternoon, Daniel arrived with little trinkets that he had hand-made for the children. Ramona got a carved wooden box engraved with a fir tree shape on the top and a mirror set inside the upper lid.

"Thank you very much Mr. Cameron," she said as she gave him a squeeze around his middle.

"Well, since we are friends enough to hug, I suggest you call me Daniel, little lady. And you are very welcome. I hope you keep your special treasures tucked away in there," Daniel confidently conversed, as if he had been around children his whole life. "And this is for you, young sir. I heard you are learning to whittle. Well now you have a box for all your projects in the making, with tool slots on the side."

"Oh, boy! Thank you lots, Daniel!" Alex cried out as he ran outside to fill up his new project box.

"And for you, Alice, I hope you don't find this too forward, but I couldn't come empty handed without something for you," he quietly said. "It is a brooch I carved from a piece of the mahogany tree I cut down to build my cabin. I hope you like bird shapes. I wanted it to represent the free adventurous spirit I saw in you when we first met."

"Oh, Daniel," I sighed, spellbound. "This is absolutely lovely. But completely unnecessary. Thank you so kindly." I showed it to Mama and I got that same sly smile out of the corner of her mouth that she had given me in the buggy as we were leaving the July picnic. I could tell she was hopeful for my happiness to return.

When the clinking of dishes in the wash tub was done after dinner, Daniel asked if I would join him outside on the front porch swing. We sat and chatted about our lives, with me eventually disclosing the fact that I was divorced. He didn't seem to mind, and in fact thought my former husband's actions despicable. He revealed that he was single, since the life of a miner didn't offer much of a consistent income for any family prospects. I spoke of my job as a boarding house keeper, my love of reading and my volunteer work at the library. He admitted that in addition to his hobbies of drafting and carpentry, he also had a similar passion, albeit his was the reading of poetry.

"In fact, I brought a book to read some poetry to you. The author is Walt Whitman, one of my favorite writers," he remarked. Daniel reached in his pocket for the book, flipped through it and said, "Let's see... this one looks appropriate."

The aroma of Papa's pipe wafted through the house, slipping through the open front window and out onto the porch, reminding me as usual, that he wasn't far off when a gentleman was calling. The amber glow from the front parlor light illuminated the open page of Daniel's poetry book. He began to read.

"Whoever you are, now I place my hand upon you,

that you be my poem,

I whisper with my lips close to your ear,
I have loved many women and men, but I love none better than you.
O I have been dilatory and dumb,
I should have made my way straight to you long ago,
I should have blabbed nothing but you, I should have chanted nothing but you.
None has understood you, but I understand you,
none has done justice to you,
You have not done justice to yourself,
None but has found you imperfect, I only find no imperfection in you,
None but would subordinate you,
I only am he who will never consent to subordinate you,
I only am he who places over you no master, owner, better God,
Beyond what waits intrinsically in yourself."

He closed the book and looked into my eyes for a response. "That was beautiful, Daniel," I replied, rather taken aback. "What made you pick that particular passage?"

"I felt that your circumstances may have left you in certain situations in which you were not treated as you should be. I just wanted you to know, as Mr. Whitman so eloquently put it, that you are a strong woman who deserves to have love in her life," Daniel said softly.

He gently placed his hand on top of my hand closest to him, and continued. "I would be honored if you would allow me to call on you again sometime, Alice. I often come to Ashland to get the best price from the mining assayer there. I have even met the bank manager, Mr. EV Carter, who has asked for my carpentry and design help with his plans for a new bank building."

"Really? You know Earnest? His wife is my best friend! We, I mean the children and I, often dine with them at their house. Anna just adores my children, especially since she has not been able to have any of her own," I gulped, realizing I should not have disclosed such personal information. Daniel glanced over my indiscretion without reacting.

"What a coincidence! It appears Mr. Walt Whitman was right. I should have made my way straight to you long ago. We seem to know many of the same folks, already," Daniel laughed. "I am hopeful I will be able to develop my drafting skills and wean away from the life of mining. You might just be the impetus I have needed to get to Ashland more often."

"That would be lovely. I am sure we would have such fun flying the new kite or sharing a cup of tea at the library sitting room. I would enjoy your visits whenever you are called to Ashland. But, you must remember, I am a working woman these days. I would have to arrange our visiting time around the hours I tend to my clientele," I emphasized.

"Not a problem. Perhaps I could be one of your lodgers when I come to visit? How much are the rooms?"

"Uh ...um ...I believe you would be more comfortable at the Ashland Depot Hotel. My lodging house has very small rooms, more suited to accommodating traveling businessmen, for just one night or two. The turnover of **clients** can be rather disruptive in such a small housing setting. And ...they, um... often have lady visitors stay into the later evening hours, which may keep you from sleeping soundly," I divulged, hoping he would understand my drift.

"Oh! I see. You DO have an interesting life! I'm sure you're right. Perhaps another hotel would be best," Daniel giggled under his breath. "By the way, do your parents know the occasional delicate nature of your lodging business?" he taunted.

"Heavens NO!" I blurted. "And, if you would be so kind as to not expound on those details, I'd appreciate keeping it that way." We both shared a conspiratorial chuckle.

With the passing of two years, Daniel and I had become quite good friends by 1898. He actually did end up moving to Ashland, changing his career focus to design and drafting. He took a room in a rental house as a permanent boarder and made sure it came with meals, since he hadn't really learned more than the cooking basics. Our town was booming with so much building, he had more work than he could handle. More of the downtown buildings wanted to be built with brick, since fire had destroyed almost all of the downtown plaza's wooden structures at one time or another.

The children loved our outings with Daniel to the park, to concerts at the Chautauqua and especially when he treated us to dinner at a fancy restaurant in town. Papa, Mama, Anna and EV all enjoyed Daniel's company as much as we did and we made sure to invite him to share in our home cooked meals often.

However, I kept an arm's length from any lawfully binding connections with him. My children were my focus and I wanted their father, currently the Station Master of Stockton, to be responsible for their welfare, and not Daniel. Therefore, it was clearly understood I would not be remarrying, which would change that financial arrangement, prior to my children becoming adults, if at all.

EV Carter shifted his focus from banking to politics, like so many in his powerful position tended to do. He became an Oregon State legislator before the turn of the century, putting the drafting of his new bank plans on hold.

Daniel's spare time, originally slated for Earnest, just opened up more time for me and my children. The children were occasionally gone for sleepovers at Anna's or Charlotte's, leaving more alone time for Daniel and me.

We were more relaxed without any perception of impropriety by inquiring eyes. Daniel and I enjoyed having the house to ourselves until the wee hours of early dawn. Before daylight kissed the eastern sky, he would slip out under the cover of the dark morning mist. I became quite comfortable in my new world of independence.

Daniel joined the Masonic Hall - Ashland Chapter, and coaxed me to many a dance, when I often wore the carved bird brooch pin he gave me, proudly displaying it on my bodice. As more of Daniel's life unfolded, I discovered his hidden talents as a musician and singer. We often played duets on my piano or he played his guitar and sang, accompanying me while I played solo at the piano.

Once, Daniel invited me to a traveling music show performing in town that touted an unusual new sound with out-of-town performers. 'Mahara's Minstrels' brought a Negro bandleader to conduct this group of colored musicians, whose music was influenced by African-American musical folk traditions. This bandleader, Mr. W.C. Handy, played the violin as well as a shiny gold cornet, which he had claimed he won in a music contest. I had no doubt as to the veracity of the story, as his talent was clearly evident. It was also said there were few equals to him as a bandmaster, with people often referring to him as a colored John Philip Sousa.

Mr. Handy had been exposed to a new type of music during his travels around the south, playing with and collecting music from many former slaves whose tunes blended rhythms from their African homeland and songs from their plantation days. Mr. Handy coined the name "Blues" for this particular type of sad-sounding class of music, often played in minor keys, as an expression of those folks feeling blue or sad. I loved the new sound and rhythm! My world seemed to open up more with Daniel around.

It was not just me that felt the effects of having Daniel nearby. On occasion, Daniel would take Alex target shooting with the bows and arrows that they had whittled together. He often included Ramona when he went fishing on the creek or horseback riding to the outlying meadows to bring back bushels of blackberries for canning jam, our favorite winter treat. We stacked many jars on the shelves Daniel built along the walls of our brick root cellar, which was above ground, and therefore not technically a cellar, but rather conveniently attached level with the kitchen porch. My perfect life finally had no master beyond myself, as Mr. Walt Whitman had so poetically predicted.

At the turn of the century, the railroad finally rolled in a rotary snow plow for the winter of 1900-1901. It was added to the lead engine, enabling it to remove snow with a corkscrew action, by throwing it far off the sides of tracks. Charles would have loved the ease of managing the Siskiyou Pass now. No doubt, he probably would have made more winter trips to see Amy, if the snow could have been so easily cleared back then. I didn't care, I was happy now.

The cleared rails brought more customers to keep me busy and updated on the latest news. In fact, I had recently heard through the railroad newsletter, that Charles was transferred to Bakersfield, in Southern California, as their new Station Master Agent. As far as I was concerned, the further away the better, as long as his monies kept coming for the children.

Alex, now fifteen, had a job after school, delivering for the Ashland Ice Company. This new responsibility gave him a way to meet more new families in town and build up a little nest egg for his upcoming adult life. He was often hired to do odd jobs through these new contacts, however, he was happiest about meeting other boys who wanted to play baseball. Baseball was a very big deal in those days, and most small towns fielded their own teams. Ashland had grey uniforms with matching caps, both of which sported a large "A" on the front. Daniel couldn't resist getting involved as well.

"Now that I'm your assistant coach, we can use the field below the railroad yard to practice anytime," Daniel boasted. His mustache had gotten fuller over his upper lip and longer around the corners of his mouth, so he truly looked the part of a mature man in charge.

"I want to learn how to throw a curveball," Alex declared. "I heard about a secret weapon developed by one of the Ashland players, the year before I was born. That Ashland team went on to win every game."

"I read about that even in Jacksonville's paper back then," Daniel added. "That Ashland team got so cocky they would put ads in the paper for a $1000 bet against any all-comers that they would win. And they always did!"

"People say, perhaps this player was the first in the West to figure out how to throw a curveball. I want to learn!" Alex insisted again. They sought out this original player, Mr. McConnell, now age 45 and still residing in Ashland, and brought him to their practices to help develop the 1901 Ashland Niner's secret weapon.

Spring brought a breath of fresh air to Ashland and when the peach blossoms were in bloom, the whole town smelled like a flower shop. Since winning recognition at the World's Fair in Chicago in 1893, Mr. Max Pracht's peaches were in high demand. His peaches were so gigantic, some of them weighed up to twenty-six ounces! It made for an overabundance of available produce for fall canning, and of course, for my pies. Yet, with all the good that life seemed to bring, fall of 1901 brought many devastating changes as well.

~ ~ ~

13  Advice and Anguish, 1901-1903

I was called on to advise and comfort Charlotte during her divorce. I didn't pry into the sordid details of the dissolution, but I did remember her husband, the former sheriff, booked a lodging room reservation with me on occasion for "a friend". I kept those secrets under wraps, not wanting to spread any unfounded rumors.

Mr. Colvig, to whom I referred Charlotte, proved to be the perfect attorney for dealing with Charlotte's circumstances. He negotiated for her to remain in her house, just as I did, after her husband left. Her parents, the Ganiards, as main figures in the Ashland community, were her stalwart supporters and very protective of Charlotte and her reputation. The attorney took care of the rest, making sure that her husband, Mr. Pelton, remained responsible and financially supportive for her and the welfare of the children.

Supporting Charlotte during her divorce took its toll on me, but my exhaustion was followed by anguish over Papa's health, which declined rapidly in the late summer of 1901. In the third week of August, Mama sent me a wire, through the railroad telegraph, to come with the children for a visit. She believed it was close to the end for Papa. She also sent word to Isaac and Mary to come to the Berry Farmstead.

"Your father is not feeling very well these days. He hardly gets out of his chair," Mama said when we were all there. She looked gaunt and unkempt. Oily strands of hair trailed out of her loose bun. Dishes were piled in the sink.

"How long has he been like this?" I asked, very concerned for them both. I feared Mama was trying to hold down the fort and do all the tasks by herself that were required on the farm. Caring for Papa should have been all she needed to do. Slumped in his chair with a plaid lap blanket tucked around him, he was fast asleep, unaware of any of us being there. Even his beard was straggly and untended.

"Things have gotten worse in the past few weeks. He collapsed in the garden just picking the green beans," Mama admitted. "He said it was nothing to worry about, just the heat. But I could see the changes in his breathing and the increased effort it took for him to do things."

"Mama," Isaac said in a definitive tone, "I will stay here for a while and get things running again around the farm. You just relax and sit with Papa. Mary and Alice will put up some cooked foods for you so things will be easier for a while."

"Oh, my goodness," Mama cried. "You children are a God-send. I've got some ham in the smoke house that needs tending. And a few too many roosters that could be roasted or dried into jerky for later. Maybe Alex could help with that?"

Mary tearfully added, "My Diadama is twenty-two now and can run the mercantile with Newell, so don't you worry about me staying around for a while too."

My older sister turned to my son and instructed Alex, "You take your cousins, Isaac Jr and James, to help with the chickens. They are quite familiar with making jerky. Ramona, Alice, you two come with me," Mary commanded, deciding to take charge.

Regardless of all our care and help, Mama knew Papa's time was coming to a close. On one of Papa's good days, she took him to the Jacksonville courthouse so they could make some permanent alterations to their estate. They changed the deed to the Jacksonville Berry Farmstead they owned for so long, into our names, with a third going to each of us siblings.

Mama bid her last goodbye to her life-long companion in October 1901. Papa was 85 years old. His obituary in the Jacksonville Times described her as *"grief stricken as she watched the life light flicker and fade away from his kindly old eyes"*.

Even though we children now owned the farm, Mama remained there for a bit, along with the anguish of her grief. She was stocked with smoked meats and jerky, canned vegetables fresh from her garden, and stacked kindling and wood to last for a few winter months.

Even so, with the onset of a difficult winter in January 1902, Mama decided, with all her children's encouragement, to move to Ashland and live with me. Alex wasn't too happy about sleeping in the parlor, and neither was Ramona, at age twelve and a half, about sleeping in a shared room with me. I wired my siblings for a group discussion about selling the farm. Although it was a hard decision, like digging up the roots of our family tree, we determined it was best for all if the old farmstead was sold.

"I am using my portion of the money from the farm that you and Papa left for me to remodel the original parlor into a third bedroom and finally add the grand parlor I always wanted. Charles denied me that request by inevitably having some excuse or another as to why his Station Master position didn't provide enough funds for such a project. We all know

now that the real reason was he had to support a second family," I resentfully restated.

"Oh, Alice," Mama said with downcast eyes. "I think I am too much of an inconvenience for this small space you have here. Perhaps I should ask Isaac if he has a spare room at his hotel in Salem."

"I won't hear of such nonsense! This is something I have absolutely dreamed of and now you and Papa are giving me the chance. You'll love your new bedroom. As the parlor, I enjoyed it as my favorite room in which to relax. I have especially loved lying on the couch and staring up at the coved ceiling's plaster-cast medallion centerpiece above the hanging chandelier. Please, Mama, not another word about leaving. You can help me decorate the new grand parlor. And I'm sure Daniel would even help to design it!"

Finished within three months, the grand parlor was magnificent. It was twenty-two feet long and fifteen feet wide with a bay window filling the full front wall facing Spring Street. Daniel twirled me around the full length of the room, dancing like a transformed Cinderella - this time as a princess, rather than as a soot-covered maid waiting for Charles - while Ramona performed her latest piece on our piano. Mama loved her newly remodeled room, especially the built-in window seat Daniel designed to replace the couch, in the nook of the small bay window. Alex took up residence in the enclosed rear porch for his retreat in the warmer months, although he surrendered to the shared space with his sister in the winter.

My inheritance provided additional capital beyond what the remodel demanded, so I bought and sold additional properties within Ashland. With direct access now as a railroad employee, rather than just as the Station Master's wife, I was privy, prior to public knowledge, to the upcoming changes and future businesses in town which were revealed in the company newsletter. Although these bulletins helped with making wise investments, they occasionally revealed some unsolicited announcements.

"Oh my goodness!" I screeched one night after dinner, while reading the latest railroad headlines. The children were already in bed, but Mama was burning the evening oil with me in the new parlor, tending to her knitting.

"Whatever is the matter, dear?" Mama replied, puzzled by my intense reaction to the newsletter.

"It says here, that the Station Master from Stockton who was recently transferred and appointed to the San Francisco and San Joaquin Railroad Company in Bakersfield, has just gotten married, Dec. 17, 1902, to Miss A. Peyton," I read aloud.

"So why is that your concern?" Mama asked.

"Because, that Station Master's name is EC Kane!" I blurted out.

"Oh.... Oh, dear. Are you alright, Alice?" her voice turned to compassion and concern.

I took a deep breath and tried to decide if I was reacting from being shocked or hurt. "I think so," I answered. "It just took me by surprise to see it in print. I assumed it would happen sometime, but....."

"But it still hurts, doesn't it sweetheart," Mama consoled me. She got up and came over to me, putting her hand on my shoulder. "It's better to know that the door is finally closed. You have Daniel in your life now, and won't have to worry about Charles coming back to ruin that."

I knew she was right, but somewhere deep inside, it still hurt. I was no longer the Station Master's wife, but remained as the rejected Mrs. Kane. "Well he better not default on the monies for the children. I don't care who else he takes on!" My anger seemed to wash over my abandonment rather quickly.

"Does it say anything else about his transfer?" Mama inquired, hoping there would be some answer to my question about his continued revenue stream.

"Actually, it does. Even though Charles is new there in Bakersfield, it says, *"His days as Station Master Agent there are numbered."* There seems to be some trouble with that railroad line paying their taxes," I read from the headline.

"Go on, dear," Mama perked up and sat in the wing-backed chair next to me, returning to knitting her wool shawl.

"I'll read the highlights," I said scanning the bulletin:

"Agents along the San Joaquin Valley line are being replaced by old-time employees of the Santa Fe Railway. There is a rumor in railroad circles that the San Joaquin Railroad Company has not fully paid its taxes and the county assessor is getting ready for a legal battle. The assessor seized seven train cars in Bakersfield and ordered they be held for auction to pay the back taxes. The railroad workers, under Agent Kane's orders, however, moved out two cars in the middle of the night."

I stopped reading for a moment to take in what that meant. Mama said what I was thinking.

"Did you say Charles stole two trains away from the Assessor?" she asked, incredulous.

"Uh, yes. I think that's what this means," I said. "Let me continue to see if they arrested Charles. The bulletin says this was a special dispatched report to the San Francisco Examiner. It goes on as follows:

"The remaining cars were chained to the track by the Assessor and he then went before a Justice and swore out a warrant charging the Superintendent and Agent Kane with misdemeanors. The railway put up bail to keep their employees at the railyard. They then addressed a letter to the Assessor commanding him to remove the cars from the yard, stating that they interfered with the railroad's business, now that they were immobile and blocking the track."

The article carries on with the Assessor sending a return communication directly to Agent E.C. Kane and Superintendent Schindler stating: *"These cars were seized for taxes and your company was notified to not remove said cars except at its own risk and responsibility. Immediately thereafter, two of the said cars were by you removed from said Bakersfield yards without my consent, and you are hereby further notified that if you fail to so replace said cars on or before 10 o'clock a.m. on March 17th, the date and hour fixed for the sale of said cars for taxes, as above stated, you will be held responsible for all damages caused by such failure. Signed, JM Jameson, Assessor, Kern Co."*

"Oh, my, my," Mama stammered. "Go on, dear. Then what happened?"

I finished reading the article aloud: *"It will be noted that Assessor Jameson not only ignored the request from the railroad to remove or unchain the obstructing cars, but proposed also to hold the company responsible for those spirited away. The Railway Superintendent gave forty-eight hours to have his yards cleared of the offending cars. It is presumed that he will attempt to get them out of his way, but the trainmen and Agent Kane will be arrested if there is any interference with the Assessor's determination to have them remain where they are until the day fixed for their sale."*

"Absolutely preposterous! How can Charles get mixed up in such shady dealings? Well, I'm glad his days are numbered at that depot," Mama sounded revolted but concerned at the same time.

"I don't know, Mama," I replied. "I hope for his sake, and his new wife, he finds another job quickly. Do you think he will stop sending money? He better not return to Ashland for a job. What a mess he's gotten himself into this time!"

~ ~ ~

14  Shocking Reveals, 1903

Monies did continue to be wired from Charles to our children, although I kept waiting for the other shoe to drop. I expected his new family would potentially draw more of his salary, leaving less for his older children in Ashland. Thankfully, after finishing high school in 1903, Alex chose to stay with the Ice Company and learn more about how to run a business. I acquiesced to his decision with some relief that there would be no further education costs for him.

Ramona was just entering her sophomore year at Ashland High School and had dreams of continuing on to college after her graduation. With the news of Charles' remarrying, I decided this was the appropriate time to tell the children the truth. I told Mama this would be the topic of discussion at the dinner table the next evening, so she could add her two cents to the conversation.

"Alex, Ramona, I would like to discuss our family's arrangement with your father," I started slowly to get them in the right frame of mind. "You have been very patient with him and his lack of connection or visits with you. I hope you know it is not because he doesn't love you both. I am sure he does, very much."

"I appreciate the birthday notes we get every year from him," Ramona said, trying to fill the hole in her heart that her father left behind. I had so wished the childhood years of my children could be filled with fatherly love, like I had in mine.

"I'm glad you get those cards, too," I said with a deep sigh, hurting along with her. "I wish he had made more of an effort to actually see you and share his life with you."

"It's okay, Mother. I understand his job keeps him from returning home," Ramona said, defending her absent father.

"But his circumstances have recently changed," I revealed, a bit nervous to continue with my reveal.

"You mean like he got married again?" Alex piped in.

"WHAT!?" I responded, so startled that I dropped the bowl of peas and almost tipped backwards in my chair.

"Father has been writing to me in care of the Ice Company," Alex continued calmly. "He found out I worked there from the guy in the depot office with whom he stayed in touch, Mr. Cap Kramer. One day, Cap told me to stop by the mailroom after I delivered ice for the Depot Hotel dining hall. Ever since the first letter, he has been holding mail for me from Father whenever it comes in the depot mail delivery, through the Ice Company address."

"How long has THIS been going on?" I squeaked, a bit louder than I intended.

"Oh, ever since I got my job at the Ice Company. Uh... let me think...since I was fifteen, I guess," Alex answered, scratching his head like it was a hard math problem.

"And you didn't think to mention this to me before, because...?" I said with a tilt of my head and a knitted brow.

"Father asked me not to," Alex stated matter of factly. "He said he didn't want to upset you."

"Why didn't you tell ME?" Ramona shrieked.

"Father thought you too young and delicate to understand such manly matters," Alex retorted.

"Well, I never!" Mama snapped. "Of all the nerve!! Such a divisive plot to split siblings and keep secrets from your mother. And now he's teaching his son that this is how a man should be? What kind of father does that?"

"Alright. Everyone calm down," I insisted. "Now that the cat is out of the bag, we are going to have some new rules around here."

Alex looked worried and Ramona sat a little taller in her chair, like she was moving up a rung in her family status. "There will be no more secrets among us. I will explain our family situation from the beginning and you can ask any questions you wish, when I've finished. Then I want to hear what each of you know. Understood?"

After the children nodded, I explained the ugly circumstances of the dissolution of our marriage, and the subsequent arrangements set out by the court for family support. I instructed Alex to share any future mail from Charles, along with his return address, with his sister if she wished to be in contact with her father. I also told Alex to keep me out of the communication, unless there were circumstances affecting the family for which I needed to be involved, like changes in finances, visits or relocations.

"Does that mean if I want to go to college that Father doesn't have to help pay because I'll be over eighteen?" Ramona looked concerned.

"Well legally, yes, dear. But I'm sure your father will be respectful of your wishes and help out in any way he can when the time comes," I explained, trying to reassure my daughter, although I wasn't truly convinced myself now, since he had just gotten remarried.

I was relieved to have finally unburdened myself of the family secrets I kept from my children for years. The only secret left to carry was the non-disclosure of the fringe benefits I arranged for my boarders. That scandal, at least, was outside of the family.

I spent more time with Mama at our Masonic O.E.S. Ladies Meetings and set her up with the Embroidery Club so I could tend to the 'delicate matters' that came with my employment.

Once I got to know the Ladies of the Night who regularly frequented my clients at the lodging house, I had a bit more compassion for their choice of career. Actually, for most of them, it wasn't a matter of choice, but rather of survival. I heard the various circumstances that landed these ladies here in Ashland, usually being coaxed by a man sending a free train ticket for them to Ashland. They were enticed by a promise of a good life with a rich miner or businessman. Upon arriving, either they found out the unfortunate truth of the man's poverty or the man decided she wasn't the girl for him and sent her out on her own, often penniless.

Sometimes women answered ads for domestic work that promised high pay but found themselves in brothels instead, with no means of escape. My fancy girls worked for themselves and usually lived above the dance hall. In order to disguise their identities or elude the law, many of the 'soiled doves' assumed fake names or nicknames.

My favorites in town were Denver Darlin' and Rowdy Kate. In their down time, these girls would sometimes come to my house for lessons in social etiquette, piano or proper dance

- not the gyrating kind familiar to them in the dance halls. I tried to teach them needlework, or on occasion how to read, lending them books from our library. These two were the sort of 'fallen angels' striving for better qualities that would make them more marriageable material.

"Mrs. Kane, you are such a gentlewoman," Rowdy Kate would say when she came over in her overalls. "I cain't pay ya, but I'm hella good with an ax. Let me cut up some kindling for your family in thanks for all you done for me."

"That would be lovely, Kate," I answered, exemplifying some proper and polite words she might learn to use down the line. Then she would go straight to work in the yard.

When Denver Darlin', or DD as her friends called her, came by the house, not on a work call, she would join me with her work gloves and apron in the garden to help with weeding and hoeing. "I just love gittin' my hands in the dirt. I grew up on a farm back in Denver until Daddy died and Mama couldn't take care of all us youngins'. Since I was the oldest, I made my way out west to this little town," DD told me. "This here job entertaining men is just to git me goin' till I can move on and start fresh in some other town. With the money I'm a-savin', I can show up all respectable-like when I git off the train in the next place."

Sometimes, like with DD, when a 'fallen woman' wanted to pick herself up and move on to start over somewhere fresh, she would bribe the local newspaper editor to print an obituary of her. Then she could move forward by creating an all-new identity. It was a hard life to live and an even harder life from which to retire.

The newspapers around the valley would often follow up the illness or death of a prostitute, utilizing the opportunity to announce the risks of her profession and dissuade others from such a path:

"It is reported one of the 'frail sisters' of the town tried to shuffle off this mortal coil last Monday night via the morphine route, but did not succeed. Suicide is the most common way a scarlet woman retires from her job, if she survives the hazards of the profession. Drug overdoses, usually from morphine, and alcohol poisoning, both intentional and accidental, are also common. So is murder. If suicide, murder or drug abuse does not befall a working girl, there is always the risk of sexually transmitted disease or illness." And that is why I tried to give them a hand.

I made sure my clientele treated these 'working women' of mine with respect. If I heard of any rough stuff or cheapskates who skipped out without paying, I made sure to put them on my "no return" list. Since the railroad was paying me to rent out rooms and connect their businessmen with ladies for the evening, I didn't need to take a percentage or cut of their pay. I was not a Madame, in that sense. My reputation in town was worth too much to me and my children. I preferred to be known as a boarding house keeper with good connections and practical information for visitors.

When railroad workers booked a room by the hour, I allowed them, while they were inside, to hang their red signal lanterns on a hook next to the rear entrance of the lodging house, which faced the depot. This was the arrangement I made with the depot, and Mr. Koehler agreed to it, so these workers could be found quickly for any railroad emergency.

Using the rear of the lodging house for red light messages was how I kept Spring Street, the main road of the Railroad District, from being known as part of the Red-Light District.

Even though Mama was getting on in years, just having turned seventy-eight a few months prior in September, she was still sharp as a tack. My second big reveal was admitting the details of my work to Mama when she eventually put two and two together and figured out there was more to my job than booking rooms and taking in lodging money for the railroad.

"I think it's very kind of you to help out those girls. You're like the mother they never had," Mama complimented me, even though I knew she didn't approve of the work the girls were doing.

"Thank you, Mama," I said. "But they like being around you, too. You're the Grandmother they never had. You are so patient when teaching them how to handle a sewing needle. I'm sure having that skill will someday prove worthwhile for them."

"I've been noticing, Alice, the "extra activity" part of that place pretty well runs itself, thanks to how you set things up. I could take over if you ever wanted to have a vacation sometime," Mama offered. "I would only need to be shown to whom you give the money to at the Depot, and where to pick up the passenger reservation list for upcoming bookings."

"Funny you should mention that, Mama," I said with expressed interest. "I just heard about this excursion near here, happening this next summer. They are headed to that new national park recently established by President Roosevelt.

It is called Crater Lake National Park because it has an enormous crater in the ground filled with fresh water. They say the water is the bluest of blues, and as deep as the mountains surrounding it are tall. I would love to take the children to see it. I think Daniel would even enjoy it. Are you sure you could handle things here by yourself?"

"First off, I know I wouldn't be left alone by your friend Anna. She'd be checking in on me every day if you asked her. And, I bet Dora would love a vacation away from Salem, and a break from working in that hotel with Isaac. She would know all about making lodging reservations and taking money. It would give me a chance to spend some time with my daughter-in-law, and help you out to boot!"

"Okay, then," I said with resolve. "I will speak with the children and Daniel and make sure it is something they want to do. I will send a wire asking Dora, too. We would probably be gone two weeks. Are you sure you would be alright for that long?"

"Oh, stop your fussing and start planning," Mama snorted and bent her head down to continue transferring stitches from one knitting needle to the other, keeping warm in front of the evening fire.

~~~

15  Adventure Abounds, 1904

S ummer of 1904 came with great anticipation and many preparations. I arranged everything with the Depot for Mama to work in my stead. My library time was to be covered by Miss Blanche Hicks, who now worked regular hours as an actual librarian. Anna was president of the library board and ran the library as efficiently as Charles had run the railroad depot. Daniel had finished his latest design and drafting project just in time for our August departure. Ramona and I had completed sewing all the canvas rucksacks. Alex punched holes in the leather cinch straps using his whittling tools, which made it easy for them to be attached to the pack buckles. My sister-in-law, Dora, arrived from Salem the day before our departure, happy to help Mama during my absence.

    Mr. Will G. Steel, who had worked for years to help create this new national park in Oregon, had gathered twenty-seven passengers for this promotional expedition. My family, which now almost always included Daniel, and I were eligible for the excursion guest list to the newly designated Crater Lake National Park because of my position with the railroad. They wanted a local spokesperson, involved with the lodging of tourists and businessmen, to experience this geologic setting first hand, and thereby encourage visitors to spread the word to come to see this natural wonder of the world.

    Southern Pacific Railroad also sent two photographers, and a reporter, Joaquin Miller, from their own monthly publication - Sunset Magazine. This was THE "Magazine of Western Living", where one expected to find photographs and articles about architecture, home improvement, cooking and food, travel, nature, and recreation. It was the perfect backdrop in which to distribute the news of this adventure and natural wonder.

Mr. Miller was about sixty-five with a long full white beard, curled up mustache, and straggly long white hair usually topped with a crumpled old cowboy hat. He was a story in himself, and had gained the title "*The Poet of the Sierras.*" Daniel couldn't wait to spend some time chatting about poetry with Mr. Joaquin Miller.

We were also joined by Mr. Charles W. Fulton, who had been elected as one of Oregon's U.S. Senators earlier in 1903. He was invited along to learn, experience, and hopefully represent the new Crater Lake National Park's interests in the upcoming national Congress.

Our trip was expected to take several days to reach the Park. The departure point in Medford necessitated that we take the train to meet the group there. On August 5th, we said our fond farewells to Mama, Dora and Anna, who saw us off at the Ashland Depot with dried fruit snacks and jerky. They all waved goodbye, but I could see Mama's smiling face had tears twinkling down her cheeks.

The "Steel Excursion" traveled in four six-seater coaches, with canvas roofs and canvas side panels that could be rolled down for inclement weather. Each coach was pulled by a team of two horses. In addition to the riding passengers, there were three bicyclists that traveled alongside the group, all the way to the Park. One of our coaches carried a sixteen foot skiff on its roof which was brought along for boating on the lake and to transport us to hike on the central island of the lake. This island, shaped like a wizard's cap had been aptly named 'Wizard Island'.

Each group's gear was stacked behind the seated area of their coach. We looked like a rather odd wagon train, especially dressed in our finest traveling clothes. I was grateful to not be the only woman aboard, happily joined by four others plus Ramona.

The expedition stopped at Eagle Point the first night, setting up A-framed canvas sleeping tents, folding canvas stools for seating, and stacked boxes for tables at which we dined. We had privacy in our tents, but little comfort on the lumpy hard ground. The flannel quilted sleeping bags provided some protection from the ground and chill night air, but it wasn't anything like my feather bed at home.

Our party spent the second night, about 35 miles from Medford, on the Rogue River at the mountain retreat of Joseph H. Stewart, a prominent Medford orchard owner. His wife made us delicious peach pie for dessert.

The final full day of travel, we passed the Rogue River Gorge, with our attention drawn to the thunderous sound of waterfalls and the rushing river. We stopped for lunch and pondered the actions of nature and how it must have carved out these spectacular scenes.

"Don't try to swim through the lava tube," our guide warned. "Some daredevils have gotten stuck and died."

We arrived in the mid-afternoon on the fourth day, dusty and weary from sitting for days in a bumpy coach, shoulder to shoulder, not having properly bathed and glad for the fresh air whipping through the open sides of the coaches.

The hired hands set up our camp, while we wandered around the edges of the campsite. The air was crisp, moist and exhilarating, passing through the wind-blown trees and cutting loose some of the layers of dust which had accumulated in the pin tucking of my blouse.

"Mama, Daniel, come look!" my teenage explorers yelled in unison from up ahead of us on the trail. "It's so big and so VERY BLUE!!"

"It's the blue of impressionist painters!" Daniel added, having recently studied this new genre of art.

At the rim of the crater crest, the view below us opened up. The lake was the largest body of fresh water I had ever seen, and in a color meant for the richness of royalty. Across the lake, a great blanket of clouds appeared to pour into the crater and yet, though it moved quickly toward the lake, the spilling portion of the cloud bank evaporated as soon as it drifted down the brink of the rim, as if melting invisibly above the lake. I could feel the warmer currents of drier air streaming up from the lake, and I imagined they must absorb the water vapor from the clouds, as they did with the mist on my face. *What a magnificent sight!*

"Can we go swimming down there? I would love a bath right now," Ramona pleaded.

I was inclined to attempt the same, but thought first. "Let's not go too far today," I warned. "It looks rather steep and precarious. We should wait for our guides to show us the best way down tomorrow."

"I'm starving," Alex countered. "I'm going to ask if I can help the cook carve the meat, and maybe get an early snack. Did you notice how he cut those slices last night? What a culinary artist he was. He made everyone feel like they got the prime cut just by the way he sliced the roast. I'm going to ask if he can teach me how to improve my knife skills. Maybe it'll help me in my whittling. I'll see you at chow time!" he voice trailed behind him as he ran back to camp.

The next day, the skiff boat was unloaded and dragged to the crater rim. Mr. Steel had named the boat "The Start", because he believed that boating on the blue water would be the beginning of regular recreation activities at Crater Lake. He picked the access canyon that had been used once before, in 1886, when the first boat ever, had originally slid down the crater wall to reach the lake. That first boat's name was "The Cleetwood", and Mr. Steel coined that name for this canyon access as 'Cleetwood Canyon'.

We walked to the rim and cautiously followed 'The Start' down the steep cliff wall which was covered with loose jagged rocks. I could feel the sharp points of some volcanic tailings pushing through the leather soles of my boots, as I gingerly high stepped over the mish-mash of rubble down the cliff. Thankfully, the going was slow behind the descending boat.

Off to the sides of the boat were two men, with guiding ropes tethered to the skids attached under the middle of the boat. Step by step, they slid the skids and lowered the boat. Another two men directed the bow with their ropes, and guided it over the ravine of hardscrabble or stopped the descent and removed large boulders from their canyon route. A fifth man managed the rear of the boat by continually lengthening his rope, which was looped around a tree on the rim, and secured inside the boat to the rear seat plank.

While climbing down the rocks, we also had to duck under the green boughs of hemlock branches. But when we caught glimpses of the blue water, smooth and glittering with sunlight, it looked like a mirage. As we approached the shoreline, the lake became more intensely blue than it seemed from the crest above. I breathed the warm air deeply into my lungs, filling them with the purity that surrounded me.

"We will take eight passengers at a time over to Wizard Island. Once there, you are welcome to trek to the top of the cinder cone or picnic on the rocky beach shoreline around the base," Mr. Steel announced.

"We would be delighted to be in your first shuttle, Will," Daniel said.

"And I would like to accompany this initial group, with my photographers, to get their first impressions for our magazine," Mr. Miller requested.

"Well, that makes eight with our guide. I'll remain here to organize the remaining folks who have also chosen this adventure today," Mr. Steel stated, casting off the rope after we all had boarded the skiff.

The serene lake surface was so inviting to touch. Some of us leaned over the boat to dip our fingers into the soft water when the guide trumpeted, "Only one at a time on each side, please! We don't want to tip."

He steadied the boat with his oars and continued to explain his warning. "Some geologists came here with Mr.

Steel seventeen years ago and measured this lake using piano wire and lead weights. It's almost 2000 feet deep, and they say it's possibly the deepest lake in these United States. It's a long way down."

As we were rowed across, in the blazing sun beaming on the bright lake, we were all glad to have hats. As an observer from the lake level, we could easily see the cross sectional layers in the angled cliffs of the crater.

"How did this lake form?" I asked our guide.

"Mr. Steel can tell you more than I, ma'am. He's been studying this place for well over a decade. All I remember him saying is this crater was formed by a volcanic eruption of a once majestic mountain peak that stood right where this lake is now. He named that peak Mt. Mazama, after his climbing club called the Mazamas, or mountain goats. That sure describes him to a "T", don't ya think?"

"Sure does," Daniel agreed. "He scrambled down that canyon just like a mountain goat; sure-footed and quick."

"How big was this Mount Mazama that used to be here before nature decided to redecorate so violently?" Mr. Miller asked, pencil poised over his notepad.

"It must have towered above the surrounding country. It filled this here crater and Mr. Steel says it went up to over 14,000 feet in height, a rival for Mt. Shasta. He said something about measuring the angle of the slopes of the land leading up to the crater rim, or some such thing, to figure how high the top of Mt. Mazama was before it busted open."

"Thank you, young man for your colorful and informative geology lesson," Mr. Miller laughed. He frantically scribbled notes and sketches, filling many pages.

We disembarked at Wizard Island onto a very rocky shoreline that was lapped by a creamy white mud of volcanic dust and some slimy algae-like ooze. The shore rocks were ringed in yellow pollen that must have floated onto the lake water from the pine and hemlock trees on the island. I opted to remain around the base with Ramona, while the men clambered up to the top cone rocks, which were varied in all shades of black to deep red.

"Mama, what's that sound? It couldn't be someone hammering in this remote place," Ramona asked me.

"Oh, sweetie, that's just a woodpecker tapping at some tree bark, looking for grubs to eat. Speaking of which, what do we have to eat?" I asked as my stomach started to growl.

"I've brought some jerky and an apple from the camp for snacks. I guess we should save the rest for lunch when our explorers return, who will most likely be ravenous, particularly Alex," Ramona replied, knowing well of her brother's appetite.

After our nibble, we carefully meandered around the shoreline of gray ash and loose reddish porous rocks, which looked like they bubbled out of a soup pot. Ramona picked a bouquet for our bonnets of golden dandelions and spikey-petaled flowers that resembled paint brush tips dipped in deep orange dye. This trip was a treat for all our senses.

Upon returning in our boat to the main lakeshore, Ramona made her second request for a dip. "May we swim now?" she asked both me and Mr. Steel.

"Certainly. But, I must warn you, the water is rather cold. The ladies change room area is the behind that tree," Mr. Steel said, pointing down shore about twenty feet away.

Once Ramona and I exchanged our skirts for our swimming bloomers, we joined the men already splashing about.

"This is colder than a creek in winter!" I screeched after dipping just one foot in the water.

"Oh, Mama," Ramona teased. "Just jump in! I'm going to soak this dirt away."

I stood at the lake edge, getting wet enough by the splashes my daughter made as she dove in. She let out a blood-curdling scream as she popped up from the pool of blue, "Aaaaaaa! This is more than COLD! This is colder than the ice Alex delivers. It is like liquid blue ice!!"

At our campsite on the last night at Crater Lake National Park, we had a campfire and sang folk songs, spirituals, and patriotic songs, some in melodious rounds that were fun, harmonious, and inspiring. The oil lamps were pitched on metal stands around the group, lighting up all our faces in a flickering amber glow. Ramona bent down to pick up her cut tree stump base to move her seat closer to the fire, when I heard her howl.

"Owww!" she shrieked, as she dropped the stump. "Something just stabbed my hand! Mama help! It REALLY hurts!"

One of the young women in the group leaped up and pushed her way over to Ramona who, although she was thirteen, was now curled up in my lap, whimpering.

"I'm trained in herbal medicine. May I take a look? I might have something with me that can help," she professed.

Alex and Daniel went over to the improvised seat stump to see what could have been the culprit that caused the injury. Tilting the lamp closer to the ground, Daniel saw the smashed tail of the scorpion sticking out from under the stump base. "I believe it was this that stung her," he reported, as he held up the predator to show it to the herbalist and me.

"Well that is unfortunate, but not something which is fatal for someone your daughter's size," she concluded. "Let me get my bag and give her something for the pain and to prevent any skin inflammation or infection."

Within minutes, this woman had mixed up a poultice of some leaves and oil and placed it over the wound area, wrapping a strip of cloth around Ramona's hand to hold it in place. Then she poured some boiled water in a cup and stirred in a few drops of a dark liquid.

"What is all that?" Ramona asked somewhat less frantic, which I assumed was from the soothing pack on her hand. "And what are those leaves you used?"

"Aren't you the inquisitive one?" the herbalist commented. "If you really would like to know, the poultice is made of leaves from the St. John's Wort plant. It has antibacterial and anti-inflammatory properties and is often used as a topical remedy for wounds and muscle pain when mixed with oil and applied to the skin."

"Amazing! You're like a nature doctor for our camp," Ramona noted.

"Well, actually I'm more like an herbal pharmacist," she corrected. "And, young lady, you might want something to help you relax and sleep through the night. Once that venom spreads a bit and your hand starts throbbing, it can become rather disturbing. I have made this tea with some valerian root tincture I brought from home. It is a mild sedative that will help you drift off and sleep like a baby, if it is okay with your mother that you take this," she said with raised eyebrows, looking up at me. "It is formulated with alcohol to concentrate the potency of the root. Don't worry, there's barely enough spirits in this to get a mouse tipsy."

    I nodded my permission and Ramona sipped the tea while I cradled her in my arms like I used to do when she was little. As I looked into her eyes, I could imagine the wheels churning in her head as they tried to absorb this information about how herbal medicine worked. Perhaps she would follow a similar path if she ever truly did decide to pursue her dream of attending college. For now, all I hoped for was for her to be alright and sleep soundly and painlessly in our tent.

~ ~ ~

16  Times of Transition, 1905-1909

Although she remained deathly afraid of camping in the woods, Ramona continued to be intrigued by medicinal cures. Time flew by as she breezed through Ashland High School. She kept active in ways other than camping, like joining six of her friends, including Mabel Pelton, on the high school girls' basketball team. Ramona's 5'8" frame afforded her the position of star forward. She loved being a star.

Alex learned more about running a business, and continued to move up in the ranks to become manager of the Ice Company. Mama and I kept busy, marking the years with annual traditions, which now almost always included Daniel.

During Ramona's senior year of high school, in the fall of 1905 during one of my evening reads, I came across a newspaper story of an Oregon Supreme Court settlement decision publicized after three years of legal battles.

Rights of ownership had finally been determined for a spectacular space object that was discovered by a settler named Hughes in the Willamette Valley, just south of Portland. Mr. Ellis Hughes had stumbled upon a huge, odd-shaped boulder, bigger than an elephant and weighing ten times as much. Since he found it while he was walking in the woods behind his land, he named it the Willamette Meteorite.

"It seems that this Mr. Hughes wanted to make some money off of this oddity by displaying it as a tourist attraction in his lower field," I summarized to Mama and the children one night, while we were all sitting around in the new parlor.

"Sounds like a smart businessman taking advantage of a celestial gift that landed in his lap, so to speak," Alex said in defense of the inventive entrepreneur from up north.

"Well, actually, it didn't land in HIS lap, or field, as it was determined," I countered. "It just so happened that one of his tourist patrons was a nosy attorney, from the Oregon Iron and Steel Company who owned the neighboring property.

"This inquisitive patron noticed and traced a ¾ mile long rut trailing back from the meteorite on display at Hughes farm, to a depression matching the same size on his company's land. The pathway showed parallel wheel grooves alongside the central rut and deep hoof prints leading from the original hollow directly to Hughes' exhibition site. The company sued for ownership of the space rock back in 1902, saying Mr. Hughes had deliberately stolen it."

"Outstanding!" Alex declared. "What an amazing accomplishment to have moved such a thing so far!"

"Really, Alex? That's what matters to you? No reaction to the theft of the object?" I scolded. He bent his head down as if he was feeling contrite, but really I could tell he was hoping I wouldn't see his subtle smirk.

"Why did it take so long to settle this lawsuit?" Mama asked, always interested in how justice was dealt out. I know she was constantly worried about Charles maintaining support for her grandchildren since his involvement in another railroad lawsuit earlier this year. At the mention of a lawsuit, my mind drifted to the most recent one involving Charles.

In a previous similar nightly reading time, we had discussed that second railroad lawsuit, except the article was from the railroad news bulletin, not the local paper. Remembering...... I recalled how piqued I was at that time by the bulletin headlines about **"Pollution of the Pajaro".** The smaller print subtitle had read:

"A lawsuit, with representative E.C.Kane of the Southern Pacific and its subsidiary, the Rialto Oil and Refining Company, is contesting an injunction by the local residents of Santa Cruz County, California."

"That man just cannot stay out of trouble!" Mama had contended. "Didn't he learn his lesson after stealing those train cars for the railroad in Bakersfield?"

"I guess not, since he's involved in yet another suit," I had quipped. The bulletin story outlined the details:

"Despite the initial popularity of the oil field and the wealth it was bringing to nearby Watsonville, pollution began to seep into the Pajaro River almost immediately. It appeared that Little Pescadero Creek, which ran just south of the refinery, was doubling as a wash from the oil wells up on the hills. The runoff was fouling the water near town and polluting and injuring the health of people and grazing stock."

"Why is Father being sued? Shouldn't the company be the ones in court?" Ramona had questioned. I remember the concern on her face as she looked up from her homework when she heard her father's name.

I had tried to explain it in a way that somewhat exonerated Charles, to soften the news about his involvement in yet another court case.

"I think he is the agent who represents the SP and Oil Company. He most likely was trying to please everyone and didn't think or know about the runoff from the project, which was designed to bring fuel to the steam trains and electric streetcars used by the Southern Pacific."

I had hoped the real reason wasn't that he manipulated the community for his company's profit. From his history with me, that seemed to be something he was easily capable of doing, but I hadn't wanted to divulge that personality trait to his daughter at that time......

"Mama, hello? What about the meteorite?" Ramona asked, bringing me out of my ruminations.

Jolted by my daughter's voice, I sputtered, "Oh. Sorry my mind wandered for a minute...."

I returned to reading about the space rock lawsuit and continued, "It says here scientists said it was the largest meteorite found in North America, and the sixth largest in the world, 10'x7'x5', made mostly of 91% iron and some nickel, weighing in at over 15 tons."

I held up the newspaper photo of the meteorite to show my audience. The black rock looked pitted with huge cavities that made it look like a monstrous glob of black Swiss cheese.

"So what happened to the meteorite?" Alex was anxious to know if Mr. Hughes got away with the fantastic feat of moving such a boulder.

I read on: *"The court found for the plaintiff, the Iron and Steel Company. Immediately after the verdict, the victorious company sent a team with horses to Hughes' property, who started constructing a contraption to transport the iron monstrosity. Hughes frantically appealed the verdict to the state supreme court, and managed to get an injunction just as the meteorite began to be hauled away. The company hired a twenty-four hour guard, who sat on top of the meteorite with a loaded gun during the full appeal process."*

"That's foolish! All this over a rock?" Ramona said, incredulous, and returned to her homework.

"It gets better," I added. I continued to read:

"A third party complicated the proceedings and stepped up to claim ownership of the space rock. Members of the Clackamas tribe, who resided in the Willamette Valley for thousands of years, knew about this specimen and had named it 'Heavenly Visitor from the Moon', or 'Tomonowos'. They wanted it back for their spiritual rituals that they said healed and empowered their community. The court finally ruled the Indian claims and Hughes's suit "irrelevant", and awarded the rock to the plaintiff."

"So the guy hauled it for nothing?" Alex said, commiserating with Mr. Hughes. I was starting to worry about my son's ethics and fearing his following in his father's skewed footsteps. "Did the company take the meteorite?" he asked.

"The Iron and Steel Company decided it should be seen by everyone, without having to pay for the viewing. They hired a ship to sail it down the Willamette River to Portland. It is to be publicly displayed at the Lewis and Clark Exposition this fall," I summed up the article.

"And Mr. Hughes?" Alex prodded.

"Well, he won't be arrested, if that's what you're asking. Although, I believe he should have some sort of legal reprimand. But alas, no. The nearby city council has decided that someday they will place a plaque in town giving Mr. Hughes the distinguished honor of being the original founder of the rock. That's more than fair, I as far as I'm concerned," I summarized my opinion for my son, hoping to aim his morals in a more upstanding, lawful direction.

When June 1906 arrived, I breathed a sigh of relief when Ramona graduated from high school. Charles had held up his responsibility of support for his children throughout their juvenile years. Despite that, I still felt a bit of a flinch when I read in the railroad bulletin employee news, that in addition to Charles' sixteen year old son Clarence, he had had two more sons, who were now ages nine and four.

It didn't matter now, I told myself. Even so, I was continually drawn to read the bulletin when his name popped up in the SP Railway News. It appeared that after the settlement of the Pajaro lawsuit, he had been transferred to Alameda, near the Oakland, California Depot where his other children were born.

What did matter more to me was that Ramona was ecstatic about her acceptance to Oregon Agriculture College in Corvallis, or OAC as folks referred to it. She still really wanted to pursue her interest in herbal and pharmaceutical medicines.

Unfortunately, she had to wait a year before making the transition to college, needing first to build a cache of funds for her expenses.

With each of us working diligently, Ramona with her part-time jobs at the library and the drug store, and with my bonuses for "repeat customers", together we made her college career possible within the year.

Eager to start her academics in 1907, Ramona was also enthusiastic to add thespian activities to her schedule. Her college experience was a whole new world for her. She came home for the holidays ebullient about her education. During her first summer break, Ramona added to her coffers by returning to her job with a promotion, as an assistant pharmacist at Mr. Bolton's drug store.

I insisted the Ramona come to our new club, where she could observe the strength and power of women when they worked together for change. The Women's Civic Improvement Club, of which Anna, Mama and I were new members, had petitioned the City Council to acquire additional acreage for Lithia Park and to include park maintenance in the City Charter. All our voices, combined with zealous citizen support, achieved that goal.

The ladies of the Club, as well as the ladies in OES, took turns beautifying the grounds of the expanded Lithia Park, sprucing up the flower beds and planting seedlings for future generations to enjoy shade trees along Ashland Creek.

Often, we attended the Chautauqua performances inside the dome-shaped building in Lithia Park, where Ramona's eyes were mesmerized as she was drawn in by the dramatic portrayals on stage.

"I love the Band Concerts and the Ballet in the Park, but the theatrical performances are my favorites." Ramona commented during her freshman summer break.

"You are more than welcome to participate with us in our Women's Civic Club performance for the Fourth of July Parade, Ramona," I mentioned when she came home. "Women promoting civic pride here in Ashland, while dancing down the street, not only boosts tourism, but it promotes a place for women to feel welcome as visitors or new residents in town. Your acting skills would be such a bonus for us!"

Ramona continued with her theatrical club all throughout college. She won many accolades and gained college distinction for her great talent. But, she was more excited about a co-performer whom she met in her sophomore year in the Thespian Club.

In one of her letters from college, she wrote about this perfect gentleman:

"...he's so handsome and polite. His name is Henry Ludwig Bergman, from Marshfield, Oregon. He is the same age as I, however he is studying business and accounting. You would be so very impressed by his family background, Mama. His father is a decorated sea captain who has run the Umpqua River Lifesaving Station since 1891. He has told me the story of how his father acquired that position after having served in the navy. I was glued to my seat as Henry described the heroic rescue. Henry relayed his father's story as follows:

"Back in January 1883, my father and his friend Robert, volunteered to man a lifeboat to rescue seven crew who were stranded at sea on the steamer 'Tacoma', which had wrecked two days earlier at the mouth of the Umpqua River on the Oregon coast. The ill-fated steamer, which was transporting 3500 tons of coal from Seattle to San Francisco, was broken

into two pieces by break line boulders and run aground by shallowly submerged shoreline rocks and sand, a quarter mile offshore. The Captain of the steamer and six others had rowed to shore, in the only remaining intact dinghy, to get aid, as their original signal whistles brought no help. Upon sending the tender back for further crew, it capsized and the oars were swept away. The remaining forty-five men were hovered on the lee side of the tilted vessel, while every wave wet them through as heavy surf washed over the deck. The keeper of the Umpqua River lifesaving station feared that any rescue boat would come to a similar fate, and refused to send one into the surf.

The decks were swept clean by the pounding waves. All lines, cargo and provisions were lost, but the crew cleverly constructed as many rafts as they could from the ship's available doors and bucket racks still clinging to the sinking shambles. All but seven men reached the shore. The marooned crew remaining onboard, desperate, helpless and freezing in the cold January waves constantly breaking over them at sea, had only a few crackers and a keg of water to sustain them by the end of the second day.

The news of the wreck took two full days to reach Marshfield, twenty-six miles south of the wreck, where my father gathered his friend and a volunteer crew to go to the Umpqua River themselves and take the risk of manning a lifeboat to rescue the stranded seven. The ocean was in a fury, but they eventually saved all the bedraggled men from drowning in the wreckage. The navy attributed the disaster to compass errors arising from lack of proper adjustment of the instruments on board an iron vessel." **What a hero he was!**

So, Mother, you can see what a role model with which Henry grew up. He's MY hero here at college. He brings me dinner when he knows my rehearsals will run late. Henry also teaches me how to manage my money so I don't end up empty handed on a Saturday when I need to food shop or pay for my laundry services. I am most excited, though, when he is picked as my leading man in our school performances. I can't wait for you to meet him!

Everything else is going well here. My classes are enlightening in so many subjects. I do want to thank you so much for all your support and financial wherewithal that enabled me to have this higher educational experience. I must also remember to send a note to Father for his small contribution as well. Please send my regards to Grandmother, Alex and Daniel. I miss you all so very much. I will be home in just a few weeks for the whole summer. Let's plan some outings to the Lake. Do you think Daniel would still like to go horseback riding with me for blueberry picking? If you wouldn't mind putting in a word with Mr. Bolton for renewing my summer pharmacist job, I would certainly appreciate the help. I love you, Mother.

Always yours,

Ramona

P.S. Would you mind if Henry accompanied me home? He said he would love to see Ashland and meet my family. The railroad will make for his easy return connection through Roseburg to Marshfield after his visit. Perhaps he could rent one of your boarding house rooms for a few days?"

17  Orphan and Widow, 1908-1909

In a blur of desperation, I scrambled to make my boarding house booked during Henry's visit. If Henry was a perfect gentleman, like Ramona had said, I didn't want him exposed to or lured by unethical women toward inappropriate behaviors. I doubted this could ever happen, for upon meeting him, he truly appeared enamored with Ramona.

The offer of a free stay at Anna's was a gracious way to have Henry avoid crossing paths with my "girls" at the rooming house across the street. We redirected Henry away from the 'delicate side' of our lodging house duties by arranging outings and tea time in our rear gardens gazing towards the southwest mountains, in the completely opposite direction of the Depot and the boarding house. Everyone enjoyed his descriptions of the Oregon coast and his family stories. We vowed to visit sometime soon.

Mama regaled us with episodes from her childhood home town as well, mostly recounting these tales for the children, as I had already heard them when I was growing up. With all her reminiscing, she yearned to visit her family. She reiterated her stories with proud independence, more than she ever did when she was under Papa's roof. The confidence she exuded was a lesson for us all. She finished her story by noting that she had amassed quite a savings from her portion of the income we shared from the lodging house employment. Then she made an announcement.

"I think I would like to take a trip back home," Mama announced mid-summer that year of 1908.

"Jacksonville?" I asked surprised. "I can go with you if there is something you need from your old stomping grounds, but I assure you Ashland has everything here that Jacksonville has."

"No, no dear. I do not mean Jacksonville. I mean Indiana," Mama corrected me. "I am getting on in years and I would like to see my friends and family from my old home and once again breathe in the wheat fields of Indiana."

"When were you thinking we would do a trip such as this?" I asked a bit concerned about leaving the boarding house for an extended time that such travel would demand.

"Oh, not us, Alice," Mama confided. "I meant me, just by myself. I want to see this country from the western rails I never got to take. Remember, your father insisted I travel through Panama to go west when I came here in 1857?"

"Yes. And that was quite an ordeal and you were much younger. Now you want to travel alone?" I exploded. "Are you sure Mama? It's so far!" I couldn't contain my concerns.

"I'll be fine. I can take one of those fancy Pullman sleeper cars and feel like I'm in a rolling hotel. I've written to my cousin Tessie and she said she'd be delighted to have me home for a while. We will have so much to talk about. And besides, when Ramona goes back to college, this will give you and Daniel some more private space without me hovering about."

"Oh, Mama," I countered. "You don't hover."

"Never you mind. I have decided to go. I will send you a wire upon my arrival in Indiana, and you can keep in touch with me that way as well. We both have the training to do such communications, as "employees" of the railroad. I'll be setting out in a week's time."

I knew once her mind was made up, I wouldn't be able to change it. "Okay, Mother. If you insist. But, I require weekly correspondence and updates on your adventures!"

No more than three weeks later, in September 1908, I received a telegram from Indiana, albeit with my cousin listed as the sender. Happy to hear from her, but confused as to why it wasn't from Mama, I opened it with a bit of trepidation.

After I read through the pleasantries of greetings, I soon came to the shocking part of the message saying that "your Mama has passed away". I felt a stabbing pain in my heart and gasped for a breath. In the note, Cousin Tessie said Mama's death was caused by 'general debility due to her advanced age of 84 years'. I was in utter disbelief. She had been full of vitality at her departure.

I felt so guilty for letting her go alone and so far away at her age. I knew I couldn't have stopped her, but regardless, I was devastated by her loss. Daniel and Alex helped me through the following days. Alex wrote to his sister and I wrote to my siblings to let them know. I penned two copies of the following letter:

Dear Isaac and Mary,

I have just learned that Mama's trip was to be her last. She departed this life last Thursday, September 3rd, in her home town of Delphi, Indiana. Our distant cousin

Tessie said it was just her time and she slipped away peacefully in her sleep. Tessie said she was sorry to lose her after just having had a fifty year reunion. Mama's remains will reach Jacksonville Saturday. It would be most reassuring to have you both there for her interment at the cemetery when I bury her beside the graves of Papa, Aleck, and Sarah. I don't know what else there is to say. I am certain Mama is happy in heaven now with the rest of our family. Please let me know if you will need lodgings in Jacksonville, or if you would prefer to stay with me in Ashland.

Regards from your loving sister,   Alice

My world was shaken to the core. I felt the absence of Mama's presence everywhere. Our dinner table and evenings in the parlor were noticeably quieter.

My son Alex filled the conversational void by speaking about moving to a bigger city where he could put his business knowledge to better use than at the Ice Company. He wanted to use his carving skills that he had been practicing ever since our trip to Crater Lake. He thought he could do what he was passionate about by combining both abilities and develop a butcher business. Unfortunately, Ashland already had two. When Daniel started discussing the advantages of relocating his business to the San Francisco area, Alex listened intently.

By the next spring, in 1909, Daniel had just finished designing Ashland's First National Bank for EV Carter and was restless about remaining in our small town. His brick and concrete designs were some of the most modern in Ashland. He had constructed adjacent buildings with brick trim motifs across their upper façades, thereby appearing to tie contiguous yet independent buildings together.

Daniel wanted to take part in the reconstruction of San Francisco, since the earthquake had nearly leveled or burned most buildings to the ground in 1906.

"I think my brick and mortar designs will be well received in San Francisco," Daniel explained. "The earthquake tremors broke the city's water lines, leaving the firefighters with no means of combating the fires which broke out from overturned stoves, or damaged electric and gas lines. All the wooden structures went up like matchboxes. It's been almost three years since the disaster, and there are still more than 10,000 buildings that need to be rebuilt. I want to get in on the redesigning of the new San Francisco."

"I can tell you've given this idea quite a bit of thought," I slowly replied to this abrupt news about his wanting to leave Ashland. I just lost Mama six months ago and it sounded like I was about to lose Daniel too.

"I have," Daniel said softly, with his eyes downcast and brow furrowed. "I just didn't want to bring it up too soon after your mother passed. But I am anxious to make the move. I have done as much as I can in our little town. It's time to plunge into the limitless unknown. I am turning fifty soon, so it's now or never."

I was breathless. Daniel had been my foundation since the year after my divorce. In our fourteen years together, I had come to depend on him more than I realized, particularly for emotional support. I tried to think of what to say, when Alex piped in.

"I believe it's a grand idea, Daniel!" Alex approved loudly. "I've been thinking of making some changes myself. Your move just might be the impetus I've been waiting for. It would really help to already know someone around the Bay Area. I really want to try my hand in my own butcher and meat business."

"What do you say, Alice?" Daniel said all of a sudden including my name to snap me out of my wallowing and back into the conversation.

"Excuse me?" I responded, still stunned by the news. I tried to form words that would sound encouraging, although I couldn't bear the thought of losing more people in my life.

"I guess it sounds logical and profitable for you both. I will really miss you two, but don't worry about me. I will be fine here with Anna and Charlotte to keep me company. And Ramona will be here in the summers, if she doesn't run off and get married before she finishes college in a couple of years," I answered in the most thoughtful and rational manner that I could muster, trying to avoid expressing my deepest sadness about their life changes drawing them away from me.

"What are you talking about, Alice?" Daniel snapped as if he were scolding me about an incorrect answer. "Neither of us are thinking of making this move without YOU! Isn't that right, Alex?"

My son nodded vehemently. I looked up confused, my head turning, from one face to the other, like a metronome.

"Wh...what?" I stumbled with my words. I was confused by this different track on which they led my train of thoughts.

"What do you mean NOT without me? Are you asking me to leave Ashland? For me to move with you?"

"Of course, mother," Alex replied, placing a hand on my shoulder. "We would never think of doing this move any other way."

"Besides, I think a real change would do you some good as well," Daniel added.

"I don't think moving to the Bay Area would be a good idea for me. You both remember that Charles lives there with his new family. I think things could get quite awkward if our paths ever crossed," I disputed. "Anyhow, I think such a move right now would be rather upsetting to Ramona."

"She could stay at OAC and take the train all the way down to the Oakland Depot. We could pick her up and you would not have to think about running into Father there," Alex tried to allay my fears.

"I'll think about it. But don't let me stop either of you two from moving forward with your plans. I just need some time to process all the changes a move like this would require. I haven't thought about this as much as you both have," I answered with a deep sigh. I was relieved to be included, but this proposed transition presented enormous changes in my housing, friends, and employment, and potential uncomfortable interactions with Charles or worse, his wife. "Give me some time to think."

When Ramona came home for her second summer break, she was very insistent that I make the move with the men to Oakland. I remained skeptical, yet started looking into options to make such a change, without burning any bridges.

I spoke with Mrs. Brundige about her living situation since her recent divorce. She, Charlotte and I were in this special club of divorcées of which no one wanted to announce their affiliation or willingly chose to be a member. We privately shared our worries and solutions to the unique problems in which a single mother found herself in our turn of the century society.

"Thanks for coming today, Josephine," I stated when I ushered Mrs. Brundige into my parlor. It was just after Ramona returned to her junior year of college that I gathered up my courage to investigate the possibility of moving. I left the heavy, carved wooden front door open so the late summer breeze could blow through the screen door and cool us off a bit, in what could be a potentially embarrassing conversation.

"I heard that your housing situation has become difficult as of late. I don't mean to pry, but rather to offer a solution."

"Yes, Alice," Mrs. Brundige concurred. "My landlord will be selling his property and the meager income from my former husband won't cover the expenses of any other suitable rental in town. My children and I will have to move to a more remote area that I can afford. This creates a problem for my younger boy who won't be able to continue with his schoolin' being so far from town. He's just about to turn sixteen soon, so I guess he's had enough learnin' to make it in the world," she described her situation, sounding completely dejected.

"Well then," I perked up my voice, as I poured her some lemonade. "I think I may have the perfect solution for all of us. I am entertaining the idea of moving to the San

Francisco Bay area sometime and was wondering if you would be able to step into my position as the boarding house keeper for the railroad property across the street. Oh…um," I hesitated slightly, hoping she would remember, "there's also the taking care of the arrangements for the other 'delicate matters' that occasionally some of lodgers request. I believe you had no problem with this previously when you substituted for me years ago, am I correct?"

"We did just fine. I actually enjoyed some of the ladies' help in the garden. They said they were used to working there with you. But, if you were to move Alice, where would me and the boys be living? I assume you'd be selling this beautiful house of yours," Josephine questioned.

"Oh, I don't think I'm ready to part with this place just yet, not knowing how I'd like or fair in a new town so far away. I would have to have some income from renting it out to supplement me until I find another job. I hear it is considerably more expensive to live in a big city. I would rent my home to you at the same rate you are paying now for your place. Would such an arrangement work for you?" I asked my friend, not sure if I was ready for a definitive answer yet.

"Well, Alice," Josephine pondered. "I think that would work rather fine. I do however, need to give notice to my landlord. When were you thinkin' about making this move?"

"I do not really know yet," I confessed. "I want to visit my mother for her birthday next week, on September 16th. I guess that sounds a bit mad since she's been gone a year now. Somehow, I find solace talking things out when I am near her. I will get back with you after I return from Jacksonville Cemetery, next weekend." I still craved my Mama's advice.

Upon my return to the Ashland Depot from Jacksonville, the day after Mama's birthday, I spotted a notice on the Depot bulletin board outside the new Station Master's office. It read:

"Former Ashland Depot Station Master, **Mr. E.C. Kane,** *has passed away at age 54, on September 16, 1909.*

It is said that he died from a failing heart. Funeral this Saturday, September 18th at 2:00p.m. at Halsted and Co. Funeral Parlor, San Francisco. Friends and acquaintances are respectfully invited to attend. The SP Railroad is offering discounted return fares for railroad employees wishing to pay their respects."

I stood staring and re-reading the notice, when all of a sudden Cap Kramer came out of the Depot telegraph office.

"Oh, Mrs. Kane," he said. "I see you read the news. I am so sorry for your loss. I know Mr. Kane didn't do right by you, but he was a darn good Station Master. Such a shame, he was so young. Are you going to be okay, Mrs. Kane?"

"I'll be just fine, Cap," I slowly replied. "How odd he died on my mother's birthday. She didn't mention that when we spoke," was all I said. Cap gave me a quizzical look, knowing full well that my mother had passed away the year before.

I turned to walk up the two blocks to my house without further explanation. A sly smile swept over my face. *I'll be more than fine,* I thought. This was the news that clinched it for me. Now I could move to Oakland and never worry about seeing Charles again. I may have become an orphan last year, and a widow this year, but now I decided to never live without love nearby. I'll tell everyone tonight to start packing.

18  Weddings and Working, 1910-1913

The 'Shasta Line' train, with Alex and I aboard, cut through rain-charged clouds at the crest of the Siskiyou Pass after it departed from Ashland in early spring 1910. We were finally headed to our new home in Oakland, California. The rainfall dripping down the windows resembled the tears I was crying inside, as I left my home state. At 49 years old, making a change like this was scary and exciting, and all the changes made me a little apprehensive.

Daniel had moved a few months prior to us and acquired the lay of the land, making our transition slightly easier. I had accompanied him on his scouting trip in November, for a quick look around at Bay Area neighborhoods and housing prices. After the New Year, he made his move to San Francisco, settling in downtown to be closer to his work. He advised us to look around the Oakland area, which was not as much of a big city and was near the railroad depot, so Ramona could travel from Corvallis with ease. The Oakland Depot, with many connections, had been the western terminus of the transcontinental railroad since 1869.

By the time we arrived, the railroad had developed a web of transit lines that connected Bay Area neighborhood stations to the San Francisco ferry pier, as well as lines that reached the newer neighborhoods in the windswept Oakland hills. Fading remnants of meadows and orchards were being platted into subdivisions, like our Railroad District in Ashland had done so many years before.

"This area looks like a lovely neighborhood," I said to Alex and Daniel as we walked around the east side of a beautiful lake in town.

"Yes," agreed Daniel. "It has a great view of the lake and the oak covered hills. I heard that this is called Lake Merritt, but it is actually a tidal lagoon that mixes its fresh creek-drainage inlet waters with the salt water from the bay during the alternating tides. They say it was officially designated as a wildlife refuge in 1870 because of all the waterfowl that frequent it." Daniel liked to read up on things.

"Oh this would be a splendid place to come for picnics," I said, dreaming of peaceful days away from my scandalous two-faced Ashland life.

"And, we could rent a canoe and I could enchant you by reading some poetry while you paddle us around," Daniel added.

"While I paddle?" I snickered. "Oh, I think not. Perhaps I'll do the reading. You can point out your recommended poems, while I point out the ducks, so you do not row over them." Alex rolled his eyes and left the two of us giggling like school children. We met him later at the Oakland Depot Cafe for lunch.

We walked around the main street by the depot, intrigued by all the different establishments. I was not in any position to buy property, but I assumed that a realty office would know of houses for rent as well as to buy. Alex sauntered into a tobacconist's shop, a newly discovered boutique for him. We reconnected after my rental inquiry.

"I've rented us a three bedroom house in that lovely neighborhood by the lake," I told Alex as he exited the cigar store. The rich fragrance of fresh tobacco followed him through the open shop door, like a railroad engine trailing a steam cloud puff. His face broke into a wide grin.

"Great! I just inquired about a position in this store," he said pointing to the shop behind him. "They liked hearing about my years of experience in managing a business. The owner said I should return after we get settled."

"I think you already are," Daniel nodded.

My weekdays were lonely with my twenty-four year old son off to work and my sweetheart busy rebuilding San Francisco. I thought it was time to boost my coffers and myself, by getting a job. I certainly could not apply for a position as a Madam anywhere in town, not that I wanted to repeat that duplicitous life. Other problems thankfully prevented me from living among those kind of scandals. I did not have those 'connections' in Oakland, nor did I have room for boarders in my rental house. I needed to do something new.

Real estate buying and selling was the only other experience I had to apply for a job. I returned to the realty office to chat about my background in real estate, from all the investments I had bought and sold in Ashland.

"Well, Mrs. Kane," the office manager said. "It appears that you know quite a bit about transferring properties, clear titles, and profit margins. Now all you will need for this job is to become familiar with our available properties and the neighborhoods that we service. Do you drive a motorcar?"

"Heavens no!" I laughed. "I am a railroad girl myself. I was the Station Master's wife, but he is deceased now. I also used to work for Southern Pacific Railroad in Ashland, managing their boarding house property. I'm sure I can acquaint myself with the Oakland area by using the branch lines of the rail network. That will also familiarize me with another selling point regarding public transportation accessibility, to tout to new buyers."

"Sounds perfect. Are you familiar with the Key System?" he asked, pulling out an employment application form and sliding it across his desk to me.

"No, sir," I replied, feeling awkward as a newcomer. "Is that a system for a universal master key to open an onsite box with the house keys to all the houses listed on the market?"

"No, but that is a good idea!" Mr. Kavanaugh said lightly, brushing aside my ignorance. "It is the name given to the local electric streetcar and rail lines connecting the East Bay to San Francisco at our ferry pier. You'll eventually learn all these nicknames we have here in Oakland. The system's routes resemble a skeleton key. The three "handle loops" represent the cities of Berkeley, Piedmont, and Oakland, the "shaft" is the pier, and the "teeth" represent the ferry berths at the end of the pier."

"How quaint and such an easy design to decipher," I commented.

"How would you like to shadow me for a few days on my rides around town, and start on your own next week?" Mr. Kavanaugh offered.

"Yes, sir! I'll be here tomorrow at ten when you open. I'll complete and bring the job papers then. Thank you, again, sir," I politely replied, standing with an extended hand to seal the deal.

Alex came home beaming one day from work, with his eyes all sparkly and his breathing more rapid than his usual walk home produced.

"What's happened to you today? You look rather flushed," I commented, slightly worried.

"Mama! Mama! You'll never guess who appeared at work today," Alex responded full of excitement.

"Appeared? Is this a trick question or about an act by that magician, Mr. Houdini?" I chuckled.

"Neither Mama. I just met the most beautiful girl. She floated into the shop like an apparition," Alex clarified. "She works for a family in Alameda as their live-in maid. She came in to buy tobacco for her employer. He's a pipe smoker."

"And does this mirage have a name?" I tried to tease out the details from my flabbergasted son.

"Yes, of course. Her name is Irma. Irma Asbill. She's originally from Humboldt County, in the northwest corner of California. Pretty close to Oregon," Alex spewed out fact after fact. "She just moved here this year."

"And you uncovered all this information whilst she was ordering tobacco for the gentleman of her house?" I queried.

"Well, yes," Alex replied, slightly embarrassed that he uncovered more than a clerk would need to make a sale. "We got to talking since we are about the same age and I rarely see a woman customer entering our establishment, so I leaped at the opportunity to assist her," Alex justified his in-depth conversation with this girl.

"I first spoke about our fine tobaccos that we keep in our special quality controlled walk-in storage room called the humidor. She asked for a tour to sample the bouquets of the aromatic tobacco leaves which just emanate from those shelves.

"Soon after a few deep breaths, she said the humidity was soaking through her cloak, so we continued her shopping in the main sales room. After she choose a pouch of our special blend, I then showed her our full line of tobacco pipes, which are mostly handcrafted. She was rather impressed with my sales ability and knowledge. She said so herself!"

"I must say, I am as well," I agreed. "So, what became of this interaction? Did you ask to call on her sometime?"

"No, not exactly. I, um..., mentioned where I take my lunch break....uh, by the lakeside park benches down the block from our shop. She intimated that she might see me there sometime if her duties allowed for another town errand. Her employer's home is, um... just a couple of stops north of here on the local train," Alex excitedly stumbled through the idea of seeing this girl again.

May flowers bloomed around Oakland, and my son's romance blossomed with Irma. They joined Daniel and me for boating on the lake, occasionally receiving a splashing from Daniel when we silently glided closer to them from behind, having been obscured by the bend along the lake's northeastern shore.

Ramona came down on the train from Corvallis for the summer of 1910, thoroughly enjoying life in the big city. She was all aglow about her romance with Henry, which was developing into something more serious as they approached their senior year. Ramona's thespian performances were winning her laurels in her starring roles as a Union-supporting southern belle in "Barbara Frietchie", and as the leading young trollop in "The College Widow". I was astounded at the broad spectrum of her talents, but I knew she loved being in the limelight, beginning with her star performance back on her high school basketball team. Henry's constant presence around Ramona's performances alleviated any concerns I may have had about her being near those late-night theatre types.

To my delight, both Henry and Ramona came down for the Christmas holiday. Daniel was kind enough to house Henry in order to keep things proper. I was done fueling any further scandalous rumors. I wanted to keep my head high in this new town. The college seniors, and Irma, joined us for Christmas dinner and the opening of presents afterwards. Poor Irma only had one day off for the holiday, making a trip to her family home in Humboldt out of the question, so she spent it with us.

Our biggest family surprise came when Alex handed his present to Irma while he simultaneously dropped to one knee and popped the question. You could hear a pin drop in the silence that followed. We all held our breath until Irma uttered the words for which we all waited, "YES!! Of course I'll marry you."

Plans were made for Ramona and Henry to return during their spring vacation time for the wedding in March 1911. I brought Irma to the fabric store and millinery shop to start the process of making her wedding attire, just like Mama had done with me so many years ago.

My connections with the realty office helped tremendously in finding a new home for the future newlyweds. In fact, I was able to locate a rental, just a couple of doors down, on the same block as my house. Together, Irma and I sewed new curtains, made pillow covers and quilted new blankets for their bed. All of this sewing reminded me of how I missed my old sewing circle with the O.E.S. ladies back in Ashland.

Although, I kept pretty busy here in Oakland. I planted crocus bulbs in flower boxes on their front porch, hoping they'd bloom a beautiful purple just before the wedding at their new house. Daniel was looking forward to visiting me in a house empty of dependents and absent of prying eyes. He spoke of marriage from time to time with me, but I always declined gracefully.

"Our lives are running so smoothly the way things are now. I don't want anything to change that. I fear that once a man lives with me, he will become complacent and distant. Presently, each time we get together it is like we take a fresh look at each other, like seeing our favorite toy once again, and we're always happy to spend time with it, or I mean you," I explained as lovingly as I could to Daniel.

"I guess with this wedding coming up, I thought we could make it a double ceremony," Daniel returned with his offer. "I do love you and would never take you for granted. But, if this is how you want it to be, I will abide by your wishes, my love."

"Thank you for understanding, darling," I replied.

"Nevertheless, I can't wait for their honeymoon to start," Daniel said. "That is a celebration I am sure you agree we can duplicate, even if we aren't married. We will have this whole house to ourselves!" Daniel winked at this consolation prize.

"Yes. However, we will have to wait a few days until after the wedding when Ramona and Henry go back to college in Corvallis," I reminded him with a smile.

The wedding was perfect. Irma's mother, Kate, and stepfather, George, came down from Humboldt for the ceremony. Irma's face resembled her mother's, round as a cherub's and with dark sultry eyes. Standing beside Kate, Irma's stepfather stood tall and thin, with a head of hair enough for two men. I discovered that Irma's father had passed away over twenty years ago. Her mother had a different last name now and went by Kate Moore, not keeping the last name of Asbill, as Irma did until she became a Kane on her wedding day.

"This is such a lovely area. George and I have been thinking about making a move out of the dampness of the rainy northern coast. How long have you been here, Alice?" Kate asked, with George beside her on the back porch of the newlywed's rental, which overlooked the expanse of sundrenched Lake Merritt.

"Oh, we just moved down here from Southern Oregon last year. It was time for a change for all of us too. Originally, I was the Station Master's wife when the railroad came to Ashland in 1884. After eleven years, we divorced and I worked the next fifteen years for Southern Pacific managing their railroad boarding house in our town. I met my beau Daniel soon after I divorced Alex's father. In fact, Daniel was the one who wanted us to move here. He is helping to design the new city buildings in San Francisco. He has been the light of my life," I explained, eyeing their reaction to my sordid history.

Not noticing a flinch, I continued. "But also, I wanted Alex to have more opportunities than were available in our tiny town of Ashland," I expounded.

"I hear he is in sales. Tobacco, isn't it?" George interjected, politely skimming over my history. I was relieved.

"Yes, he loves business and sales. He hopes to become involved in the meat business someday. He learned as a teenager how to butcher and carve meat in different ways and cuts. He's got his eye on this Sacramento company, Virden Packing, which is opening up a meat packing plant just a few miles from here, the end of this year," I boasted about my son's potential.

"Well Irma is so excited about becoming his wife. They seem so in love. I suspect we will all be grandparents in the near future," Kate said with a wink.

Irma's parents had bought a kitchen table and chairs for the children's wedding gift. Alex used his whittling skills to make a handsome carved mahogany bed frame for their new double bed. Daniel and I bought them a red velvet couch and matching loveseat for their living room. Ramona was the lead chef for the entire reception dinner, plunking Henry in the roles of her butler and waiter.

After the wedding, everything changed. Within three months, my daughter swapped places with my son as my new housemate. Ramona and her sweetheart Henry had graduated in June 1911, just a few months after Alex's wedding. They were apart for the first time in three years and Ramona seemed lost without her best friend. I suggested, as a distraction, she look for a job. Now that she had a college degree, she could put her skills into action.

"I have, Mama," Ramona snapped back one evening during our after dinner parlor chat. Then, after she saw my raised eyebrows, she confided the true reason. "I knew that I should start helping out around here and I want to save money for trips to Marshfield to see Henry."

"Okay, dear. But don't worry about your expenses here. We are doing fine with our Ashland rental income and my realty job wages. Will Henry be coming down here sometime?" I tried to sound reassuring and compassionate.

"Oh, yes. He said he will take the overnight train to Oakland on every bank holiday that falls on a three day weekend. He also promised to be here for my twenty-third birthday in September. Did I tell you that he already has a position as a clerk in a bank?" Ramona bragged about her beau.

"That's wonderful, dear," I responded. "Now what about your job?"

"Oh, I forgot to tell you. I start next week at Collins Brothers Pharmacy here in Oakland. They are right across from the streetcar stop, one mile up from here."

"Excellent!" I remarked, glad for the financial help.

Throughout the summer, Ramona and I continued our post-dinner conversations accompanied by knitting and sewing projects of baby clothes for the upcoming newest Kane family member.

Alex and Irma were nervous and excited about becoming parents. Irma's parents had indeed decided to make the move to the Bay Area. I helped them find real estate near the water's edge, something they preferred, since they were used to an ocean view on the north coast. They purchased a small two-story older Craftsman cottage in Alameda, just across the bridge over Oakland Harbor. Irma beamed having more family around to dote on her.

Alex talked his way into that job with Virden Packing Company, in Fruitvale, a mere two miles from home. He started as a salesman, traveling and promoting Virden products to shops around the San Francisco Bay.

Alex worked his background to his advantage. He had knowledge of the benefits of railway shipping from listening to his father's stories and had experience with preserving arriving produce and meats from his deliveries with Ashland Ice Company. He combined this information into a suggested arrangement with the railroad and his packing company. He outlined how a business like a packing company could ship quicker and fresher using the rails, if they could get a discount with them to move their products. He brokered a deal which benefited both companies. Mr. Virden was rather impressed by Alex's gumption to take the initiative and make things more efficient and profitable. Alex quickly moved up the ladder to district salesman.

After the New Year was ushered in, most of 1912 revolved around the new baby. Alex and Irma's first born, Keith, came in February. His eyes were as blue as the bay, and his hair curled around his smiling face, framing his dimples. With four grandparents now available, Irma had more help and advice than she needed. This came in handy with Alex's new traveling position, which made for late night returns from work, often arriving home after Keith was asleep. Grandmotherly donations of prepared meals and occasional babysitting strolls gave Irma a chance to catch up on her chores and much needed sleep.

Also that February, Daniel and I joined a new society which met in Golden Gate Park. The paper announced a headline stating "Southern Oregon Society Planned" for former residents of Oregon and descendants of Oregon pioneers.

"Let's go!" I declared to Daniel one Sunday, after we brought and shared brunch with my son and his new family.

"Sounds good to me! It says that in addition to the promotion of the social spirit among the members, the society will seek to aid the exposition project through advertising among the towns of southern Oregon," Daniel read, then commented further. "Maybe we'll find some other Oregonians here that we already know, or maybe the society advertisements will ignite a spark for our friends to visit."

The society was an outlet for the music and dancing that we both missed. We learned about news from back home that was never reported in the big San Francisco papers. It appeared that Anna Carter was ever so busy with her library. Along with the Ashland Women's Civic Club, she fought for and succeeded in obtaining funding for the new Ashland Carnegie Library. I immediately wrote to her for all the details. Her reply was as follows:

S.K. DeMarinis

Dear Alice,   *May 20, 1912*

I do miss you so. I wish you were here to watch the new library being built. There has been such controversy over whether or not Ashland should build a library with tainted money offered by the industrialist Andrew Carnegie. After convincing the council, we formally applied for the $20,000 Carnegie Grant, but the reply Mr. Carnegie sent said he would only give $15,000, and only if the City of Ashland would provide a site and a maintenance fund. Well that sent everyone into a tizzy!

The East Side Boosters pointed out that with the town center moving up the boulevard, they wanted to build the library in a growing part of town. Others wanted it on the hill near the Chautauqua dome. One old fogie wrote his opinion in the Tidings as such: 'I am one of those old fogies who thought a library was for the use of the people, to help educate, etc., but I am woefully mistaken; it is for an ornament to the city and to enhance or increase the value of some lots for their owners, it does not matter where or how inaccessible to the people.'

Well, with Lottie Wilkins offering her corner lot on Gresham Street for only $3500, the East Side boosters sweetened the deal by raising $1700 to help defray the costs of the site. That was what clinched the deal. It is now catty-cornered to my house, across the main boulevard. It will open this summer. I am still on the library board, and Blanche Hicks is now head librarian.

The Women's Civic Club is also calling for a 'Votes for Women' campaign. They have to rally the men to put a vote on the ballot. So many changes around town. Wish you were here to help move things along.

Congratulations on the new grandbaby! Hope to see you soon,

Warmest of regards,

Anna

At Christmas time, we were again blessed by witnessing another man hand a gift to his sweetheart on a bended knee. Henry slipped a ring on Ramona's trembling hand as he proposed. Another resounding 'YES' echoed around the Christmas tree, floating on the scent of my apple pie which hung sweetly in the air. The engaged couple made plans for Ramona to meet Henry's parents in Marshfield before the wedding during the upcoming spring, sometime in March. They planned the ceremony for a couple of months later, in May of 1913, to be held in my new California backyard.

~ ~ ~

19  Sewing Circle Secrets, 1913

"Oh, Mother. You should have seen their house!" Ramona declared when she returned from her Oregon trip to coastal Florence in March 1913.

She rattled on about her soon to be in-laws. "Sitting on the center of their ornately carved fireplace mantle, was a shiny goblet. Henry's father, they call him 'the Captain', showed me this beautiful solid silver loving cup, standing nine inches high and seven inches across. The cup was given as a retirement gift with an inscription on it which said: Umpqua River L.S.S., Oct. 1st, 1911, presented to Keeper John Bergman by his crew."

"Oh, goodness." I said. "Solid silver? What an honor!"

"Yes, but that's not all. He also showed me a real gold medal that was given to him by a rare and special act of the United States Congress for his leading the rescue of those men stranded on the sinking steamer I told you about."

"Now that's something of which one can be proud," I admitted. "Be sure to remember these stories for your children, so they understand what a great man their grandfather was."

"Oh, Mama. Aren't we getting a little ahead of ourselves?" Ramona skirted the subject of babies in her near future.

"I guess babies have been on my mind since I spend so much time with baby Keith. I do hope you and Henry come to visit often after you move back to Oregon. I wouldn't want to miss out on spoiling your children too, when the time comes."

"Well, Mama. Maybe by then, Alex's children will be grown and you will move back to Oregon to be near us," Ramona taunted. I laughed. Another move seemed daunting.

In April, Irma's mother Kate invited us to join the Alameda Sewing Circle she had discovered in her neighborhood. I missed the O.E.S. embroidery club meetings I used to have at my house in Ashland and jumped at the chance to add a women's circle to my busy life and work schedule.

"They meet every other Saturday when Alex is home from work, and I bet he would love to have some father and son time without us ladies hovering," Kate suggested. "How about you, Irma and Ramona take the streetcar and I'll meet you at the stop by the Presbyterian Church hall? We can all go in together," Kate said to me on her last visit to see baby Keith, in Oakland.

"I'd love to come." I answered. "Are the members all our age, or are there young ladies there too, like our girls' age?"

"Well, I've only been to a couple of meetings," Kate answered. "But it looked like a nice mix of ages. I don't know anyone yet, except the woman I sat next to named Amy. Bring your latest project, the ladies often trade threads. And we can probably get some ideas for summer jumpers for baby Keith."

Ramona was anxious to have help with sewing her wedding trousseau. I was half way done with her wedding gown and needed a little extra help with the beading on the white satin bodice. The ceremony was in five weeks at my home, just in time to have a canopy of spring flowers blooming over the gazebo in my yard, and prior to Mother's

Day Sunday. Ramona picked a date where she could add a tribute to all the mothers who would be there for the wedding. Alex wanted to have baby Keith's christening done at the same time by Rev. Father Gee. The table talk at the sewing circle seemed to revolve around weddings.

"My son is getting married as well," Amy chirped in when she heard us speaking of Ramona's upcoming nuptials. I looked up to see who was speaking and took a glance at the woman sitting next to Kate. For some reason her face sparked a faded memory of someone I had seen before. I couldn't place her face, and she was much older than the image in my mind. With so many new faces in this big city, it was more than likely, that certain features would remind me of someone I had seen before.

She continued, "His wedding is in June, so I have a little more time than you to finish my project, their wedding bedcover quilt. Most of the ladies here are sewing for local orphans, unless they too have some special occasion to mark with their seamstress talents."

However, at the first meeting in May, Amy had quite a different, chilling story to share. "It was an awful, harrowing experience for my son and his fiancé. The Sunday following our last meeting, he and his betrothed were walking over a foot bridge in a park near San Rafael when it gave way. They both fell twenty-five feet into deep water. My son struggled, with great difficulty, to keep his fiancé's head above water. They were both rescued by a man who dragged them to safety with a long pole."

The crowd of women all gasped and squealed at the tale. A few women asked if they were hurt or seriously injured.

"No, thank goodness. My son Clarence is very stout and his fiancé is now in love with him more than ever, for saving her life. She says he's her Hero. He is a newspaper man and wrote a story for the paper about the thrilling experience. He always seems to know how to turn lemons into lemonade."

As we all gathered at the exit to leave the hall, the janitor called over the crowd, "Mrs. Kane! You forgot your sewing basket!" I turned around when I heard my name called, thinking it odd since I didn't remember introducing myself to him. But at that same instant, I saw Amy raise her hand in thanks and walk over to retrieve her basket. Then, at that very moment, it all clicked.

That nagging feeling of familiarity fell into place. THIS Amy was Amy Kane, Charles' second wife! Clarence was THAT Clarence, Charles' second son! Twenty-one years later, her face had aged from the photo I had placed on our fireplace mantle the day I told Charles to leave.

The color drained from my face. I started to topple and fortunately, Ramona caught my arm. My breathing became shallow and staccato. I grabbed my chest to contain the pain.

"Mother, are you alright?" Ramona asked with a furrowed brow. She obviously had not paid attention to or heard the call of the janitor.

"Let's just go," I answered, my words skipping over my exhaling air. "I need to get home and lie down. All of a sudden I'm not feeling so well."

On the streetcar ride home, the girls made sure I had a seat. Ramona asked again about my health. I took a few deep breaths and gathered my words. Irma leaned in to hear me, holding on to the pole next to Ramona as we bumped along.

"Well, dear," I began. "You remember the story I eventually told you about your father having an affair and marrying another woman?"

Ramona looked puzzled as to why I was bringing up this story at this very moment. "Um, Yes. But why are you asking me this now?" She gave me a stern look, tilting her eyes towards Irma.

"I don't mind if Irma hears this. She's part of the family now and she should know our history, no matter how scandalous," I curtly answered. "It's true. When Alex and Ramona were just young children, their father had an affair. I found out about this 'other woman', and the son she had had with my husband, which triggered my divorce lawsuit." I paused for a moment to take in another deep breath, and waited for a response from Irma. None came, so I continued.

"So today, as it turns out, I just realized that that 'other woman' is the Amy with whom we have been sewing these past weeks. And her son, Clarence - who is about to be married in June - is the child she had out of wedlock with my husband in 1890. What a horrific coincidence! I am mortified. There is no way I will return to that group again!"

Now it was Ramona and Irma's turn to have the color fade from their faces. Their mouths were agape and they kept looking from each other and back to me to see if I was joking. All they could say, in unison of descending tones, was, "Oh, Mother! Oh, my goodness! Impossible! Oh, no, mother...."

"I'm afraid so," I admitted, clutching the armrest of the trolley seat for support so I could to continue explaining my appalling revelation. "The custodian of the hall called her by her proper name, as we were leaving. After I heard the Kane name connected with Amy, it triggered me to rehash her stories and I realized that the names and dates in her family history matched the ones involved in your father's timeline of his philandering ways."

Ramona's mouth opened into a big "O", with no words forthcoming. "Don't tell Henry," I added, glaring at Ramona. "He shouldn't know such things about our family before you two are married."

Then, I noticed Irma's face looking more concerned than Ramona's and said, "I doubt Alex would ever follow in his father's footsteps and wander from you, Irma! But, I've learned with most men, it's a good idea to keep a close eye on them anyway."

~ ~ ~

20  Wedding Time Again, 1913

Sitting half in sunlight and half in shadow, Captain Bergman had the posture of man in two places. It appeared as if his thoughts were also divided, as his eyes stared out over the lake and onto the bay. Henry's mother, Kathrine, was plainly dressed in a pale blue pinstriped dress with dark blue buttons accenting her white sailor collar and matching cuffs on her ¾ length sleeves. She sat next to her husband with her hand on his knee, watching her son go over the final wedding details with the Reverend.

Henry's brother John, Vice-President of Lane County State Savings Bank, and his wife Lena, along with his sister Mary and her attorney husband Fred Hollister, had also come from Oregon for the wedding. John resided near his parents in Florence and Mary was from a neighboring coastal town called North Bend.

My family, the bride's entourage, sat on the other side of the lavender wisteria-covered wedding arch. Irma had fifteen month old Keith on her lap and sat between me and Alex. Irma's parents, Kate and George, joined the bride's side, but were mainly there for the christening of baby Keith, which had been prearranged for immediately following the wedding ceremony.

Isaac, Dora and Dot took the train from Portland to join us and had planned a tour afterwards, around San Francisco. I was overjoyed to see them and introduce them to Ramona's new family. They sat behind us and craned to see

Dot, still a single woman at thirty years old, positioned to precede the bride down the stairs of my back porch. She held a basket of orange blossom flowers, ready to toss and create a fragrant path for Ramona's bridal walk.

When the piano and violins started playing the chorus refrain of *"All That I Ask of You is Love"*, Dot started her descent, followed by the bride emerging through the back door like a flowing angelic vision. Ramona, in her slender, white satin beaded gown and tulle veil dotted with attached fresh orange blossoms, was escorted down the back porch steps; one arm wrapped around Daniel's elbow and the other carrying a bouquet of lilies of the valley and orchids. I hummed the words to the familiar wedding song in my head and smiled:

> *"All I ask is love,*
>> *All I want is you;*
>> *And I swear by all the stars,*
>> *I'll be forever true.*
>
> *All that I seek to know,*
>> *All that I want above,*
>> *All that I crave in this wide, wide world,*
>
> *All that I ask of you is love."*

Vows were exchanged and the bouquet was thrown. Of all the guests, I happened to be the one to catch it. When Daniel winked at me, I quickly turned and set the flowers into a vase on the food table at the base of the porch.

The festivities were not over until the services of the Reverend were shifted to the christening of baby Keith. The new bride and groom stood as the godparent sponsors of their nephew, alongside the baptismal basin George brought up to the arch for that ceremony.

Kate cornered me at the reception and struck up a conversation that quickly became uncomfortable. "How come you haven't been back to the Alameda Sewing Circle, Alice?" she asked so politely, but I could tell she thought it may have been something she said or did.

"Oh, Kate, dear. It's nothing really that's keeping me away. It's just that I was done with Ramona's wedding gown and now in the summer, I prefer to work on my other projects here, outside in my yard at home. Maybe I'll return again in the fall," I lied. I wasn't sure how close she was with Amy and I didn't want to upset her association with her women's group.

Henry and Ramona left for their weekend honeymoon in San Francisco, while the rest of the Bergman family stayed between the two Kane houses on our block. We said goodbye to my brother Isaac and his family because they were headed home after they finished their train tour of the Bay Area.

During the absence of the bridal couple, we had a chance to get to know Henry's lovely family. They repeatedly invited us to visit the Oregon coast whenever we liked. The Captain, as he preferred to be called, still spoke with a German accent, having arrived in America as an adult, when he was twenty-two years old. He had a wealth of stories and legends to share about the nearly fifty shipwrecks he participated in rescuing. Though he had many adventurous days along the treacherous Pacific, Alex was most interested in his original business, the Seaside Packing Company. For ten years, he ran this first salmon packing establishment on the Columbia River, prior to his thirty years as a lighthouse keeper.

"Ja. Ve made lots of Geld, uh money, selling za fish. Ve learned how to schmoke it and zen ve cudt sell it packed up for shops farzther avay," Henry's father told Alex. It took me a while to get used to his pronunciation of English words, but my son seemed to have no problem. It appeared that he was making mental notes for his work.

"I work with meats, mostly," Alex contributed to the conversation, as he carved the turkey for our shared dinner one night. "I would be interested in learning about smokers and how to build small smokehouses. I'm thinking about opening my own meat market next year."

"You are?" I chimed in, chopping the vegetables for the salad. "When did you decide this? Will you be leaving Virden Packing then?"

"Oh, never, Mama. I just think it would feed my passion and my family better. It would be an easy side job once I set everything up and hire and train the right butcher. I already have the connections with the food shops in town, so my client base is ready made. You'll see," Alex comforted my concerns with his detailed plans.

When Ramona returned with Henry from their honeymoon, they joined the rest of his family for the long train ride back to the central Oregon Coast. Henry had already found a house for them in North Bend near his sister Mary, and reiterated that we were to visit soon.

Daniel had surprised me with a vacation of our own that summer. "Don't forget to bring your swimming costume and tights for the beach. There are bathhouses on the beach for changing into your bathing clothes while maintaining your modesty," he said.

Our travels landed us at the Santa Cruz Beach Boardwalk Amusement Park and Pool. The connections were easy from the Bay Area, using Southern Pacific trains and Santa Cruz trolleys. The trolley stopped right at the beach by Santa Cruz's natatorium, just blocks from our hotel.

"Aren't we swimming indoors in that high arched pool building?" I asked, confused about beach bathhouses and pointing up to the name on the arch, which said "The Plunge".

"Oh, sure. We'll swim both in the ocean and indoors. I bet we'll want to be in the heated salt water pool after a quick dip in the very cold bay. Another plus indoors is their forty foot slide dropping into the main pool. Get ready to be splashed!" Daniel warned.

"And you as well," I retorted. "Where will we stay?"

"I booked us an ocean view room at that hotel," Daniel said, pointing to the nearby Sea Beach Hotel. That will make it easier to change our outfits for the different evening activities along the boardwalk. Did you know they built a carousel here two years ago?"

"I think I heard something about that. Does this carousel have that Brass Ring Toss Challenge?" I wondered if I had read about it as an East or West coast new amusement park feature.

"Yes. That's definitely here. And we will most certainly take a ride. I look forward to the challenge," Daniel confidently added. "How about you?"

"No. I don't think I need to fall off a horse, even a wooden one. I'll cheer you on for the perfect toss."

The weather was perfect for summer fun at the beach. I actually enjoyed splashing around the ocean in my short swimming skirt and sailor blouse top. It was so much easier to move about the waves with less fabric than in my old bathing costumes, which always weighed me down.

After changing into dry clothes, we pieced together a picnic lunch from the snack booths. Then the carousel challenge was on.

Daniel grabbed a seat on the outermost carousel horse, leaving me to sit on the inside sleigh seat for the ride. I laughed at Daniel's crazy antics when he reached for the brass rings, which rolled down the tube dispenser on the wall, with every merry-go-round revolution.

"Here, hold this one. I want to keep it as a souvenir of today. I will get another one, on the next go around, for tossing into the clown's mouth," Daniel screamed over the loud music that paced with the rise and fall of the wooden, painted animals on the circular machine.

When we got off, I was slightly dizzy. Daniel asked me to give back the brass ring to him. "I want to put it somewhere safe. And.....I, um.....want to give you a different one."

I pulled the brass ring from my dress pocket as he simultaneously pulled something from his jacket pocket. When he took the brass ring from me he said, "Here. I think this one will fit you better."

He slipped a silver filigree diamond ring onto the fourth finger of my left hand. It made rainbows in the sunlight that danced on his face.

"Oh, Daniel," I gasped at the ring. "What is this for?"

"You! Silly woman," he quipped. "Now that both of your children are out of the house and married, I thought it was time we did the same. I said I would honor your wishes, but I thought I'd ask one more time. Will you marry me, my darling Alice?"

Speechless, and pensive, I finally formed the words to answer him. "Yes. I would be honored to now become your wife and not be known anymore as the Station Master's abandoned wife. You are truly a man I can trust and love without fear of losing you."

"Great! Let's plan a fall wedding close to your birthday in October. That will give everyone a good reason to visit and we can surprise them with the ceremony," Daniel concluded.

We confirmed our commitment with a kiss. My life was finally filled with love and happiness again, for me and my entire family. At that moment, my world was perfect, and I held on tightly to the love of my life.

~ ~ ~

21  Bay Area Blowout and Back, 1913

An unexpected knock at my front door made me jump. It was only 4:00pm. on a Monday afternoon. I wasn't expecting Daniel until 6:00pm for dinner. The summer evening light in early September was perfect for an intimate backyard dinner, with a gentle breeze blowing off the bay up towards the Oakland hills.

"Alice Kane?" a gentleman inquired when I partially opened the door. Most of my body stood protected by the door, only my face peered out.

"Yes, I'm Mrs. Kane," I answered. "May I help you?"

"Um, I would like to come in, if I may. I'm Mr. Daniel Cameron's supervisor, from the construction project downtown," he informed me. "My name is Johnson, Gus Johnson. I'm the other half of Anderson and Johnson Construction."

"Oh. Please, do come in," I stepped aside and pointed toward the living room. "Is this about Daniel's request for vacation time in October? I bet he didn't tell you it was to be for our honeymoon. I know he's had a fair bit of leave requests recently, but we have had many family events happen in the past year requiring his presence. Did he tell you he walked my daughter down the aisle at her wedding in May?" I babbled on.

I sat down and got a closer look at the agony in his face and realized this visit was more of a serious nature. "Oh, pardon me, you look like you have something rather important to discuss. Please, continue."

"I don't know how to say this any other way than to just come right out with it. Mr. Cameron is no longer with us," Mr. Johnson said, twirling his hat nervously in his hands.

"Wh....What?" I couldn't understand what he meant. "What do you mean? That's impossible," I said dismissing his proclamation with a wave of my hand. "I just saw him this morning and he said the project was progressing nicely. Why has he been dismissed? Tell me, please.........." I rambled.

"My foreman and Mr. Cameron were meeting today to review the blueprints for our project. There was some confusion about the design of the window arches. They were standing at the base of the building when the third floor wall beams were being put in place. It must have been the extra weight that made things happen," he recapped the event as he was told.

"What do you mean, 'happened'?" I screamed. I inched towards him, my hands grabbing the arms of my chair. Mr. Johnson slowly and methodically continued with his story.

"When we started this project, we removed the prior wooden building's rubble and debris that was strewn across the site by the earthquake. Mr. Cameron, uh, I mean Daniel, designed a more fireproof building made of a block limestone base, with a façade of brick and tile framed over steel beams," Gus rattled on.

"Get to the point!" I yelled, impatiently.

"Yes ma'am. What I'm trying to say is that by the time the building reached its current height with placement of the third story, the weight of it appears to have collapsed an unmarked three foot wide clay sewer pipe, in place prior to the earthquake, running under the whole northeast corner. The building's footing sunk into the collapsing hollow cavity of the pipe, and beams started to fly off the structure. Mr. Cameron and my foreman were head down, making notes on the blueprints, when they were struck and killed. I am so very sorry Ma'am. You were listed as his next of kin. I thought the only decent thing to do was to tell you in person."

I slumped back into my seat. My head dropped to my chest and I started to wail and scream. The sounds emanating from me were not recognizable as human. Shortly after, Mr. Johnson muttered something to someone who came in the front door. Through the blur of my tears, I saw Irma and baby Keith in her arms. I assumed she heard my screams two doors down, at her house and came running. I heard them talking and the next thing I knew I was falling asleep in my bed after being given some medication by my daughter-in-law. I was grateful for the chemical fog that produced no dreams, turning off my world for a while.

"Really, Mama," Alex and Ramona said together, standing by my bedside. "You have to get up sometime. It has been three weeks since you have been outside. We don't know what to tell the realty office, or anyone else, for that matter."

I was confused as to what Ramona was doing in Oakland, but I eventually understood that Irma and Alex summoned her to bring me out of my funk.

Alex and Irma, overwhelmed with their toddler, had just announced that they were going to have another baby next June. I was so paralyzed by Daniel's death that days were eclipsed and time was befuddled in my brain. The children were speaking about how they wanted to celebrate my birthday, which I then realized was only a week away.

"I think after we toast to your birthday next week, you should move back to Oregon with me," my daughter declared. "Alex and Irma will still have Kate and George to help out down here and I would love the company back home. The coast is such a good place for relaxing. The ocean waves will lull you into peace. I walk on the beach often to clear my thoughts."

"Oregon... I would love to be back in Oregon," I mumbled, remembering all the good times there with Daniel.

"Well then, it's settled. When you feel a little stronger we will get things going for your move. I will speak with your boss at the realty company and explain our decision," Ramona announced.

"I'll set up packers and movers and reserve a special train car for transportation and delivery directly to your door in North Bend," Alex added helpfully. "Just let me know when would be best for you, Mama."

I sat up and opened my eyes wider to focus more on what was being decided. Ramona continued to clarify the details. "We have plenty of room in our home, Mama. Henry and I bought a three bedroom house and haven't filled it yet with the pitter-patter of little feet, as you well know. He is so busy at the bank, for extended hours sometimes, I would be grateful to have the company. I'm sure the Captain would enjoy introducing you to his pioneer friends and the important people around town."

"Hold on there, my sweetheart. I know you are trying to help and bring me back to the world of the living, but let's just focus on my move first and let things settle for a while," I said to Ramona, exhausted just thinking about it.

Within a couple of weeks, everything was set in motion. I dragged myself through each day, using all my energy to pack one box of mementos or personal items, and then take a stroll to the lake and back.

One day, Irma's mother Kate came by to check on me and visit with Irma who was still in the nauseous stage of her second pregnancy. She joined me on my afternoon amble to Lake Merritt.

"Are you going to be alright, Alice?" Kate asked so kindly as we walked.

"I'm not sure yet. Daniel was such a strong pillar in my life, it's hard to believe he's gone. We had finally decided to get married. I don't know if I told you that. It was going to be a surprise announcement at my birthday party," I finally admitted to someone.

"Oh, my! That makes this even harder to imagine how difficult things must be for you right now," Kate confided. "Do the children know about what you and Daniel had planned?"

"No. It does not seem to matter now," I sobbed. After a few more steps in silence, I took a deep breath and continued speaking. "I know Ramona is just trying to help. She hovers over me like a mother hen. I think the best thing for me will be those walks on the beach. Plus a change of scenery that does not remind me of my recent days with Daniel every time I turn a corner, will help me move forward in my life. Or, at least I am hoping it will," I said trying to convince myself and Kate that things would be okay.

My departure was within a few days and I wanted to let Kate know the truth about Amy Kane and her history with the Station Master of Ashland, and when he was posted more recently in Oakland. I began to unravel the story on our way back from the lake.

"Kate, I need to tell you something else," I hesitated trying to gather the courage. "It's about that woman who sits next to you at the Alameda Sewing Circle."

"Oh, you mean Amy?" Kate asked.

"Yes, that's the one. Do you know her last name?" I gently pried, hoping to subtly broach the subject.

"No, not really. Everyone just goes by first names there," she said. "Why do you ask?"

"Well, the janitor knows her name. He called out to her once when I was there. It is Amy Kane," I blurted out.

"That's odd. Are you two related somehow?" she innocently inquired.

"Not by my choice," I replied. "She was my husband's second wife. Actually, she was his mistress first, while we were still married. Her relationship, and her son Clarence, whom she had while I was still married to my husband, was the impetus for my divorce in 1895."

"Oh...OH! Oh, my! ALICE! Are you sure?" Kate asked, hoping I was mistaken.

"Oh, yes. I am definitely sure," I clearly stated. I knew my Charles moved to Oakland to be the Station Master there soon after we divorced. I put things together after I heard the janitor in the Sewing Circle hall call her name. She had mentioned her husband had passed away a few years back, and her face looked somewhat familiar to me."

"You met her before?" Kate asked incredulously.

"No, not in person," I clarified. "I saw a photograph of her and my husband, with their son Clarence when he was about four or five. She called Charles, "Ellsworth". His name was E. C. Kane. In Oregon, my husband always went by his middle name, Charles. I guess he used his first name, Ellsworth, for his double life in California. She sent that photograph to him at the Ashland Depot, completely unaware that he was already married and the father of two other children."

"How do you know she didn't know about you?" Kate wanted to understand the whole story as I knew it.

"I inadvertently opened a letter addressed to him when he was late coming home from work one day. It explained her desire to get married and her confusion about the story Charles had told her about the railroad regulations for long-distance marriages being frowned upon for Station Masters. Of course that was a lie he had to concoct to maintain his dual life. After our divorce, he moved closer to her and eventually married her and had two more sons. I don't believe he ever told her about us."

"How do you know all this?" Kate asked.

"I don't know if I ever told you that after Charles left, I was employed by the railroad to run their businessmen's overnight lodging house. It was a cheaper alternative to the tourist's grand Depot Hotel. So, with that connection, I was privy to all the railroad news and bulletins, which printed such employee announcements and assignments."

"This is all too much. I don't think I can go back to the Sewing Circle now," Kate harrumphed.

"Oh, don't lose out on your women's circle because of me, please," I said encouragingly. "Amy seems to be a very nice woman, proud of her sons, and completely unaware of the history of her husband. It's all water under the bridge now."

"She should know. Her children should know that they have half-siblings right here in town. It could be healing for everyone, especially for your son to meet his brother. They could fill in gaps in their childhood stories," Kate explained. "Would you mind if I explained who you are to Amy?"

"If you think it would help, I don't care. I'm leaving. I have more overwhelming and heartbreaking issues to recover from right now," I said, sinking back into my reality without Daniel.

About a month after I arrived in North Bend, Oregon, I received a letter in the post from Kate, in Alameda. She recounted the scenario of the inevitable interaction she had with Amy, at her next Sewing Circle meeting on November 1st:

Dear Alice,   Wednesday, November 5, 1913

I hope this letter finds you feeling better. We all miss you around here and think of you recovering quickly by taking your morning constitutionals on the coast beaches.

I had to write to you with updates from the Sewing Circle. I did in fact speak with Amy last Saturday. She asked what happened to 'that Alice and her lovely daughter Ramona?' I thought it a perfect lead in to clear the air about your connection. I said, "Oh, you mean Alice Kane? Her fiancé recently passed away and she moved back to Oregon to be closer to her daughter and new son-in-law." She was sorry to hear about Daniel and wanted me to send her condolences.

Then, recognizing that you had the same last name, she asked further about you. I said you were originally from Ashland, where your former husband was the railroad depot Station Master until 1895 when you divorced him and he moved away. I could tell at that point that Amy was trying to calculate dates and places to cross-reference with her husband's history.

At that moment, she stopped sewing and asked, "What was her husband's name, do you know?" I answered with the name you called him, "Charles Kane, I think." I told her you said he preferred to use his middle name, since his first name was so unusual.

She looked uncomfortable, but continued to pry for more details. She looked a little peaked and stuttered when she finally mustered the courage to ask, "Do...do you remember what his first name was?"

I didn't want to lie, so I told her the truth. "Yes, in fact I do. It was Ellsworth. I only remember it because it was so unusual." Amy instantly dropped her sewing project and doubled over in her chair after that. I asked, "Are you OK? You look as if you are about to faint."

She gathered her belongings and said, "Just some stomach troubles, I have to go now." I never got to express my hopes for healing old wounds and getting the children to meet. She stormed out of the Hall faster than a steam engine going downhill. I am afraid I didn't handle this delicate conversation with the utmost grace.

And, an even worst part comes next. I just read a bold headline in this morning's paper: *"Woman Dies Suddenly at Home in Alameda."* I felt terrible when I read that 'Mrs. Amy Peyton Kane has passed away after suddenly taking ill a few days ago'. It mentioned that she is survived by three sons, Clarence, Ellsworth, and Jack Kane. It also said she was the widow of E.C. Kane.

Oh, Alice! Do you think the realization of her two-timing husband is what killed her? Could the shock of such a revelation actually send someone to their demise? I feel responsible. I will never forgive myself. If I had known this would be the result of my conversation, I would never have opened my mouth. I was only trying to help. Forgive me, dear Lord. And God, PLEASE, ask Amy to forgive me too. What was I thinking?

I didn't want to add to your distress, Alice, but I thought you should know. That no good Station Master ex-husband of yours continues, even after his death, to leave a track of destruction wherever his train rolled on through.

Sorry to end on such a sad note. My next letter promises to include more upbeat news about our grandbaby on the way, and how their big brother and Dad seem to be handling things. Irma is glowing and growing.

With healing hope and best regards,

Kate

The Station Master's Wife

After reading Kate's letter, I hoped that this story would never be retold. I didn't wish any misfortune on the three other Kane boys fathered by Charles. I wrote back to Kate and asked her and Irma to remain silent if they ever crossed paths with those boys. I saw no reason to ruin their memory of their father, or mother for that matter. I only hoped the sins of the father would never be repeated by the actions of the sons.

~ ~ ~

22  Coast Connections, 1914-1918

"Where Rail meets Sail" - was on the arch over Main Street when one drove into downtown North Bend, Oregon. It was a timber and trade town, serviced by motorcars, railways and shipyards. I chose to remain in North Bend, a neighboring town north of Marshfield, with Ramona and Henry until I figured out what I wanted to do and where I should live for the next phase of my life.

Their house sat facing Coos Bay and the timbered hills due east. It was a short drive out to the expansive ocean beaches with their cliff promontories, blazing sunsets, and endless stands of massive forests. Golden sand dunes were cut through by rivers emptying into the ocean waters that were teeming with fish and boat traffic. Settlers had been drawn to this part of the southern Oregon coast since 1857.

Henry had purchased an automobile from Mr. Tower in town and made a habit of taking us on Sunday picnics at the beach. Sometimes Henry's brother John and his wife Lena would join us. Henry's parents often traveled south with them from Florence, Oregon for the hour and a half drive by motor car to visit with us and regale us with their pioneer stories.

The "mosquito fleet", the moniker given to the conclave of small boats on Coos Bay, delivered people and products to places for pleasure, culture and shipments to other parts of the world. I learned how to take the ferry across Coos Bay to Eastside when I joined the ladies branch of the Masonic Hall there, called the Millicoma Club.

Walking around the Millicoma Marsh green-edged trails was particularly invigorating and the crisp fresh salty air was rather rejuvenating. I saw beaver building dams, which slowed the Mosquito Fleet and forced them to divert course, or worse, occasionally dynamiting the disruption in the flow of the waterway. I discovered new shore birds, waterfowl and raptors I had never seen inland near Ashland.

Now that I was back in Oregon, I longed to visit my former home town of Ashland. I convinced Ramona and Henry to accompany me to a party in March 1914, to which my friend Anna had invited me.

"It will be fun to get out and travel," I assured them. I was trying to pull myself out of my grieving past and into a more agreeable future. I knew seeing Anna would help.

"Well, Alice," Henry said, "As assistant cashier for over a year now, I will have my two week holiday time from the bank coming up soon. My brother John is the vice-president, so I'm sure there will be no problem with my absence. How about we drive to Ashland?"

"Sure. That sounds like an adventure just getting there," I said.

"Splendid!" agreed Ramona. "We'll head out the end of February and go by way of Eugene. Henry has a high school friend, Mr. Charles Farris that moved there from here. They've been in communication about doing some lumbering business together here on the coast, just north of the Siuslaw River that cuts through Florence, near the Captain's property. I'm sure he'd welcome a visit to discuss things in person with Henry. I will send a letter requesting an overnight visit on our way to and from Ashland."

Anna Carter was beside herself when we drove down Main Street and parked in front of her house. She came running out at the sound of Henry's car horn, which resembled a bellowing moose, "Aooo-gah!"

"Oh, Alice!" Anna cried, totally exhilarated. "It's so good to see you again! I'm glad you are back in Oregon. We will get together more often now, I'm sure of it! Come on in, all of you!"

EV and Anna were superb hosts. They never had had any children and I didn't want to be impertinent and question why. I was just glad they had enough room for all of us to stay. They held a lovely dinner party given in my honor, with all my old friends in attendance, and for everyone to meet my daughter and my new son-in-law.

"What do you think of our new Carnegie Library?" Charlotte Pelton asked. "We had quite a row in Ashland deciding if we should build it and where."

"I heard. Anna wrote to me and told me all about it," I replied. "I think it is wonderful to have such a permanent edifice dedicated to books. You know we are starting to build a Carnegie Library in Marshfield this year. You'll have to send me the latest titles that I should suggest for our shelves."

"The Women's Civic Club has been very busy working on town improvements like the library, but our most recent endeavor involves the bond that we supported and has just been passed by the City Council," Anna boasted. "The Parks Commission has just engaged the landscape architect, Mr. John McLaren, to design improvements and trails throughout the expanded acres of Lithia Park."

"You mean the same gentleman who designed San Francisco's Golden Gate Park?" I remarked astounded.

"Yes, indeed," Anna continued proudly. "He has sent preliminary drawings that the Council has shared with the Women's Civic Club. It looks so inviting with the sinuous pathways and multiple access points from the road, plus he included quaint foot bridges crossing Ashland Creek. He even added an Auto Camp, at the upper end of the Park, to the design.

"I adore the inclusion of a cascading waterfall into the new pond by the entrance of the Park, and the bench seating surrounding it where one can sit and watch the ducks and swans," Charlotte added. "Our ladies will be managing the seasonal flower beds, making the entrance look like a Monet painting, Donations are pouring in from the businesses on the Plaza.

"Well, if it turns out anyway similar to Golden Gate Park, it will be magnificent," I commented. "Daniel and I loved walking through there." At the mere mentioning of his name, I began to sniffle. I thought it best for everyone if I changed direction of the conversation. "Oh, did I mention that my son Alex is expecting another baby in June?"

The ladies were as relieved as I to steer the talk toward new life, rather than death. "How are Alex and Irma doing with all these changes? Are they still ever so much in love?" Anna queried as she passed the green bean and almond casserole to the guests down at the other end of the table. I knew she grew both of the main ingredients in her garden.

"It's hard to tell," I confessed. "They were all fussing about me, more than worrying about themselves, as I had to deal with so many difficult changes in the past seven months. I believe they'll be fine. **Irma**'s mother, Kate, and her husband George, are nearby to lend a hand when needed. I do worry however, about Alex spending so much time on the road with his district salesman duties. He's even planning on opening a couple of meat markets in downtown San Francisco soon. He says they should double his income and help with his increased family expenses. I hope **Irma** doesn't feel too neglected. I know what it is like with a husband on the road."

While we ladies continued our gossiping, EV and Henry found common ground in discussing bank business. I overheard them mention a new currency called traveler's checks. This money was not associated with a patron's account, but was as good as cash. Their bank conversation continued throughout dinner.

"Our patrons manage to get better results with American Bankers Association traveler's checks," EV Carter pronounced proudly, revealing his remarkable acumen in data analysis he had developed as a bank manager. "They are accepted in the smaller towns across the country, whereas the other popular brand, American Express traveler's checks, are more negotiable in bigger towns where they have an office."

Henry, being somewhat of a novice in the banking field, tried to add what details he had garnered from listening to his brother, the vice-president of his bank. "Yes, I've heard that, too. However, due to our relatively isolated location, many of our bank patrons require these more well-known American Express checks when they travel longer distances, sometimes overseas. Our bank can earn interest for a longer period during which checks are uncashed, while not having to pay any interest to the check holder. Basically, these notes become interest-free loans. "

"Quite true," EV replied. "I will have to mention that to our board. However, it's does pose an increased risk for the bank. Once we purchase these unsigned checks from the distributor, they sit around like cash in the bank vault until they are sold. We managers have to keep a closer eye on things now."

"Hmm. I guess you're right. Hadn't thought about that," Henry added pensively, but quickly turned the conversation back to dinner. "Now what's for dessert?"

Even though it was early spring, Anna had requested that we pack our swimming costumes for this visit. On Saturday afternoon, she gathered up a bundle of towels, instructed us to pack our swim gear, and we readied the motor car for our surprise swim, which I feared would be too cold for my fifty-four year old bones.

"Now, Alice," Anna teased. "Do you really think I would do that to you, or me?" She looked over her steaming teacup at me with a quizzical expression. "I wouldn't want anyone to submerge outside in this brisk weather! Trust me, it will be a treat."

Henry packed up the car with our day bags full of towels and swimsuits, and we drove past my house on Spring Street. This reminded me to check in with Mrs. Brundige later, about the rental and lodging-house duties. We headed toward the railroad and as we turned left, I noticed a distinct smell of rotten eggs. Suddenly, a huge one hundred foot long building emerged into view, with a dozen tall windows, sporting a big arch at one end. The sign read "Ashland Mineral Springs Natatorium and Sulphur Baths".

"When did this pop up here?" I asked overwhelmed by the sheer size of the structure.

"This opened in the fall of 1909. I think you were house hunting with Daniel in San Francisco when the grand opening happened." Anna answered. "I remember you were so busy when you returned, packing up your house and making arrangements for the lodging house, that you probably didn't even realize this was here."

She continued with more details. "Wait until you see the inside! There are two pools that run the length of the building, one for men and the other for the ladies. Don't you worry, the water is nice and warm from being fed by natural artesian hot springs. The waters are more than for just soaking, the pools have a forty foot slide, springboards, high dives and even trapeze rings."

"What is that part attached to the pool building?" I asked confused.

"Oh, that Pavilion wing is even better. It has a huge maple wood dance floor surrounded by seating for 500 people. The activities on that floor rotate between orchestra-led dances and a roller skating rink with accompanying music groups," EV bragged. "We love it."

"Now Sutro Baths in San Francisco has some serious competition!" I claimed. Henry and Ramona had already entered the bathhouse, while us 'old folks' were catching up.

After returning to North Bend, I started to acclimate to the coast in the ensuing couple of months. However, Ramona and I were soon called to travel again. Irma had just given birth in June to my first granddaughter, whom they also named June. We took the train down to Oakland within days of the news reaching us.

The new baby was radiant and had bright blue eyes like her father's, and wisps of brown hair. Irma looked bedraggled and her body had given in to the fullness of a maternal figure. Alex, at twenty-nine, had more lines on his face than I remembered, and lacked his youthful glow.

"So tell me about this market you have set up in San Francisco," I begged Alex to keep him engaged in conversation. I could tell he was about to fall asleep as his head bobbed forward and the evening paper dropped to his lap while he was reading after dinner.

"Oh....uh, what?" Alex excused himself. "Did you say something Mother?" He folded the paper, trying to make his actions appear intentional.

"Yes, dear. I did," I reiterated. "The meat market downtown. What made you decide to add that to your workload?"

"Well, as you know, Mother," Alex began explaining a little bit defensively. "I've always wanted to have my own butcher shop. My meat carving passion was sparked way back on that 1904 excursion to Crater Lake. So, when a corner store in downtown San Francisco became available to rent, I nabbed it for my first meat market. It is one block from Grace Cathedral. The church going crowds file in after every service buying my specialty cuts for their Sunday dinner." Alex livened up when he bragged about his new companies.

"How fortunate to find such a spot," I said approvingly.

"Yes, I know," Alex agreed, not realizing his conceit. "And, by next year, I hope to open a second shop. I have my eye on another location uphill from there, but close enough so that my butchers can share the stock as it comes in from the ferry docks. It is just a quick boat ride from the Alameda docks to the Ferry Building Terminal in San Francisco, and then a half mile trolley ride to the entry door of my shop on the corner. It has double display windows framing the entry and I named it after the streets it sits on, the 'Pine and Jones Market'."

"It sounds like you have put a lot of thought into this venture. I'm very proud of you. Do you still have time for picnics and boat rides at Lake Merritt?" I gingerly asked trying not to intrude into his married life.

"Oh, Irma's so busy with the children right now, I thought I'd get the shops going and then we'd have more family time, and money to do such things," Alex answered, insisting his rationale worked best for everyone involved. I hoped he was right.

Ramona and I concluded our visit to California with a family dinner, joined by Kate and George. Alex showed off his carving prowess making the turkey meat appear to fly off the bone. He cut it so feathery, it dissolved in your mouth.

After helping out as much as we could, canning strawberry jams, tomatoes, and butter beans, plus making trays of dried fruits, Ramona and I showered the children with clothes and toys before we left. I loved being a grandmother. I wished Ramona would soon add to the fold.

News that Panama Canal opened in the summer of August 1914, reached coastal Oregon by early fall. It triggered my recollection of the story Mama told of her travels from Indiana with my siblings Isaac and Sarah, traversing the jungles of Panama to connect with the steamer headed north on the Pacific side of the Americas. I automatically started to feel itchy remembering the descriptions of all the mosquito bites they received on the four hour train ride crossing the Isthmus. Now, with the Panama Canal open for Pacific shipping vessels to connect with the Atlantic side, Marshfield's timber trade was booming and continued well into 1915.

 Henry's father, the Captain, was still very connected with the shipyard in North Bend and the lighthouse crew in Empire City, a few miles west at the mouth of the Coos River. Captain Asa Simpson, an old friend and sea-faring colleague of his, had originally opened a timber cutting mill in North Bend around 1855 to serve the lumber needs of the Gold Rush building boon and development around San Francisco. In 1899, he handed off his shipyard and shipbuilding business in North Bend to his son, Louis Simpson, or LJ as he was known around town.

 LJ was very much enmeshed in the development of our town since 1903 and in fact he was our mayor until 1915. LJ completed building his seaside home estate in 1915, and then stepping down as mayor, he and his wife Cassandra moved there. Cassie, as she preferred, named this new estate on the ocean promontory cliffside, Shore Acres. It was about fourteen miles southwest of North Bend. LJ spared no expense in building the three-story mansion which included an indoor swimming pool, a ballroom, spacious formal gardens tended by five resident gardeners, a modern farm, and a dairy herd.

 As an old friend of the family, the Captain was invited

to Shore Acres with his whole family in 1916. I tagged along as one of the elders, aged fifty-six now, with the Captain and his wife. The four Bergman siblings - Henry, Carl, John and Mary, brought their spouses. We walked through an entry hall paneled in Oregon myrtle wood, with a Louis Comfort Tiffany electric lamp designed especially for the residence, suspended over the vestibule. The evening setting sunlight cut through the chandelier and veiled our faces in rainbows as we arrived.

"Welcome to our humble home," Cassie sarcastically announced as we handed our coats to the butler. It is so nice to finally meet the whole family that my father-in-law, Captain Asa, had spoken of so highly."

"I'm sorry we never had the opportunity to meet him before his passing last year," I mentioned as a condolence. We were brought into the ballroom and seated next to an expanse of floor to ceiling windows, which overlooked the waves crashing on the ocean rocks below the cliff upon which the mansion sat. Ramona seemed to immediately connect with LJ's step-daughter, Isabella, who visited often from her home in Washington State.

"Oh, he was a real card!" Cassie laughed, holding onto her father-in-law's memory. "You would have enjoyed his tales. My favorite quote of his was when he spoke of how he made his fortune. He'd say 'there was far more gold growing on the trees that lined the West Coast, than anyone could ever dig out of California's increasingly stingy mountain soil.' I guess he was right!" Cassie said fanning her arm across the length of the ballroom.

"Well, now that the railroad has finally connected the Coos Bay region to the inland Coquille and Willamette Valleys, your lumber products will have an easier time being distributed," I commented.

"That's so true, Mrs. Kane, or may I call you Alice?" Cassie asked.

"Certainly. In fact, I am no longer married to Mr. Kane, and thankfully not referred to as the Station Master's wife any more. However, I am so used to the Kane name, I keep it when needed for formality. But under these circumstances, please do call me Alice," I disclosed.

Steering the conversation away from my divorce and back on track, I added, "My former husband used to run the depot in Ashland, so I am familiar with how beneficial a railroad coming to a town can be."

When the dinner bell was rung, we filed into the banquet room to be seated at the long elaborately set table. Cassie insisted that the women and I sit at her end of the table and the men gather at the opposite end, nearer to LJ. I enjoyed her unconventionality and her company.

Cassie raised her empty crystal goblet and tapped it with her knife. "Excuse me, everyone," she blurted out loud enough for the full length of the table to hear. "I must apologize for the lack of alcoholic beverages tonight. It seems that Prohibition Laws are taking effect in Oregon this year, in 1916. We could have dined in our neighboring state if we chose to imbibe, since this restriction has not become a federal law as of yet. But, since we are here, please do enjoy our apple cider or **marion berry** juice alcohol-free cocktails to your heart's content."

The talk at the table shifted back and forth like a tennis ball between the two sides of men and women. Topics were discussed regarding women's suffrage, production of personal liquor caches, regulation of gambling and the pros and cons for abolition of prostitution.

My least favorite issue of deliberation was the talk of the United States entering the Great War. LJ was torn between the benefits he could reap from the increased demand for manufactured lumber and the misfortune of lives estimated to be lost to make the world safe for democracy. I just hoped that my son and son-in-law were too old to partake, or become casualties in such destruction and devastation.

President Wilson eventually asked Congress to join *'a war to end all wars'*. U.S. troops began arriving on the Western Front of Europe in large numbers in 1918. Although Alex was thirty-three, and Henry was thirty, they both had to register for the draft. I kept my fingers crossed that they would call on younger men without families to help win our battles overseas.

Closer to home, Henry was recently promoted to the position of Vice-President of the Lane County State and Savings Bank in Florence, when his brother John became the President. Their younger brother Carl stepped into Henry's position as assistant cashier. It was a bit of a distance to travel daily from North Bend to Florence, so Henry stayed at his folk's home in Florence during the work week.

"I worry about you working so hard, darling," Ramona would say at our Sunday picnics at the beach that Henry insisted on keeping as a tradition. "Your father says sometimes that you get home rather late, often after dinner."

"Don't you concern yourself with my extended work hours, dear," Henry comforted his wife. "I'm simply getting adjusted to the new responsibilities that come with this position. I am just so grateful to have some consistency with the same secretary who was passed on to me from John. Harriet, I mean Miss Weatherson, has been an angel showing me the ropes."

Ramona pondered this reply and sympathetically added, "I wish I could be there to help you too. Did you look into buying some property on which to build our new house?"

"Yes, dear," Henry said somewhat condescendingly. "My father and I have been looking at properties just north of the Siuslaw River in Florence, near Heceta Head. I hope we can find some land and start building within the year."

"Alright, Henry," Ramona submitted. "Mama and I will have our own fun here in North Bend. You just get some more rest, you look pallid."

I chimed in to brighten the banter on the beach. "Have you two heard that Cassie and LJ's daughter, Isabella, got married?"

"Really?" Ramona sounded more upbeat. "When and to whom?"

"This past February to Mr. Tower, the automotive dealer in Marshfield." I reported. "I heard it was quite a small wedding in Portland, for only the immediate family. Her father, Mr. Stearns, from Washington, gave the bride away. They are setting up their home here in Marshfield so you may get to become closer friends. She's about your age, too."

"Yes. Well, I guess Henry's new long-distance job will give me ample time and opportunity to do just that," Ramona smiled slyly. I hoped she was only kidding me and teasing

Henry. He reached over and planted a kiss on his wife's lips to assuage any concerns either of us may have had.

The ocean waves began to crash and pound louder at the shoreline and the stinging mist of salted sea air reminded me of how quickly a calm scene could become a storm. As we packed up our picnic, I prayed for their lives to reconnect soon. I was suspicious of his kiss, hoping it was truly heartfelt and not one to allay any guilt.

Early that fall, Mr. Louis J. Simpson decided to run for Oregon Governor in the election. He was nicknamed the *"handsome stranger",* courting the state's newspaper editors at his Shore Acres mansion. His platform was for 'Development of Oregon' and 'National Women's Suffrage.'

In early October, Louis and Cassie invited all the prominent business owners in the Coos County area to a fundraiser event for LJ's campaign. The entire bank staff came from Henry's bank in Florence. LJ talked to them about his time on the board of the Bank of Oregon which he had started in North Bend, back in 1903-04.

"We've got our own 'family bank' set up in Florence," Henry flaunted his position in the bank.

"I heard," LJ replied trying to work Henry's comment to his advantage. "I was hoping that since I've known your family so long, that your 'family bank' would be willing to make a substantial contribution to my campaign."

"Certainly, LJ," Henry declared confidently. "Keeping our financial institution all within the family makes our investments more secure. We have very few outside prying eyes reviewing or able to manipulate our books. As the VP, I keep track of everything. Of course, I couldn't do it without the help of my secretary, Miss Weatherson here," Henry said as he scooped up her arm and brought her around from his side for an introduction to LJ.

After the brunch, which was served outside on the circular lawn in front of the mansion, we all gathered to dance in the grand ballroom. I noticed more than once, the music brought Miss Weatherson into the arms of Henry, swirling her around on the inlaid parquet maple floor. Ramona was smiling, so I ignored my gut wrenching response. It was probably a left over from my being the Station Master's discarded wife.

~ ~ ~

23  Dumb and Dumber, 1920-1923

The Great War was finally over. Those two years passed with little disruption on my home front. LJ didn't make it into the Governor's mansion in Salem, but continued to fight for the development of Oregon. He worked with Ramona's brothers-in-law, John and Fred, petitioning the Oregon legislature for monies to build a coast road from Astoria to Curry County, not only for benefitting business and commerce trade, but also for military transportation when needed, as seen just recently during the war.

The Government moved slowly and John Bergman, as bank President, traveled often with LJ to lobby members of the Oregon State congress in Salem, leaving his brother Henry in charge of the bank to learn more of its inner workings.

Ramona finally moved to Florence when her new house was finished and I was able to build my own home on the Coos River, after I decided to sell my house in Ashland. While I was decorating, Ramona was getting pregnant. She had her first born in 1922. Baby Patricia was a gift I thought would never arrive for Ramona. She had been married almost a decade by the time the baby came.

Unfortunately, when God giveth, he also taketh away. Henry's brother, John, only thirty-eight years old, succumbed to pneumonia that same year. Thankfully, his wife and their six year old adopted daughter survived the ravages of the disease as it coursed through their household.

The bank was in turmoil but Henry's brother-in-law Fred, Mary's husband, being older and having been the attorney for the bank and more familiar with documents and legal arrangements than Henry, was appointed by the Board to the position of bank President. Henry complained that he felt somewhat slighted, but with less responsibility, he took advantage of his vacation days.

By 1923, things were settling in to place for the bank and our family. Henry offered us an escape to Ashland for a fall getaway. This time he arranged for us to stay at the Lithia Park Auto Camp Deluxe. Baby Patricia would have been a handful to impose upon my friends.

"Don't you worry ladies," Henry assured us. "The American Motorist magazine describes all the Auto Camp facilities available to camping tourists. In Ashland, they have electric lights with individual switches for each tent area and hundreds of trail lights strung in the trees so it is safe to meander after dark to the wash houses. The tent cabins are spacious with cots for comfort, and a picnic table outside for each site. Campers are invited to use the community cook house with gas stoves, and they say there is a nearby grocery store with mineral water to purchase. There's even a laundry wagon that picks up wash each morning and returns it the next day. That's as good as a hotel and for only 50 cents per night!"

"Baby Patricia will love playing in the creek," Ramona added, remembering similar childhood playtimes in Ashland.

"I will watch her while you two love birds stroll around that beautiful Lithia Park and Gardens," I inserted as a suggestion to encourage the spark of marriage between them.

"I'll arrange for my vacation leave to be in the beginning of October. The weather is usually still summer-like and perfect for camping without mosquitoes," Henry concluded.

I added my two cents to the itinerary discussion. "Maybe we can celebrate my sixty-third birthday with a trip to the circus. I've heard from Anna that the Circus will be in town the second week of October. It would be so fun for Patricia to see the clowns and the elephants. I remember how much you loved it, Ramona, when it first came by train to Ashland, back in 1891."

"This will be magical for us all," Ramona smiled from ear to ear. Henry had already turned and gone once the decision had been made and the dates chosen. It seemed like he scheduled another meeting, rather than being excited about a vacation.

Our drive took us through Eugene again, stopping to visit with Henry's friend, Mr. Farris. He and Henry discussed the timber land they recently purchased near Heceta Head. A small portion was owned by Mr. Farris, as an investing partner. Henry had bought six million board feet of fir timber near Siuslaw National Forest for $12,000. He was in a contract with logging and timber companies, planning to make a profit from the harvest, while designing a community development site for the area once it was cleared.

Communities were popping up all along the West Coast and requiring more lumber for commercial and residential buildings. It sounded like a sensible business venture, with an almost guaranteed increase in returns above the purchase price. I felt reassured that I had invested the profits from my house sale in Ashland with the bank that was headed by my son-in-law and his family.

Once we were in Ashland and settled in the Auto Camp, we visited with Anna and EV, who insisted that we take a tour to Crater Lake. "So many improvements and amenities have been added to the Park since the first excursion you took in 1904," Anna said.

"For one thing, the roads are drivable by motor car now. The trip takes less than a day to get to the crater rim. They even built a lodge overlooking the edge of the crater rim eight years ago," EV recited. "In the past two summers, they have expanded the original lodge and added plumbing. Most of the rooms in the new annex even have private bathrooms!"

"Let's put that on our itinerary, then," I agreed.

Once the excitement of Patricia riding a circus elephant subsided, we set off for a five day tour of the 'newer' Crater Lake National Park. We all were in awe of the magnificent views and surrounding peaks of the Cascade Range. Colorful birds flited from tree to tree, as if painting nature when they landed on a branch; like dipping the tips of the conifer needles in blue, red and yellow dots of quickly disappearing color. Ramona was most happy to sit in a chair and not on a tree stump outside. She made sure to avoid all contact with scorpions by having lace up boots for both her and the baby.

By the time we returned to Ashland on October 21st, a most dramatic event was being talked about all over town. A report of the crime was described in the *Tidings*. EV summarized it as he read the highlights in the paper.

"It seems the train heading south from Seattle to San Francisco, the SP No.13 "*Gold Special*', has been robbed about ten days ago, while we were at Crater Lake. The train acquired its nickname because it had once hauled large quantities of gold from the surrounding area mines. Rumors still spread that it would always be carrying gold, in addition to the passengers it now carried. Four men had been killed when the unwitting robbers tried to abscond with the supposed shipment of cash and gold, which usually had been transported in the mail car," EV reported. Then he read directly:

"The bandits had jumped on board as the train slowed to enter the Tunnel 13, to test its brakes at the top of Siskiyou Pass. Climbing over and into the engine cab, they ordered the engineer to completely stop the train inside the tunnel.

"Unfortunately for everyone, they had no idea what they were doing when they used too much dynamite to open the barricaded mail car. The entire end of the mail car was blown to smithereens, instantly killing the mail clerk inside and setting everything inside ablaze, including any insignificant amount of paper money that may have been on board.

"To the thieves' surprise and disappointment, they couldn't see or find any gold through the smoke inside the mangled mail car, stopped inside the tunnel. They couldn't move the train out of the tunnel because of the twisted metal tracks and mail car pieces which resulted from the explosion. The engineer, brakeman, and the fireman who rushed to see about the explosion were killed in the confusion of the daunted robbers who were angry and wished not to leave behind any eye witnesses. The murderous villains escaped on foot, without any loot for their efforts."

"Oh, my!" I responded when I heard about this dreadful tragedy. "They haven't been found yet? It's been almost two weeks!"

"No, not yet," EV replied, looking up from the newspaper article. "But, it says here they have brought in a crime specialist, a detective who looks **closely** at all the evidence."

"Well haven't the police already done that?" Anna asked, rather disturbed. "Why are they wasting time with evidence when they should be hunting down the criminals?"

"Seems like this fellow can direct their investigation by fitting together evidentiary **clues** like puzzle pieces. Says here," EV read further from the Tidings,

"Detective Heinrich, looked over a pair of overalls left by the bandits, deduced from the pitch stains on the garments that the wearer was likely a lumberjack, and from the wear pattern on the buttons, that he was left-handed. He also found a strand of hair that helped him determine the approximate age of one of the assailants."

"But the most damning thing he found was, *"a crumpled up old mail receipt in one of the pockets. Heinrich has been able to track it through the Post Office back to the purchaser. The hunt is narrowed specifically to three brothers named DeAutremont, two twins about 23, and their younger brother, 19,"* EV finished his review.

"Fascinating!" I exclaimed. "To figure all that out from tiny details is extraordinary. However, should we be worried being so **close** to the crime scene? Do you think they are still nearby?"

"I highly doubt that," Henry said. "If I were them I would high-tail it out of town as quickly as possible. Hope they weren't counting on that heist for travel money." Henry giggled at their dumb luck.

The next morning, Henry went to the Peerless Rooms Diner down by the depot for his morning coffee and to read the newspaper in silence, taking a break from the wails of baby Patricia. When he returned, he told us about a peculiar incident that transpired while he was there.

"I was sitting by the front bay window when the bell above the door jingled and this scrubby looking bloke entered," Henry began. "Thinking he was a railroad fellow, I didn't pay him much mind. I did think it odd, though, that he had a bag full of groceries with him at this early hour, but I assumed he had just finished a night shift on the recently arrived train and was headed home with food for the day.

"He sat down at the table across from me, curiously not removing his newsboy cap which was pulled down low over his forehead, and began to sip his coffee. When he started to read the same newspaper headlines that I was perusing about the train robbery, he choked, almost gagging on his beverage, and coffee spewed out in a spray over the wanted photos in the paper. His hand jerked, spilling his drink, and he squealed from the hot liquid splashing onto his lap. He leaped up, took the newspaper, grabbed his groceries, and ran out of the diner. I guess he was rather upset by the news of the recent train crime..., and the hot coffee in his lap," Henry reported.

"Did he say anything to you?" Ramona asked nervously.

"Nope. But he gave me an awful hard stare when he saw me looking at him when he screamed. Something about that kid wasn't right," Henry relayed.

"Kid? How old was this fellow?" I asked for details, playing my own sort of detective.

"Oh, I'd guess in his early twenties, or so," Henry frivolously answered. "Why, what does that matter?"

"It could have been one of the train robbers!" I shouted.

"No. Impossible. It's been too long for them to still be hanging around here. That would be stupid. And besides, no one's that dumb to come to the town where everyone is looking for you," Henry justified.

"What if he didn't know yet that the police figured out it was him?" Ramona wondered. "Then that type of reaction to the headlines could be expected."

Returning home to North Bend, many hours away from this Great Train Robbery, as it was sarcastically nicknamed, made me feel safer being so distanced from all this criminal activity. My mail had collected over the past few weeks at the post office, and I plopped into Charles' old winged-backed chair when I got home to begin with the most familiar letters first, the billings and event notices could wait. There was a relatively thick envelope posted from Kate, **Irma**'s mother, in the middle of the stack. I was drawn to read it first:

Dearest Alice,   October 15, 1923

It is with a heavy heart I write to you today. I will preface my news with some of my history. I have never really told you about Irma's father and I, and how things ended for us. He was an abusive man who yelled horrific things at me and Irma, up until he left when she was seven years old. He had a history scattered with bouts of uncalled for violence. Unbeknownst to me before we were married, he and his brothers got into trouble when they were scouting land to settle. He alone massacred over forty Indians to claim a valley, rather than negotiate or offer to buy them out. His temper continued to flare, with no provocation, throughout our marriage. After I divorced him, and married George, I found out that he had died. I tell people of his death, instead of revealing my dirty laundry. I am afraid Irma must have modeled her method of dealing with anger after my former husband.

Things have not been going well between Irma and Alex, for quite some time now. I know neither of them would burden you with such news, but as I am there visiting often, I have heard and seen for myself how much discord resides in their home.

Irma has told me she has filed a divorce suit yesterday against Alex. She described an altercation which occurred this past Thursday night, between herself and an unidentified young woman, found in a compromising position with Alex......

I couldn't continue. My heart sank. The letter fell to the floor. My worst fear that 'the sins of the father would become those of his son', was now coming true, but instead, with my own son! It wasn't with Charles' second, third or fourth sons. Alex was following Charles' philandering ways. *How dumb could he be?* I felt dizzy and swooned sideways, collapsing into the wing of Charles' old high-backed chair.

24  Downhill Dealings, 1923-1925

I woke up in a sweat. My brief dozing had allowed my racing heart to settle somewhat. Newspaper clippings had tumbled out of the envelope from Kate and lay in a pile on the floor beside my chair. I sat up to finish reading the letter from Kate, but my eye was caught by a headshot of Irma framed by a headline in one of the articles laying on the floor, which Kate had enclosed. I picked it up and read it before continuing with her letter.

"WIFE SAYS SHE TRAILED SPOUSE, Files for Sensational Divorce" - Mrs. Irma Kane, of Alameda County, charges that her husband, Alexander Kane, associated with other women"

How could this be real? Under the headline was a photo of Irma in a modern bobbed haircut; soft curls peeking below the brim of her tilted cloche hat. She looked determined and resolute. I was drawn into the article which was subtitled with '*Mrs. Kane will tell of alleged battle with other Woman*'. I forced myself to read further:

"*The fray came as a climax of an evening of sleuthing on the part of Mrs. Kane and Henry Blum, a private detective. Mrs. Kane and Blum are alleged to have followed Mr. Kane, who is a salesman for the Virden Packing Company and owner of two meat markets in San Francisco. According to Blum, Mr. Kane met a young woman and the two motored to an apartment house on Pine Street, in San Francisco.*

"Mrs. Kane and Blum followed the two into the building and there, after pounding on the apartment door until it opened, Mrs. Kane set upon the young woman, striking and scratching her and pulling her hair out. Blum states that when Mrs. Kane appeared, Mr. Kane fled the scene."

I couldn't imagine such a spectacle! *How could my son, or Irma for that matter, be doing such things? And then for Alex to run away when confronted? What was he thinking?* I was riveted by this story and compelled myself to continue:

"In her suit for divorce, Mrs. Kane charges her husband with associating with other women and says that he frequently boasted to her of his conquests. When she remonstrated with him, he urged her to seek the company of other men, she declares in her complaint.

"It is further alleged that Mr. Kane beat his wife and that on several occasions, he cursed her and called her vile names. He likewise unjustly and falsely accused her of being unfaithful to him, she avers."

Could this all be true? Was Kate correct in assuming her daughter was prone to extreme reactions like her biological father? I certainly prayed so, for at least some of these accusations to not be true. I continued reading to the end of the **clipping**:

"Mrs. Kane says her husband's salary is more than $300 a month and that in addition to this he has income from his two meat markets, one of which is on Pine Street, down from the apartment building where the women's battle took place. Mrs. Kane asks for payment for alimony, attorney's fees and court costs, in addition to custody of the two children of the couple, Keith, aged 10 ½ , and June, aged 9 years.

"A restraining order preventing Mr. Kane from disposing of any of his property, including cash in a San Francisco bank, was issued yesterday by Superior Judge J. Koford."

Suddenly, at that moment, I realized that I had stopped breathing again. I forced myself to take some deep inhalations before I fainted once more. This dire news was so distressing to my core, that I could feel my heart pounding. I was waiting to read the part that it was all a joke. But not even in the rest of Kate's letter, did that kind of news unfold:

……… So, dear Alice, I am at a loss of what else to say. Enclosed is the article I clipped from the Oakland Tribune for your first hand review. For now, their children are safe at home with Irma, and Alex is staying elsewhere. I will do what I can to ease our grandchildren's minds about the pending changes in their lives. Please forgive me for being the bearer of such tragic news.

If there is any chance you could talk some sense into your son, I will try to do the same with my daughter. It takes two sides to have an argument, as well as two voices to come to a mutual agreement. Maybe as mothers we can make a difference.

I believe you can reach Alex through his work telephone number or address at Virden, if you wish to contact him.

Best regards with hope in my heart,   Kate

I was grateful for having a week between receiving this dreadful news and Ramona's next visit from Florence. I was feeling the emotional scar of my own scandal resurfacing all over again.

When Ramona arrived, I let the story unfold about her brother, as we sat having hot tea on my back porch overlooking Coos Bay. Crisp autumn winds blew over the blankets on our laps, mixing the steam from our tea with the puffs from the smokestacks of the Mosquito Fleet ships passing by.

When I was finished telling the tale, questions poured out of my daughter. "Are you sure? Have you spoken with Alex?" Ramona was aghast, grateful her children were visiting their Aunt Mary.

"It's not really a conversation I would want to have at the downtown telephone exchange building, since I don't have a home phone line. Nor do I think Alex would want to discuss this on his work phone," I confessed, at a loss for what to do about this situation, and my heart breaking inside.

"This sounds awful. How could he do such things as Irma claimed? Why did she wait so long to confront him before things got so out of hand?" Ramona wondered aloud. I could tell she believed marriage was all about truth and communication. I hoped she would engage the same beliefs in her own marriage, if any irregularities were ever to arise.

"Perhaps she didn't want to admit things were that bad? Or, perhaps she turned a blind eye to all the clues leading up to her final revelation. I know I did the same with your father, when I believed his explanations of his unusual behavior or circumstances. Marriage is a commitment made of trust and love. When one bond is broken, the other shortly follows, I'm afraid," I sadly admitted.

"We should have their children come here for the Christmas holiday," Ramona suggested. "I remember after Father left, how good it was for us to get away and spend the summer at Grandfather and Grandmother's homestead in Jacksonville. Do you think Kate and George would want to bring them up here? Do you think Irma would let them go for a while?" Ramona queried hopefully.

"I'll write to Irma and Kate and share our concerns and wishes," I answered. "I hope our sympathy will come through in our request. I don't want to make things any harder for anyone right now." I thought, *my tears were enough for us all.*

Christmas on the coast was decorated with bountiful boughs of cedars and firs across the storefronts and houses. My grandchildren Keith and June were brought to North Bend with Kate and George for the holidays. They played with their little cousin Patricia and snuggled up with me under soft downy feather comforters, to hear my bedtime stories.

Kate and George, who found lodging at the Chandler Hotel in town, joined us when we boated on the bay, and on our occasional outings when we went to the beach to watch the whales migrate south along the Oregon coastline. The Captain even arranged for a special tour of the lighthouse for all the children. Our special holiday dessert was the Bergman family's favorite, Gooseberry pie, handpicked and made solely by the Captain, and served at Christmas dinner at my house. All of my grandchildren managed to smile and forget their woes, while visiting Grandmother Alice's retreat.

It took another year and a half, until 1925, for Alex and Irma to settle their divorce. Keith and June did end up with their mother in Oakland, and Alex accepted a transfer to the Sacramento division with Virden Packing Company. He sold his meat markets in San Francisco to pay the bills and to afford himself a fresh start.

Alex eventually straightened out his wandering ways and knuckled down as a devoted dad. Together, he and Irma made arrangements for the children to have summer vacations with Alex in Sacramento, and he visited Oakland often for his job and to see the children. Virden put up Alex in company housing for his business meetings in Oakland, making it convenient for him to see his children more often than just at summertime. Irma calmed down enough to deal with Alex in a cordial manner in front of the children, but we all knew she would never forgive him.

I was saddened that lingering effects of Charles' behavior were manifested in our son. I remembered that Alex never seemed to be that upset by our divorce or the reasons behind it. I had no idea he believed such gallivanting around was an acceptable behavior, or one to emulate. Just then, I recalled Alex's reaction to the man who stole the meteorite and felt feeling guilty and ashamed that I had not addressed his **inclinations** to get away with something when he was still a moldable child. I feared his scandal was trailing behind in the wake of mine.

My days of subsequent travel to San Francisco were infrequent and limited to the transition times between the end of school and the beginning of summer, when Alex came to get the children for their off-school months. **Irma** was gracious enough to let me stay in her guest room for that week when I was there.

On one of my walks to Lake Merritt, accompanied only by my son, I spoke with him as a concerned parent. "Alex, dear, please sit down. I would like to speak with you," I said, when we sat on the benches under the pergola at the tidal lagoon, with its towers of algae billowing up along the shoreline, like the stomach acid bubbling up in my **throat.**

"How are you faring by yourself in Sacramento? I worry about you eating well and being distracted by vices not appropriate for a family man."

"Thanks for your concern, Mother," Alex replied with a mixture of defensiveness and dejection. "I plow through, keeping my nose out of trouble these days. Work keeps me busy and I've found new diversions."

"Oh?" I asked, hoping they were suitable. "What kind of diversions?"

"Don't worry, Mother," Alex answered, patting me on the knee. "I have joined a men's baseball team. I guess I got some good influences from Daniel, if not from Father. I've also found some summer leagues for the children. Keith plays baseball and June plays in a girls' softball league. We have team picnics and some of the families go fishing together. I'm really trying to change and make up for my mistakes."

"That all sounds so wonderful, Alex," I applauded his efforts. "Maybe Irma will be more amenable to sharing the children with you more often than summers? Or, maybe you could move back to the Bay Area after everyone's emotions calm down."

"I don't know, Mother," Alex sounded doubtful. "I think I really made a mess of things. It may take quite a while, probably years, for my mistakes and hurtful words to not be all **Irma** remembers when she looks at me."

I understood exactly how **Irma** felt, having faced a similar situation with Charles. Daniel being around helped enormously, but I remember flinching every time I read about Charles in the railroad bulletin. I didn't push the subject, but sat quietly looking at the ducks gliding on the lake.

Alex broke the heavy silence. "So, Mother, maybe you could visit me and the children in Sacramento sometime? Or, come with us when I leave after my last meeting at Virden this Friday?"

"Oh, I don't want to be a bother," I said, unsure how I felt about being around my son for very long, and in a place where I knew no one. "Maybe next time, dear."

~~~

25  Transformations, 1925-1927

In that same year of 1925, my little coastal town was booming from the continued profits of local lumber merchants, boat building and shipping yards, and the sales from the woodworking shops. New concrete buildings in town sprouted up, like the Hotel North Bend and Keizer Memorial Hospital.

Government "essential use" restrictions on building materials after the Great War were finally easing up, allowing for recreational projects to resume. The most exciting change in Marshfield was the conversion of the concrete and beam Motor Inn Garage and Service Station into a movie theatre for the latest silent films.

An architect, who had attended O.A.C. - a bit before Ramona and Henry did, was hired to convert the garage into an Egyptian style movie palace. This style was all the rage since the discovery of King Tutankhamun's tomb in 1922. This Egyptian style architecture flaunted columns as if they were gateways to Egyptian temples, painted in geometric designs and stripes of gold, blue and red.

Inside, the old garage was exquisitely transformed into an Egyptian showplace with luxurious carpeting, velvet drapes, hand-carved chairs made in the image of a seated Pharaoh, and wrought iron and parchment light fixtures.

One extraordinary feature that stood at the base of the stage, was the Wurlitzer pipe organ, for which the new owners paid $32,000. Mary and I loved going to see these moving pictures starring Charlie Chaplin or Laurel and Hardy. The best part was the resonant sound of the deep organ tones when they reverberated in my bones, especially during the frightful scenes.

The magic of the organ tones bellowed on each side of the stage through two organ loft openings, hidden behind large lacy panels painted with two kneeling bodyguards strumming the shape of a huge lyre, similar to the actual image at the entrance of King Tut's tomb.

I allowed myself the luxury of attending these silent movies, with their accompanying vaudeville stage acts, about twice per month. My mind was entertained and distracted from all the distressing events in my life. I guessed that was why most people read books or now chose to see stories come to life on a screen.

By the end of the year, my life was brightened even more by Ramona's most recent news. "Mama?" Ramona said when she came for her weekly visit. She now drove a motorcar by herself and could make the trip with Patricia easily in under two hours. I always enjoyed those weekends, especially having my three year old granddaughter around.

"Yes, dear," I said while I was showing Patricia how to roll a skein of yarn into a ball. She wanted to learn how to knit a cap and a cape for her dolly.

"Mama," my daughter said a bit louder. "I have something to tell you." I looked up slightly worried, but I could see a grin spread across her face. "Mama, we're going to have another baby!"

"Oh...Oh! That's wonderful Ramona!" I squealed. "When is this one due?"

"Not until next June," she answered.

"And that's a good thing," she immediately added. "Henry is just getting started platting out the Heceta Beach subdivision. He's hoping to have many of the lots sold before the baby comes."

"Well, I better get started quilting!" I motioned toward my sewing room. "Do you want to pick out some of your fabric swatch favorites?"

Henry and his family were some of the most influential citizens in the county. Since his brother John had passed four years ago, and his sister Mary's husband, Fred Hollister, was getting more involved with his law practice, naturally Henry was the logical choice as the next president of the bank. With this relatively new title, his extensive holdings in real estate and constant attention to business matters, he was away from home more than Ramona would have liked.

She tended to Patricia and her aging in-laws, and managed the household as best as a pregnant woman with a three year old could do by herself.

The birth, in June 1926, was easy for Ramona, as a second delivery usually is. Baby Ray was a happy, chubby little boy, the spitting image of his father. Patricia adored her baby brother, except at bedtime when he cried in their shared bedroom. She was grateful when her mother took baby Ray to sleep in her parent's bed. Henry was not.

Henry's interrupted nights made for long days at work, his exhaustion dragging him slowly through his duties. His bank, Lane County State and Savings Bank, was one of the most solid and influential financial institutions in the city of Florence. As a long standing member in the community, as well as a member of the prominent Bergman family, Henry garnered his investors, contractors and real estate news through his connections in town.

However, towards the end of 1926, the Heceta Head lots weren't selling as expected. So, Henry devised a plan to protect his standing in the community. I was visiting their family for my birthday celebration in October, when Henry, Ramona and I had this discussion.

Henry cleared his throat and started with, "I've been thinking. It would be better for everyone if I transfer the title of the Heceta Beach property into your names. If I keep an arm's distance from the slow return on this investment, my bank reputation should be protected."

"But, Henry," I queried. "Why would you need my name on the deed, in addition to Ramona's?"

"Because, Alice," he calmly responded. "You are one of my biggest investors at the bank. If you put your name on it, then my other patrons won't be worried if things take so long to pay out to you, rather than me. Your apparent investment would just be added to your portfolio. "

"Henry, dearest," Ramona chimed in. "What actually is the problem with the sales? Do we need to worry about our financial situation? With two children now, I hope these delays won't send us to the poor house."

"No, no, dear," Henry assured her. "Things aren't that bad. They have just slowed down a bit. Everything will pick up when the weather turns bright again. We will need to do this paperwork however, before Alice goes back down to North Bend in a few days."

"Alright, Henry," Ramona answered. I nodded in agreement and went back to tickling baby Ray's belly. Later, I swaddled him in the quilt I made for him when we all took our evening walk down by the Siuslaw River.

Our coastal winter was rather mild during January 1927. I often took walks through the marsh trails or along the shifting sand dunes at the beach. Everyone was right. The ocean had a way of calming and bringing peace whether from loneliness or grief. Whale watching was a uniquely calming pastime for me. Crisp cool air brought blue skies when the coast was clear. But when Mother Nature wanted to show her strength, our world could be turned upside down with violent winter squalls and downpours that could drench you to the bone in a matter of seconds.

One late afternoon in January, Mary, Ramona's sister-in-law, knocked on my door. She lived near me in North Bend and was often my communication link with the family in Florence, since I still had not put in a telephone. Mary informed me that Ramona had called her at the insurance office where she worked, to say that Henry's bank had been robbed that afternoon.

"Oh goodness! Is everyone alright?" I shrieked.

"Not to worry. No one was hurt in this criminal caper. However, Ramona seemed quite nervous," Mary reported.

"How is Henry taking it?" I inquired.

"Not too well," Mary continued. "He is mostly worried about his secretary, Miss Weatherson. She was the one who told the authorities about the robbery. He said she was quite shaken by the whole ordeal."

"How did it happen?" I was concerned as well.

"Miss Weatherson said she had been held up by a lone bandit and locked in the vault, but had opened the door with a screwdriver and escaped," Mary reported. "Sheriff Taylor has directed multiple posses to start combing the coast area in search of the robber. They said that several thousand dollars was taken."

"I hope Ramona starts locking her door now," I said, with worry and concern for her safety.

The next day, Friday, January 28th, Mary came by again to update me on the robbery investigation. I had locked my own doors for the first time ever, and was taken aback by the loud knocking on the front door.

"Alice, it's me! Open up," Mary yelled through the heavy cedar door, sounding urgent in her request.

"Oh, good afternoon Mary," I said, albeit somewhat confused by her anxiety. "Sorry to take so long. I have begun to lock things up since you told me about the bandit on the run. Why are you here? Have they found the man?"

Mary stood on the porch and repeated the news from Ramona's latest call, not wanting to stay long or chat inside. "No, but they are definitely leaving no stone unturned. They have gone to Ramona and Henry's house today to interview Henry about any details he may have.

"The sheriff said he already questioned Miss Weatherson and released her from further interrogation. However, they told Henry they had more questions and would be back tomorrow, considering how late the evening hour was, and all," Mary reported.

"Let me know as soon as something is found out!" I cried as she turned to leave my porch.

"Certainly. I just wanted to stop by on my way home from work to keep you updated," Mary said waving as she walked to her car.

The next time I opened the door for Mary, four days later on Tuesday morning, February 1st, she was standing on my front porch with her suitcase and umbrella.

"Where are you going?" I questioned my recurrent guest, as she stood there with a depressed look on her face.

"Nowhere without you, Alice," Mary replied in a somber tone.

"What are you talking about? Come in, Mary. And why do you have luggage with you?" I demanded, pushing the screen door ajar for her. I was afraid she was escaping from a scandal at home. This seemed to be the pattern in my life.

"I've just gotten another call from Ramona this morning. She is beside herself. Henry has disappeared," she stated dismally, setting her valise down just inside the door.

"What? What do you mean disappeared? How long has he been gone?" I demanded further clarification.

"I'll tell you on the way," Mary said. "Please, pack a bag for a few days and come with me to Ramona's. She has asked for our support and our help with the children."

Ramona hugged us when we arrived, served us dinner as if she was an emotionless robot, and then put the children to bed. I could tell she was about to break down into a puddle of tears when she returned to the living room.

She then began her tale of woe. "The sheriff asked for a second meeting on Saturday, with Henry. That morning here in Florence was overcast and filled with a cold damp air. I had woken up early to take care of the children," Ramona recited.

"I decided it would be best if I took the children to his parent's house to give him some quiet privacy to speak with the authorities later that morning, when the sheriff was scheduled to return. Henry, who looked like he didn't get a wink of sleep, grumbled when I bent down to kiss him goodbye. He nodded and mouthed a silent 'thank-you' to me, as I slipped out the bedroom door."

She continued, "When I returned later that afternoon, Henry was gone. There was no note or explanation as to his whereabouts that I could see on the kitchen table, or anywhere else. But, after settling the children down for their afternoon naps, I decided to take advantage of this quiet time and slip into slumber myself, for a brief moment of peace. It was at that moment, when I entered our bedroom that I noticed Henry's closet door was open and most of his clothes were gone." Ramona started to cry and sniffle into her handkerchief.

"Maybe he had to attend an out of town bank meeting or something after the interview with the sheriff," I interjected, hoping for the best, but felt the nausea building from another imminent scandal.

"I thought that at first and for the next couple of days. Thank goodness for my in-law's help in the past two days, while I nervously waited for Henry to return or call. But the Captain and his wife are so old, they can't keep up with the children. That's why I called you two this morning," Ramona paused. "I don't think Henry is coming back."

"Why do you think that?" Mary asked gently.

"I didn't panic or think that until a friend of Henry's, actually another employee at the bank, came," ...*sniff, sniff*...., "to the front door with a message for me this morning," Ramona sobbed and spoke in staccato breaths. "I have been immobile ever since.

"What did this friend have to say?" Mary begged for details about her brother. She looked pale as a ghost, hoping to hear he was still alive.

"He said he spoke with Henry just before he left town. He was with that secretary of his, Miss Weatherson," Ramona finally spilled the story. "He said Henry told him that Miss Weatherson robbed the bank!"

"Wait! What?" I screamed. None of this made sense.

"Not only that," Ramona added, "but that Miss Weatherson, or Harriet as we all know her, admitted to it! Our family has known her for over ten years, since she was a teenager and her mother was one of the first patrons of Henry's bank. That's why Henry hired her. I couldn't believe it!"

"Then what happened?" Mary asked after the color returned to her face and she caught her breath.

"Harriet, um...Miss Weatherson, said, 'It's true. I'm so ashamed,' the co-worker recounted her story to me. Then this co-worker said Henry requested him to contact me after they left town. He also said Henry hid some money away for me to survive in his absence and this colleague let me know exactly where the cash box was buried. His instructions were for me to keep the money, but send the traveler's checks from the cache to his friend, Mr. Charles Farris in Eugene. He said I'd know how to contact him," Ramona explained.

"The Mr. Farris we stayed with when we went to Ashland a few years ago?" I tried to clarify the players.

"Yes. That's the one," Ramona nodded when she answered.

"Why would he want you to send traveler's checks to this Mr. Farris? Aren't those the kind of checks Henry spoke about to EV in Ashland? The kind that are untraceable to an account?" I asked confused.

"Yes. I guess he didn't want me to know where he was headed so as to protect Harriet from the police," Ramona said trying to make sense of this preposterous story. "Henry most likely realizes they will question me next. Mr. Farris will probably be his go between, so when he gets Harriet settled, Henry will let him know where to send the checks and then give them to Miss Weatherson. After that, I'm sure Henry will return."

"Why is Henry helping her? What are you going to do?" I asked flummoxed by the whole ordeal.

"I'm certainly not going to keep any money that Henry may have hidden. Why would he do that and where did he get that money? Did he stockpile, hoard or embezzle funds from the bank over time? Maybe he knew about this robbery in advance and was trying to protect me and the children with a buffer of money in case he was accused of anything. But, I'll have no part of this scheme!" Ramona said clearly. "And I will certainly NOT send any funds, checks or communication to implicate Mr. Farris!"

"You should call Carl, my other brother," Mary offered. "He's the Vice-President of the bank and he will know what to do... I hope."

26  Fleeing from Florence, Early 1927

Carl had gone to the secret hiding place under the cover of darkness, getting drenched by the storm that came in the middle of the night. Ramona had frantically summoned her brother-in-law after our conversation. Carl knew his brother well enough to formulate a theory and calm Ramona on the phone, at least until he arrived the next morning. Mary took the children to the park when he arrived, and the three of us remaining, all sat in the living room to talk.

"This metal box was buried under six inches of dirt, covered by a thick pile of pine needles, at the base of the tree he indicated in his message, just like you said," Carl announced. He had brushed it clean and set it on the kitchen table to open it.

"Oh my goodness!" was all I could muster when Carl lifted the lid of the dirty box, which smelled like compost.

"That's a lot of money!" Ramona estimated. "How much is that all worth?" She began to unload the cash bills, the gold pieces and the traveler's checks.

Carl started to make piles as he counted the loot. "I count $1120 in gold, $2206 in cash, $3570 in American Bank traveler's checks, and $1680 in American Express traveler's checks. That comes to...." Carl scratched some figures on a pad of paper, "$8,576.00!"

"We have to go to the bank and return these funds," Ramona decided. "Will you please come with us, Mother?"

Later that afternoon, Wednesday, February 3rd, after redepositing the funds back in the bank coffers, a bank official, Mr. Voget, and policeman came to Ramona's house. They wanted to speak further with Carl.

"What is this about?" Carl asked politely, but somewhat concerned.

"Following the return of the hidden funds from Mr. Henry Bergman, we have been reviewing the ledgers in the loan department," the bank manager, Mr. Voget, stated. "It appears that you, as the Vice-President of the bank, should have been aware of the banking laws that prohibit making loans when the bank reserves are well below the limit for such activities. Is that not true, Mr. Bergman?"

"Of course I am aware of such laws," Carl responded indignantly.

"Then, how do you explain these documents which authorized such loans?" Mr. Voget continued with narrowed eyes and squinted brow, sliding a pile of papers towards Carl.

"I don't know," Carl said after cursorily reviewing the papers. "Perhaps these were the ones that passed through my brother's approval, not mine. We tended to split these duties when the load of potential loan clients increased."

"I'm afraid we are going to have to charge you, as well as your brother, in violating these banking laws and blatantly disregarding your fiduciary responsibilities as a banker," Mr. Voget said, pointing to the police officer who was dangling handcuffs.

"I will come in and straighten things out," Carl said defiantly. He was indignant and he slowly spit out more words.

"There is no need for those," he added, tilting his head towards the cuffs.

When the room was devoid of men, I spoke with my daughter. "Now what do we do? It seems Henry has dragged his brother into this mess right along with him," I said with compassion for those in the fallout of this debacle.

"I am going to telephone Mr. Farris in Eugene," Ramona answered. "Henry will answer my call and explain things straight away, if he is still there."

Ramona rang for the operator to connect her to Eugene at the identifiable number belonging to Mr. Farris. I was glad she knew how to do such things. These telephone techniques were still so foreign to me.

"He's not there!" Ramona shouted when she hung up the earpiece. "He left with that woman!"

"Did Mr. Farris say anything more?" I begged for more details, hoping for answers that would comfort my daughter.

"Oh, yes. He did," she retorted. "He said he knows nothing about any bank problems, illegal loan practices, or where they went. Henry didn't confide in him about anything bank related. He just said he and Miss Weatherson were taking a trip together and wanted to borrow his Studebaker motor car for a few days. He also said Henry asked him, and a friend of his, to cash out a couple of traveler's checks Henry had for some road money. He assumed Henry hadn't realized how expensive it was to travel these days. He left with about $550....he said."

"What IS that man up to?" I pondered out loud.

Suddenly, there were loud voices on the porch and heavy knocks on the front door. I picked up baby Ray, heavy for an eight month old, and clutched little Patricia to my side. She grabbed the hem of my skirt, since nowadays skirt lengths were right about the level of her hand. Ramona peeked through the folds of the lace curtain, pulling it slightly to the side towards the overlaying floor length thick floral draperies framing the bay window.

"It's a bunch of reporters!" she cried. "I don't have anything to say to anyone. Let's go upstairs. Take the baby. I will carry Patricia. Go now! Please, Mother, go!"

People started gossiping about a relationship between Henry and Harriet once the news blasted the story of their disappearance after the robbery. Some even believed they ran away together to Mexico.

The next day, Mary shared the news from a call she received from her husband, Fred, who was still at their house in North Bend. "The sheriff, accompanied by the county police, were asking if Fred had seen Henry or knew of his whereabouts," Mary recounted. "He told them he hadn't seen or heard anything of Henry other than what the newspapers had reported. They asked if Fred knew another longtime friend of Henry's, Mr. E.S. Downing. They were going to his home next, in Coos Bay, to question him."

"I don't know what's happening," Mary whimpered. "Oh, Lord, this is getting serious. WHERE is my brother?"

Ramona turned beet red after hearing about the conversation. "That's probably my fault," she admitted. "I mentioned to the Sheriff that Henry is probably around Coos Bay or went to Eugene. I told them I knew he'd give himself up since it was Miss Weatherson who robbed the bank."

Ramona added that Carl had suggested to the police that maybe he sailed for China, a couple of days ago, from the Columbia River on the vessel which their cousin was an officer on board. Carl said he took that trip last year around this same time.

None of those suppositions or leads panned out. Of the $40,000.00 believed to be embezzled from the bank, the investigators now believed that $20,000.00 was taken prior to robbery by Henry to make good on his losses incurred in his real estate operations. Further incriminating evidence was uncovered when auditors noticed that in 1926, Henry deeded his house to Ramona in December, as well as re-titling his Heceta Head property to her and me back in October.

So, now the plot thickened. Those changes weren't just to make the bank or Henry look good. Henry was planning this heist and getaway for a while. It seemed he didn't want to leave Ramona or me in a lurch. He knew if the bank failed, we would have an asset to sell. *Thanks, Henry! But I would rather have an honest son-in-law. Not a son-in-law that does the dance most men do in my life. What is it about another woman outside a marriage that is so alluring?*

I felt so bad for my daughter whose life looked like a re-run of the Station Master's wife's. A different story, but the same villainous type of husband. Oh, and the babies, too!

Sheriff Taylor, of Eugene, was put in charge of this case. He made the long trip to Florence to speak directly with the investigators and with my Ramona. I hadn't left her side since this whole fiasco began. On the day of the appointed interview, I was sitting within earshot, and had a perfect line of sight to the living room, feeding the children lunch at the dining room table.

"Thank you for meeting with me, Mrs. Bergman," the sheriff started out so politely. I feared the interrogation that might follow.

"Certainly," Ramona sounded composed. "What is this about?"

"I wanted to give you some updates on our investigation, and ask if you have received any communications from your husband."

"No, I have not heard from Henry. I am so worried. Do you think he is alright? Has he finished helping poor Harriet? She has gotten herself into so much trouble," Ramona's compassion unwittingly poured out.

"Did you say Harriet?" the sheriff looked taken aback.

"Yes, Harriet, um, I mean Miss Weatherson, my husband's secretary," Ramona clarified with her more proper name.

"It sounds like you know a little more than you told the police the last time you spoke with them," Sheriff Taylor said, leaning a bit closer to Ramona, scooting to the edge of his seat, flipping open his notepad with his pencil in hand.

"Well, um, not really," Ramona stumbled looking for the right way to say what little she knew. "It was just something I was told by that colleague of my husband's, when he divulged the location of the hidden money cache my husband left for me. Which, by the way, I returned immediately!"

"Yes, I heard about that. Thank you very much for your honesty in that situation," he complimented her in a condescending tone. "So what was the other 'something' you were told, Mrs. Bergman?"

"That man passed along further instructions from Henry for me to send along the traveler's checks from the cache, to his friend in Eugene. My family has stayed at this friend's house in Eugene, on occasion, so I know his address."

Ramona took a deep breath and continued with vehemence. "I, of course, did nothing of the sort! I returned ALL the monies directly to the bank. And a fat lot of good that did for my brother-in-law! They turned around and accused him of being involved."

"Mrs. Bergman, please calm down," the sheriff said, patting her knee. I was incensed at his forwardness, especially now that skirt lengths were barely covering the knee. "The auditors are just trying to not leave any loose ends. Mr. Carl Bergman will have justice on his side when all is finally settled. Now please, tell me about this Eugene man. What was his name?"

"Mr...Charles...Farris," my daughter stated clearly, spitting out one word at a time.

"That's very interesting," he said as he started to write in his notebook. "That is the name we connected with an abandoned car called in from Fresno, California. A car with an Oregon license plate, was reported left at a garage there. The Chief of Police contacted the Department of Motor Vehicles in Salem, and they contacted me, as they usually do with open investigations."

He stopped to flip some pages and check his notes, then continued. "Well, not exactly abandoned. The driver said he would be gone from one to six weeks, and prepaid in cash for the storage fee. That odd indeterminate amount of time, and being all paid in advance, was what provoked the garage mechanic to inform the police. The mechanic said he gave a lift to this middle aged man and his young pretty lady friend to the Fresno train station. We traced the plates back to a Mr. Farris in Eugene."

"What does that have to do with Henry?" Ramona looked shocked. I knew she didn't want to tip her hand and tell about Mr. Farris lending Henry his Studebaker.

"Nothing......until now," the sheriff noted. "You have connected the dots for us. It seems Mr. Farris was with your husband after the incident, and he may know something to help our case."

"Oh," Ramona exhaled with a sigh and slumped back into her chair. "I am glad I could help." She looked pale and drained realizing what she had inadvertently done. "Do you think Henry and Harriet are alright?"

"Oh, I think they are both just fine, Mrs. Bergman," he said with raised eyebrows and a nod. "Would you mind giving me Mr. Farris' telephone number, if you have it? And if you don't mind, I would like to have your number as well, just in case I have further questions or updates. I'll leave you mine to call if you hear anything that might help resolve this case."

Ramona got up and walked to the writing desk in the corner of the living room, right next to the kitchen. I looked at her nervously and the spoonful of mashed potatoes I was shoveling into baby Ray's mouth, missed its mark and plopped like a bomb on the floor, the mess exploding onto my shoes.

"Here you go. Please keep in touch if you find Henry," Ramona said as she escorted Sheriff Taylor to the door.

27  Fugitives Found, Spring 1927

A week later, on Valentine's Day 1927, the newspapers printed a bold headline, another in the long line of articles about the Florence bank robbery. This one touted a finality, almost.

"Florence Pair is Caught in Safford, Arizona" - Henry L. Bergman, President, and Miss Harriet Weatherson, Cashier at Bank, Almost Intercepted".

The subtext below stated: **"Trail is followed. Detectives Discover Abandoned Car at Fresno** - Two Will Face Embezzlement Charges." I was anxious to read what happened:

"The Burns Detective Agency followed a lead to a mechanic's garage in Fresno. Details were given of the vehicle driver and passenger, which matched the description of the Florence pair of missing bank officials. Information pointed detectives to the local train station clerk, who also identified the couple from photos provided. Tickets were reported to have been purchased to Los Angeles, and then on to Safford, Arizona. However, by the time agency operatives arrived in Arizona, the couple had already fled the area, evading the detectives.

"The Studebaker car, which was recovered in Fresno, has been identified as the property of Mr. Charles Farris of Eugene, who was contacted to come retrieve his vehicle. It is reported in drivable condition."

I couldn't believe this! Henry was on the run. He truly did abscond with bank funds, and that woman. This was worse than the story I had to suffer through as the Station Master's wife. My 'poor Ramona' was all that kept turning over in my mind. We suffered together while we waited for the next news.

The following week, Sheriff Taylor telephoned Ramona. After she hung up the black bell-shaped earpiece, she collapsed into the kitchen chair, her head flopped onto her crossed arms on the table. Tears rolled down her cheeks.

"What did he say, dear?" I tried to sound consoling. I sat next to her and laid my hand on her arm. I was grateful the children were upstairs for their nap time.

"They've found them and taken them into custody."

"What? That's good news, I hope. Maybe Henry can do some explaining to clear up this whole mess. At least they're not injured, are they?"

"No, they're fine. And Henry is saying he didn't do the things they said he did. They both denied any implication in the robbery now. He and Harriet said they would prefer to waive the two weeks in an Alabama jail while waiting for extradition papers. Instead, they proposed returning to Oregon in the custody of Birmingham authorities, to immediately face any charges. Sheriff Taylor said that won't happen. He is going to get them himself."

"So they are in the deep south? Alabama, you said? How did the Sheriff find them? Did they contact the police once they saw their faces on 'Wanted Posters' in the Post Office stating the allegations against them?"

"No. Not at all. The sheriff said they were tracked by letters they sent to Harriet's mother and to Mr. Farris in Eugene. Each of the recipients turned the letters they received over to authorities. I assumed they were being monitored, like I am.

"Henry used an alias, James Sylvester, as the return address name when he sent a letter to Mr. Farris. He asked Farris to send him some more money cashed from the traveler's checks he expected that I had sent to him. By the time that letter arrived, Sheriff Taylor had already been in touch with Mr. Farris, due to my piece of information that connected Henry to him. After reading Henry's message, Mr. Farris then understood that Henry could possibly be involved in the robbery and he immediately turned over the written communication to the authorities.

"The mail was postmarked, from Safford, Arizona. When the detectives were directed to interview the Postmaster at Safford about this Mr. Sylvester, they discovered a letter had been sent from a 'James Sylvester' requesting his mail be forwarded to 'General Delivery' at the post office in Longview, Texas."

"I'm confused. So they are in Texas, not Alabama?"

"No. They moved on from Texas before the detectives drove there. After these **Burns** operatives interviewed the mail clerk in Texas, they found out that Henry, or 'James Sylvester' had sent another letter, this one mailed to the Postmaster in Longview, Texas, asking that any mail for him be forwarded to 'General Delivery' in Birmingham, Alabama. That time, the detectives *called* their **Burns** Agency branch in Alabama to stake out that post office, rather than chasing Henry and

Harriet by driving the distance and possibly missing them again."

"And? Were they there?"

"Well, the Alabama Burns detective asked the Birmingham postal counter clerk to nod at him, if and when anyone came in requesting mail for 'James Sylvester.' That operative stood watch in the post office lobby corner, pretending to casually be reading the paper. Within a couple of days, the private investigator got the nod and was able to follow Henry back to his new apartment. Armed with the address, he notified the police to come arrest them."

"Goodness! That is quite a cat and mouse tale. When will they be coming home? I hope things can get back to normal when they return."

"I don't think so, Mother," my daughter sighed. "That's not all to the story. Harriet's letter to her mother also helped narrow down their location, but the information it contained is even more lamentable. The sheriff told me what Harriet wrote to her family, so I would be aware of the situation upon their return.

These are words I can't easily forget. She said: *"I am gone for good. I hope to be able to be good enough to Henry to make up for the home he had to lose. I know he is a married man with two children, but I love him and I believe he loves me. We have been ostracized in Florence for our intimate conduct, and we are looking forward to a new start somewhere completely different and far away from Florence."*

I made the sheriff read it to me twice, since the first time I heard it, I could not take in any word after *"be good enough for Henry"*.

"Oh, my dear Ramona," I sobbed with her. "I can't believe this is happening to you. Goodness gracious, you just gave birth to his son less than a year ago! How could he do this? Was that why he said he had to "work" such late hours all these past years at the bank? What is wrong with men these days? Perhaps it's just men on any day," I thought back to Charles' and Alex's excuses for being gone so frequently. The similarities made my stomach churn and my heart race.

Ramona just kept whimpering. She looked so despondent. I was grateful to have watched Ramona use the telephone, so I was able to call the Captain and his wife to let them know their son had been found.

"I believe the sheriff said it would take about two weeks or so to bring them back to Oregon," I answered when they inquired when Henry would be home. "But I don't think he will be coming back to Florence. They said he would be arraigned in Eugene and have to stay in their jail until the trial."

"Zat cowardly son of mine!" the Captain bellowed. "Why didn't he just come to me vit his financial concerns before doing somezing as schtupid as robbing a bank, und HIS own bank, to boot!" I was finally getting better at understanding the Captain's accent now.

I could hear Henry's mother crying in the background over the telephone wires. Her words in between her wailings included, "Wait till I get my hands on that boy! He'll have a no good whipping worse than he ever had as a boy, even if he is almost a foot taller 'an me."

"When you both have had a chance to settle a bit, why don't you come over here and share some time with Ramona and your grandchildren. I'm sure she would love the help and support."

"Of course, Alice dear," John, Sr. replied. "Just give us a couple of days."

I hung up the earpiece into the silver horseshoe-shaped side lever of the wooden telephone box on the wall. Motioning for my daughter to come to me, I wrapped her in my arms, escorted her upstairs and helped her into bed.

The little ones were confused as to why their mommy wasn't joining them for dinner, but I let them play with the rolling green peas to take their minds off any irregularities.

After everyone ate and was tucked into bed, I opened the newspaper to read anything else that would take my mind off this despicable affair.

Then I saw the other headline in bold: *"**State Trial for H. DeAutremont**" - Arrested in Manila in connection with the holdup in 1923 of a Southern Pacific train in the Siskiyou Mountains, just south of Ashland, Hugh DeAutremont will face trial on murder charges in the courthouse at Jacksonville."*

Oh, my, I thought. Wasn't he part of the band of brothers that robbed the train while we were visiting Ashland in 1923? It took this long to find them? Well, I should read how this bandit was tracked down, rather than reading more about my son-in-law's on the run escapades:

"Hugh DeAutremont joined the U.S. Army in hopes of avoiding capture, and changed his name to James C. Price (purportedly using the name "James" in honor of his boyhood idol, Jesse James). He was stationed in the Philippine Islands. A few months after the train robbery, when another army

enlistee returned stateside, he saw a Post Office Wanted Poster with Hugh's picture. After being identified by this army corporal, it took four years to extradite Mr. DeAutremont back to the United States. Renewed posters have been circulated in hopes of locating his twin brothers."

Well, isn't that dandy! Those Post Office Wanted Posters are certainly doing their job. I'll have to keep an eye out for the twin brothers and the outcome of this trial. I wish it was the only trial to watch, but I know I'll read more about Henry's, too.

Within two weeks, Sheriff Taylor returned with Henry and Harriet. The Oregon sheriff described the old Southern customs he observed to the local newspaper reporters:

"When I went to Montgomery, the state capital of Alabama, to obtain the extradition papers, the governor was in conference. I was told to wait outside his office, in the lobby. During this interval, a darky waiter made several trips into the sacred precincts of this Chief Executive, bearing a tray with a number of glasses containing what looked uncommonly like mint juleps," the sheriff was quoted as saying, in the local paper.

He continued with his description of the suspects. "Miss Weatherson was cold and placid from the time she was taken into custody in Birmingham. She asked if her mother and sister would be meeting her when they were dropped off in Eugene, unaware she would be held in jail until trial, unless bail was posted. Mr. Bergman was quiet most of the time, however he did inquire about his wife and family, unaware that Mrs. Bergman had reported and returned the hidden stash of funds he left for her."

On Monday, March 7th, the papers carried on relentlessly with bold headers spotlighting the bank robbery and its suspects. They spoke of Harriet's uncle pleading with her:

"An announcement was made on Friday night that Mr. George Knowles, uncle to the accused, would furnish bail for her at the amount set of $20,000. However, it is said that Mr. Knowles, who is bitter against Bergman, made a condition that Miss Weatherson make a clean break of the whole illicit affair. As of press time, no bail has been posted, and it is expected that she will enter a plea of not guilty."

Then the story proceeded to discuss Henry's side. *"Mr. Bergman acknowledges the charge of embezzlement of the Florence bank funds. He is expected to turn over any and all of his individual property to the bank and his creditors, saying he is anxious to do anything he can to right the wrongs he has done. If his claims against the Pierce Logging Company and the Willamette-Pacific Lumber Company should pay out as expected, then the losses of the depositors and creditors should be reduced considerably."*

Finally, with this last piece of information about lawsuits against his logging and lumber companies, I started to understand why Henry had shifted things around last October. He was working with uncooperative contractors who most likely set his finances into a tailspin. He was trying to protect the project, his name and Ramona's future by switching titles into her name. I just wish he hadn't shifted his emotions to that young woman, as well.

Memories of the deep hurt I felt when I found out Charles had another woman in his life, started to surface again, making me nauseous. Having my Mama and Papa around was what kept me and the children sane. And, of course, when Daniel joined the picture, the wound seemed to fade some.

But, my Ramona had much littler children, and only one parent able to really help. I hoped Henry's family would pitch in and thwart the barbs that would fly from this scandal. My daughter was still in shock and didn't believe the rumors the paper had printed. She had gone to Eugene to see Henry herself. She wanted to look into his eyes and find out the truth. I, of course, volunteered to be with my grandchildren. Deep down, I already knew the truth.

Ramona returned from Eugene in a state of oblivion. Even though she met with Henry, I don't think she let sink in what he actually said. Cautiously, not wanting to pour salt on a wound, but very interested in his explanation, I asked her to tell me what happened.

"When I walked into the county jail, I crossed paths with Mr. Downing from North Bend, who was coming out from briefly speaking Henry. He said Henry seemed very penitent and eager to make amends. Mr. Downing was hopeful that Henry would be able to furnish his own $20,000 bail, so that he could go to Florence, and aid the state receiver now in charge of the bank, to straighten out the bank's affairs. Mr. Downing said Henry's knowledge would facilitate the work and be a great advantage for the depositors of the bank. He hoped I could influence him to do as he requested.

"I thanked him for coming and hurried in to Henry. I was so happy to see him, I ran into his arms and gave him a big kiss. I didn't care who was watching, I really missed my husband after worrying about him for over a month."

I could see Ramona was not ready to accept the reality of the situation. "I admire your strength," I hesitated in contradicting what mattered to her right now. "I'm sure Henry will do what's proper when the time comes at trial. I know he loves you and the children, and that is all that matters right now."

"Exactly, Mother," she relaxed on her patterned brocade brown twill couch. "I even spoke with Harriet when I was there."

"Really?" I replied, trying to keep my judgement at bay. "What did she have to say?"

"Oh, we were very pleasant with each other. I sat on the bed with her in her small separate jail cell. We chatted about how wonderful Henry was and how he cared for us both. She was sorry for how things developed, particularly when Henry's finances took a downward spiral. She said he couldn't bear to speak of such losses with me, so I guess he turned to her in his time of need. She said she always considered Henry her hero and this was her chance to finally help him." Ramona seemed resolved with this explanation of things.

"Well she certainly did more than help with his ledgers and finances," I crudely responded. "I think you are being just a bit too nice about all this, Ramona. Remember the outcome of her actions, no matter how altruistic she may have been originally. She did snare your husband and run off with him to start a new life."

"I know. But I'm counting on Henry seeing the error of his ways and returning home when all this is straightened out at the trial. He won't need her anymore. I will be his shoulder to lean on and the rightful one to help with his troubles."

Right then, I knew it would take a lot more for Ramona to understand the betrayal she faced. As her mother, I would be there for her when she did.

Ramona and I made the curvy drive through the coastal mountains to Eugene for Henry's trial, scheduled for Wednesday, March 10th. Mr. Farris felt so bad about the financial mess Henry had created, he offered to put us up so we could save money on a hotel. We all sat in the packed circuit court room, appreciative that Henry's sister Mary, and her husband Fred, took the children during the week of the trial. I could not believe the sensational event this had become.

Henry was dressed in his pinstriped suit, and stood tall when the judge asked for the defendant to rise. When asked how he pleaded, Henry's chin dropped toward his chest and he muttered a plea of "Guilty, Sir" each time when asked to reply to the charges of his two indictments.

One accusation was for embezzlement and one was for making bank loans when the legal reserve was impaired. Henry also admitted his guilt to the charges of larceny of a Studebaker. We knew he wanted to protect his friend, Mr. Farris, from any further involvement. Mr. Farris breathed a deep sigh after this, grateful to avoid any charges of collusion in these crimes.

We listened to the attorneys battle and barter for leniency. Mr. Bryson, Henry's attorney, told the court that "my client is willing to turn over all assets and is willing to travel to Florence to help the receiver with the books to straighten out the affairs of the bank, if the court so decides to delay his sentencing a few days for such matters."

Then the District Attorney prosecuting the case stood up and yelled, "That's all bunk! The books are being transported here to Eugene. This is obviously a delay tactic on behalf of Mr. Bryson's client to visit his home one last time."

"How discourteous!" Mr. Bryson rebutted. "My client is only trying to help with the liquidation of the bank finances."

I jerked when the judge slammed his gavel on his desk coaster. His other hand immediately shot up like a crossing guard stopping traffic, and halted the argument between the lawyers. He announced sentencing would be delayed for two days, allowing for any input from Henry to help untangle the bank's financial situation, although any ledger reviews would be held in Eugene, under guard, since Henry was considered a flight risk. Ramona gasped at those words.

On Friday afternoon, March 12th, the judge's gavel hammered once again against his desk, after his pronouncement of Henry's sentence. Henry, aged 39, was sentenced to thirteen years for his crimes, to be served in the Oregon State Penitentiary. Ramona was allowed one last visit prior to his transport to prison.

"At least your Uncle Isaac is no longer the Warden. If he were, I would probably be killed by the other inmates thinking I would have favoritism," Henry told her. Then he added a final contrition, "I am sorry for all this. Take care of yourself and the children. I never meant to hurt you like this. I just needed a change and Harriet so helped me with that," Henry said as his final words to Ramona.

Upon returning to our room at Mr. Farris' and hearing Ramona recount her husband's parting words, I asked, "He didn't say he loved you?" Those were my final words to Ramona. I could tell my comment really made her ponder mixed thoughts about Henry. Her silence spoke volumes.

~ ~ ~

28  Convictions, Summer 1927

Even though Harriet pleaded 'Not Guilty' the next week, the judge said she was educated and knew the ropes and knew what she was doing when she participated in the making of the loans and embezzling the funds. Her ruse of a 'fake robbery', as well as her conduct involving a married man, led the judge to his decision.

Upon returning to Ramona's home in Florence, I read the account of Miss Weatherson's trial in the paper to my daughter. Ramona was still in a daze. The courtroom scene was described in the article as follows:

"I hereby find you 'guilty' on all counts as charged", the judge proclaimed. "You will begin your sentence, of six years, at the Oregon State Women's Prison beginning this coming Monday, March 21st." The sound of the gavel was like a nail being pounded in her coffin. Miss Weatherson collapsed into her defendant's chair.

Miss Weatherson's lawyer had tried to stress the point that she did not get a nickel out of the bank's funds, and that Mr. Bergman had confirmed this in his final statement to the court before he was sentenced. This plea fell on deaf ears. The judge had already made up his mind based on the overwhelming evidence and improper behavior.

Upon nearing the prison gates, Miss Weatherson, age 27, turned deathly white and tears flooded her eyes. She was booked into the women's ward and it is expected she will be assigned work in the accounting department."

"Are they insane? They are really thinking about putting her to work in prison accounting, after what she did?" I rhetorically asked Ramona.

My daughter could care less about what happened to Miss Weatherson. She sat there holding a letter from Henry in her hands, rereading it over and over, looking for any inkling of love hidden in his aloof ramblings about prison life. He mentioned that he had been put to work in the flax mill on site and met many of the other laborers, some of whom seemed pleasant enough, considering their situation.

"Henry says he will probably ask to be transferred to an assignment in the office department after he learns all the prison routines," Ramona said somewhat complimentary of his ambitions, and hopeful he remained safe in jail.

"I hope he avoids being assigned to the dungeon or mingling with the fellows who spent time there. Your Uncle Isaac wouldn't even show us that part of the State Pen when we were there. So, did Henry mention his son's first birthday? Any suggestions he would give him for presents?" I tried to point out Henry's world and his distancing from the family.

"No, but he did say he'd write again when he gets the chance."

"That will be nice to hear from him again. Oh, look!" I tried to reroute the discussion to the world that we lived in, rather than Henry's. "The paper has a disturbing article about the railroad to Ashland. According to Southern Pacific, they will begin, in April, to redirect their California trains through a cut-off to Klamath Falls to get north to Eugene. Trains will cease northern through-routes into the Rogue Valley completely."

Ramona snapped out of her fog when she heard the name mentioned of the area where she was raised. "Won't that affect Ashland? I mean, won't that detour the passengers away from stopping and visiting in our hometown?"

"It says some rail service will still go to Ashland. One train will be run out of Portland to Eugene where it will be divided, with one section coming to Coos Bay and the other going to Ashland."

"But that will take so much longer to get to Ashland from California, if people have to go to Eugene first and then back south again to get to Ashland. Passengers on their way north, who used to stop for lunch or shopping because of the layover, won't make the effort to double back to Ashland just to see our little community."

"I know, dear," I commiserated with my daughter's assertions. "I guess SP was thinking more about the through passengers to Portland, than the layover tourist dollars that Ashland will miss. The railroad says that the new route through Klamath will save nearly four hours between San Francisco and Portland, and reduce the time from Los Angeles to Portland by seven and one-half hours. The fast trains will have an extra $3.00 fare attached."

"Fast trains?"

"Yes. The trains will maintain a faster speed when they don't have to cross the elevation of the Siskiyou Pass or deal with heavy snows at such altitudes during winter. They will go east of Mt. Shasta City to Klamath Falls and then head north through the high flat desert finally turning west to Eugene near Oakridge."

"That must have cost a fortune to build the new route!"

"Well, I remember your father telling me how expensive it was to maintain the Siskiyou Pass. The costs were exorbitant for hiring labor and materials to repair twisted tracks from snow slides and down trees, or the extra work created by the train plow to remove the snow drifts. I learned a lot of behind the scenes details as the Station Master's wife."

"Snow couldn't be the only reason for such a huge shift of the route of the line, could it?" she asked. I was glad to see Ramona engaged by other concerns aside from Henry. I kept talking about Ashland.

"No, not just that. There were extra engines they had to supply to haul passengers and freight over the Pass, too. Charles told me it took an extra six engines to make it over the hill even in good weather. Sometimes, he had to close the track altogether because of weather issues. But I think the final blow that sparked them to start building the new route in 1923, was that train robbery near Ashland, when those delinquent brothers blew up the mail car and killed those four train employees. I'm sure they didn't want to ever slow a train down again, especially in a remote place like a mountain pass, to check train brakes."

"Well it sounds like the trains will be going so fast, no one will ever get on or off, except at the stations where folks are watching all around."

I joined the family in Florence for my grandson Ray's first birthday in the beginning of June 1927. Everyone was there, except his father, of course. Even his Uncle Alex came up from Sacramento, bringing baby Ray's cousins, Keith and June, who just started their summer vacation with their father. Alex, who had rekindled his passion for whittling, brought a hand-carved rocking horse for the baby. June brought some of her old dolls for her little cousin Patricia, age five, so she wouldn't feel left out during the present giving.

"These are such special gifts, Alex," Ramona said as she hugged her brother. "I'm so glad you came. Things have been so topsy-turvy here with Henry gone, it is nice to have a man around the house."

"Happy to be here, sis," Alex smiled. "I am actually glad that you invited us. I was needing to be around family too. My life is so fragmented with the children so far away and they don't really feel at home when they visit me. I wish we all lived closer to each other."

I was standing behind Ramona when I overheard my children bonding again. This made me happier than I had been in years. Alex appeared to have turned his life around and back onto the straight and narrow.

"Mother, I see you eavesdropping," Alex said prying over Ramona's shoulder. "Come over here and let me give you a big hug." I giggled and let him scoop me up till my feet dangled above the floor.

"Yes, it is good to have you here, Alex," I admitted. "I have much to discuss with you after these festivities. But for now, will you carve the meat for lunch?"

After the birthday luncheon, Alex came outside to join me on the porch overlooking the river, and lit up his pipe. I noticed the ornately carved ivory bowl as he filled it with his aromatic cinnamon tainted tobacco.

"Is your pipe bowl carved in the shape of a sea captain's head?" I asked leaning over from my wicker rocking chair to get a closer look.

"Yes, it is. I picked it up from my old tobacco shop in Oakland, when I retrieved the children from Irma's house. I bought one for the Captain as well. I couldn't resist. Do you think he'll like it?"

"That is so thoughtful of you, Alex," I commended him. "I am glad to see your world involves thinking about others now. You have certainly made some changes for the better now that you are single."

"Thanks. That means a lot coming from you, Mother," Alex replied.

"Well, I can see the transformation in you. You are setting a good example for your son. Keith is how old now? Sixteen or seventeen?"

"He turned seventeen this past February. And June turned thirteen this past week. Maybe we could do something special for her birthday too, while we are here?"

"Perhaps Ramona could take her fishing to her favorite spot on the Siuslaw River. You know your sister. She has been hooked on fishing ever since Daniel took her to his favorite spots on Ashland Creek."

"June would love that. It would be great for her to have a female role model who does outdoorsy things girls aren't encouraged to do. Has Ramona gotten over her fear of scorpions?"

"No, not ever. She just laces up tall boots for nature outings, no matter what the weather. I suspect her feet start to mold in summer."

"Good one, Mother," Alex giggled and bubbles of smoke followed his laughter. "What did you want to speak with me about, that you mentioned earlier?"

I took a deep breath and settled back into the rocker. An osprey swooped over our heads and down towards the river. His nose dive produced a wriggling fish in his talons, as he headed back up to his treetop nest. I struggled for the words to begin, like the fish struggled for his life.

"Alex, dear," I started slowly. "You are aware of this mess that happened to your sister. All the sordid details have been skimmed over so as to not upset the family. But I've been thinking about having her leave this town of Florence and move closer to me. The gossip here is so hurtful and the financial situation will be getting worse as the courts start selling off Henry's assets. These investments of Henry's used to bring money into Ramona's coffers, but when they are sold, there will be nothing left but the house she lives in."

"What about all the land he transferred to you and Ramona before he and the cashier.....um, before the bank issues came to light?"

"That property development seems to have stopped since the trial. No one wants to deal with either Mrs. Henry Bergman or her mother. We own empty platted land with no money to develop it. Our only option is to sell."

"Why don't you then?"

"The sale of such an undeveloped property won't bring in enough to pay me back for my deposits I lost in the bank failure, much less support Ramona for any length of time." The osprey whistled as it took flight from its perch.

"Weren't there other investments that brought in money?"

"The bank has garnered all of Henry's assets, and the ones that are still owned jointly with Ramona are causing more trouble."

"More trouble than losing your husband and income? What kind of trouble?"

"Well, it turns out a lumber company who did work on some land of theirs near Mapleton, up the Siuslaw River from here, is filing a lawsuit for over $30,000 against the timber company for some products they were promised. And, they are naming Henry AND Ramona as part of the list of defendants in their claim. The mess keeps snowballing and I am not sure your sister can handle this and the children all by herself."

"Then it sounds like a good move to me," Alex concurred.

"I will need your help convincing your sister to do the right thing. She continues to believe in Henry and that things will return to wedded bliss when he gets out. She's blinded by the memory of love and needs a real kick into reality by her big brother. Please spend some time with her. I'll take all the children on a picnic by the bay lighthouse tomorrow."

"OK, mother. I'll try my best. But you know how stubborn she is."

~ ~ ~

29  Moving On, Autumn 1927-1928

The next headline that was plastered in bold across the country's newspapers was about the capture and trial of the brothers who robbed the train in 1923 near Ashland. It took four years, but they finally caught all three of them.

Triggered by the new wanted posters distributed after the younger brother was extradited from a South Pacific army base, it only took two more months, and a large $15,900 reward, for the older twin DeAutremont brothers to be found.

For their cover identities, one of them had bleached his hair white blonde, and the other had married a seventeen year old. They both grew bushy mustaches, but all these changes failed to disguise them. Under the names of Elmer and Clarence Goodwin, they had eluded authorities for four years. They were located and identified in Ohio by a one blind-eye steel mill supervisor, who worked with them.

On June 24, 1927, the three of them were tried and convicted at the Jacksonville courthouse on four counts of first degree murder, two counts of malicious destruction of property and attempted theft. They were all headed to the Oregon State Penitentiary for life imprisonment.

In a letter that Ramona received from Henry that August, she learned all about the new friends in his world of State Pen criminals. She read his letter to me and her sister-in-law Mary, when she came to visit us in North Bend.

Dear Ramona,

I met these twin brothers working with me at the flax mill. I started talking to the one named Ray. No one in here admits or discusses what brought them here. We pretty much stick to talking about what we like to do and the weather for conversation.

This guy's hair was two toned, with brown roots growing through a head of bleached blonde hair, but he soon had his head shaved to not get such odd looks from fellow inmates. His face looked familiar when I spoke with him, eye to eye, but after he shaved his head, I definitely remembered where I'd seen him before. He was the kid, now a young man in his late twenties that I saw in Ashland at the coffee shop when that train was robbed. Remember?

Your mother was the one who thought that kid could be one of the murderous brothers, but I didn't believe it. Well, it was! Once I realized this, I told him we had met before. We swapped stories of being on the run, although he was better at it than I. He evaded the authorities for over four years!

I am glad to be in one place for a while. It gives me time to think. I've decided I don't want to be in the banking business anymore. For now, I'm hoping to use my training in accounting here. I have requested a transfer to the *financial department in the prison. Heavy labor is hard work in the flax mill.*

Give the children a hug for me. Again, I am sorry for this mess.

Regards, Henry

"I told you that kid was one of the train robbers!" I announced after Ramona finished reading Henry's letter. "I can't believe Henry talked to this reprehensible man. He must really be losing his mind in there."

Ramona looked forlorn and non-responsive to my outburst. I wish I could take back what just blurted out of my mouth. I should have thought about how it might make Ramona feel. Then she spoke softly to both of us.

"Mama, Mary, I've been doing some thinking as well," Ramona sounded somber. "My situation isn't going to get better waiting a dozen years for Henry. And, I'm not sure he'll even be coming back to me. Not once since he left in January, has he said "I love you" to me. I think he has moved on, for whatever reasons or circumstances ultimately led him in that direction. I must accept this as a permanent change. I have to start thinking about the children. Alex spoke with me earlier this summer about selling my house."

"Oh, I'm so glad to hear you say that," Mary agreed. "I didn't want to initiate this subject, but Fred thinks so as well. Selling your house in Florence will pay off the debts you share with Henry. We were thinking it would be lovely to have you and the children join us in our house here in North Bend.

"We have so much space in the old billiard room downstairs. It is so large, practically the length of the house. You remember when you and I started the first library in there for North Bend, back in 1914?"

"Yes, definitely," Ramona reminisced in her mind. "You had all those shelves built for the donated books and we kept the fireplace going whenever we had library hours."

"And we even had Mayor Simpson give an opening speech on the porch before he cut the ribbon across the basement door. Thank goodness the Carnegie Library was completed the next year. I got tired of hosting and cleaning up, especially after children's story time."

"Well, that room would certainly be big enough for me and the children, as well as toasty warm. But what about Fred, Jr.? Won't it be a bit annoying to a seventeen year old to have us around?"

"I'll give him a 'what for' if he gives you any trouble. Besides, he will be graduating from high school in a few months and heading off to college soon. Don't you give him a second thought," Mary ruled.

"And I will be nearby to help babysit, if you want to get a part-time job. You do have a college degree, remember darling?" I added to motivate her to move on.

"Alright, I'll do it," Ramona decided. "Will Fred be able to help get my house on the market? And, do you think maybe Fred, Jr. could help with the moving?"

"Consider it done!" Mary concluded. "After the move, but only when you are ready, I would love it if you would give me a hand working in my insurance company office. We have a secretarial position opening up soon, since Mrs. Evelyn Miller is expecting her baby in November."

"I'll think about it. Let me get through this move first and settle in." Ramona's face looked less tense, although a veil of sadness remained.

The transition from Florence went smoothly for Ramona. She said goodbye to her in-laws and told them to visit when they could. Her house sold within two months, and the move was completed by Halloween. Christmas was celebrated in full style, with Irma giving her permission for Alex to bring their children to join the rest of the family in North Bend for the holidays. Even Isaac and Dora came down from Salem, accompanied by Dot, now a grown woman of forty-five who preferred to be called Laura, with her husband Carl.

The Christmas tree was decorated with red velvet bows, hand painted ornaments, and multiple strings of popcorn garlands that Ramona and Alex had taught everyone to make. Cinnamon spice floated from the kitchen, as the tea kettle whistled. I sat at the head of the long table Mary had set up that spanned two rooms, crossing through the archway that divided the living room and the dining room. Before dessert was served, I clanked my wine glass with my spoon, calling everyone's attention to silence.

"I just want to thank everyone for gathering together here at Mary and Fred's, for this holiday," I broadcasted. "It has been a long time since all of my family was in one place. This is the best Christmas gift for an old woman like me."

I winked at my brother Isaac, including him as another even older elder. "We have all gone through hard times, some more recently than others, but with each other and our love, we will all persevere. Merry Christmas to all!"

"Here, here!" was the sweeping response.

"I also want to welcome my daughter to her new home," I raised my glass towards Ramona. "I hope the community here will extend open arms to you, as it did for me, helping to unfold your next chapter of life."

"Thank you, Mother," Ramona lifted her glass to toast with everyone else's.

"And I hear congratulations are in order to my son, Alex. From what he has told me, he has been promoted to district manager of Virden, starting in February, in Fruitvale, only ten minutes from Oakland. Hopefully he will move back to Oakland next year, and be closer to his children."

"Yes, please!" both Keith and June chimed in together.

"Now what's for dessert? And have we picked a 'present-servant'?" The non-Berry family members looked perplexed by my question. So I peered over my eyeglasses and nodded to Ramona to explain.

"Grandfather Berry always let me be the 'present-servant', so I guess I should explain the duties and pass on the title," Ramona announced. "This job requires the one with the title to pick the person who opens their present first, then the present-servant finds their present under the tree and brings it to them. Then that person picks to whom the server brings the next present, and so on. I think anyone under eighteen should put their name in this Santa hat, and I will draw the winner for this year. Next year, that person will draw. Okay?"

Everyone's great excitement and anticipation was settled when Patricia's name was drawn. She was so happy to be the center of attention that she almost knocked over the tree getting the first present.

Cousins Keith and Fred, Jr., ages fifteen and one-half, and seventeen, respectively, were happy with their whittling kits that Alex had given them. Laura had a special gift for Patricia that she had saved for over thirty-seven years. Since she married Carl so late in life, she had no plans of having any children and thought Ramona's family could use something precious right about now. It was the handmade doll that Papa Berry had made for her when Charles and I visited during Isaac's time as Warden at the Penitentiary. Both Ramona and Patricia cried when they saw it. Papa's gift lived on.

Ramona had one last present to hand out, and she gave the box to Patricia to bring to me. I unwrapped the yellow ribbon and opened the small box to find a small handmade silk purse tied with a yellow ribbon. I thought it looked familiar, but it wasn't until I loosened the ribbon cinch, that I saw the silver dollar inside.

The date on the coin showed it was minted in 1895. Tears started rolling down my cheeks. "This can't be the same coin and purse that my sister Sarah gave you when you were about seven or eight, is it?"

"Actually, it is, Mother," Ramona answered, also with weepy eyes.

"But, how?" I wondered aloud.

"As you remembered correctly, I was only seven. Aunt Sarah said it was a Christmas present that would be a gift given twice when we spent it. I was too young to use it, so I kept it. I figured now would be the best time to have it be gifted again. You have been my anchor throughout my life, and I wanted to repay you for that. I know it should be more than a dollar, but I thought this particular coin might be worth more to you. Merry Christmas Mother, from your whole family, including those all here and those who have gone."

That was the best Christmas I had in many years. I slept so soundly, I didn't even hear the night's stormy winds that blew across the bay.

Ramona started working with Mary at the insurance office after the New Year of 1928 began. She was the fresh face people met first when they entered the building. Unfortunately, the Coos Bay Times reached almost every household in North Bend and Marshfield. It seemed that everyone in town had read about the Florence Bank Robbery and Henry's ignoble behavior. By mid-June, the local gossip mongers to start telling wilder tales of Henry's escapades than the already inexplicable truth, and dragging Ramona under the bus with him.

"They are assuming that I had something to do with the robbery, Mother," she would say when we shared dinner at my house. Ramona didn't want Mary to know that her past history with Henry might interfere with her work, or worse, with maintaining the insurance clientele.

"Don't listen to such rubbish, dear," I countered. "They just want to have something to blabber about. You are a strong independent woman now."

"I don't know if this is the right place for me. It will only be harder in the fall when Patricia starts elementary school. The children of those chatterboxes may tease her and she will hear things about her father that no young child should know until they are older."

"I understand, dear," I said. "Perhaps we should think about moving back to the Bay Area, nearer to your brother. No one will bother you there in such a big city. And I know the best places to live and still have connections with a great realty company, remember?"

"You mean you would move with me?"

"Of course, my darling," I answered, soothing her anxiety. "I have been thinking about being in the warmer weather as I get older. This climate is beautiful, but the wet weather gets straight into my bones. California is so much sunnier."

"I don't know if I am strong enough to begin again, in such a new place. I've put roots down in Oregon, particularly here, for over fourteen years. A single woman, with two little children, isn't supposed to do things like starting over again."

"Huh," I harrumphed. "If you want to hear about a woman not supposed to do things that she just up and did, I should read this article to you about Amelia Earhart. Did you hear what SHE just did?"

"No. I've been pretty swamped with work and motherhood," Ramona mumbled. "I flop into bed after the children are asleep. I don't have time for the newspaper."

"Well, Amelia is going down in history as the first woman to fly across the Atlantic Ocean. This was just announced after she flew an airplane from Newfoundland, on the East Coast, on June 17th and landed the next day in Wales. They said her flight, which she co-piloted with a man named Stultz, plus another man, a flight mechanic named Slim, took twenty hours and forty minutes, compared to steamship vessels taking a week or more."

"Now that's a big difference. Not only the time, but for a woman!" Ramona commented on Amelia's achievement.

"She said she had to fight through rains so thick she was flying blind at times. She admitted to having flown over Ireland and not even knowing it until they landed in Wales, and on almost an empty fuel tank to boot."

"Well she was either very brave or very daft."

"A little of both, perhaps," I laughed out loud. "However, the point is, she did it! It is said she will inspire future generations of women to do things that have never been done by women before. I think making this move to the Bay Area is an example of you blazing a new path, for you AND your children. You can be a pioneer, like Amelia."

"I suppose when you put it that way, it doesn't seem so insane."

"Good. I will put my house up for sale next week, and start making inquiries about housing near Alex. I am glad he has moved back to Oakland. We will all be together again soon. I hope Alex is as excited about this as we are."

~~~

30  The Final Whistle, 1929-1931

The house was filled with screams of laughter every time my granddaughter June came to babysit for her cousins, Patricia and Ray. Ramona and I bought a two story home in Oakland, early in 1929, from the proceeds of the sale of my North Bend house. She kept her dwindling savings she hoarded from liquidating her assets, to keep her family afloat. I made sure the new Oakland house deed was titled in thirds. One third for each of us - me, Ramona and Alex. Eventually, my third of the house would pass on equally to my children to do with what they pleased. Alex was renting and I hoped he would take my place in the house when I passed on.

The current living arrangement with Ramona and I was ideal for both of us. I had the ground floor bedroom. This made me very happy and safe, knowing I would not have to be climbing stairs as I aged. My bedroom had an adjacent 'master' bath with indoor plumbing, plus a second door, opening into the hallway, for others to enter and use these facilities.

Ramona and the children occupied the entire second floor in the three upstairs bedrooms and second bathroom. When searching for the perfect home, I insisted that the realtor find us a home with a back porch overlooking Lake Merritt, where I had such fond memories with Daniel.

Ramona started a new job as a stenographer in an auto sales company in San Francisco. Her commute was simple, with the train and ferry connections almost dropping her door to door.

"I filled out the application form for my new position listing myself as a "widow", Ramona reported. "It just seemed easier to explain than being a single mother. Do you think they will find out the truth?"

"Ramona, it basically IS the truth. Your husband is gone and never coming back. That makes you a widow. I think you'll be fine. Maybe you'll even have a more sympathetic environment in which to work. There's no paperwork trail that will connect you to Henry down here. It's not like they have one big ledger book in the sky where information can magically be transferred from one place to another. That will never happen."

"I feel bad. But this is the way I can finally admit to myself that Henry is gone and I can start over. Do you think he'll come looking for me after he serves his time?"

"A lot can happen in eleven more years. Let's just be thankful for today," I emphasized our good fortune.

Mary and Fred were sorry to see us leave North Bend, but they still had all their friends there to keep them busy and entertained. We kept in touch by mail and telephone, which Ramona maintained was a necessity and that one be installed in our new house. The *Coos Bay Times* and *Lane County News* occasionally had clippings on the 'Florence Pair', as Henry and Harriet had become known. Mary forwarded them to me, asking for my discernment regarding passing along any of these articles to Ramona. I kept most of them tucked away in my cedar chest at the foot of my bed. Maybe with a little more time, after the wound was not so raw, I would show them to my daughter.

The first and only one I mentioned to Ramona was about Harriet. One early Fall evening in 1929, after the children were in bed when we were sitting on the back porch sipping our warm tea and listening to the symphony of crickets and frogs, I broached the news.

"Do you want to hear the latest about Harriet?" I mumbled looking straight ahead at the falling leaves in the yard being tossed around by the evening breeze.

"Now what?" Ramona hissed her reply.

"She's been paroled," I reported.

"What? It's only been two years! She was sentenced to six!!" Ramona reacted stunned and perturbed.

I put down my tea and faced my daughter. "I know, dear. It doesn't seem quite fair. But, she is no more a concern of yours. She won't be in your life ever again. I just thought you should know." It was the last time I told Ramona anything about those two. I didn't want to open an old wound and have her hurt all over again.

Patricia started elementary school that September. With Ramona at work, I became an authorized guardian for dealing with school drop offs and pickups. It felt good to be useful again and part of a family household. During the day, when baby Ray and I weren't strolling along Lake Merritt, we both enjoyed our afternoon naps.

Alex's rental house was just down the block from our house, making it easy for shared dinners and the availability of his helping hand for those heavy chores around our house. Alex, and his seventeen year old son Keith, made quite the pair of manly helpers when it came to putting on a new roof and planting new white and red oak trees in the yard.

I was so happy to hear that Irma had calmed down enough to allow joint custody of the children with Alex after Virden had transferred Alex back to the Oakland area. I presumed, after Irma heard about Ramona's story and how much worse things could be with a cheating husband, she eased up on Alex. He, at least, was trying hard to make things right with his family. On his weeks with the children, he often brought them to our house to visit and play with their cousins, and pamper their grandmother with hugs and help.

In December of that year, 1929, Mary sent more articles, although this time, about Henry and his unbelievable, but likely parole. It seemed that a strong effort for his parole was underway among his friends. I discussed this development with Alex while Ramona was putting baby Ray and Patricia to bed. Thankfully, Keith and June were at their mother's house.

"Alex, dear," I started sweetly. "Would you mind if I ran something by you for your opinion? I'm not sure if I should mention all this information to your sister."

"Sure, Mother, but just a minute," he replied. Noticing how nippy the evening air was, he went back inside and grabbed my lap quilt I had recently finished over the Thanksgiving holiday. That holiday break afforded Ramona more time to deal with her children, leaving me available to tackle and finish my own projects. Alex came back out, laid the patchwork quilt over my exposed, but stockinged legs, and sat down on the porch swing next to my wicker rocker. "What's on your mind?"

"Thank you dear," I complimented him on his thoughtful and observant behavior. "It's just that I received these articles about Henry from Mary, Ramona's sister-in-law. I'm not sure it is in Ramona's best interest to know about Henry's goings-on."

"Go on, Mother. What did she, or rather the newspaper articles, say?"

"There has been some attempt to hasten Henry's parole. A petition was presented to Oregon Governor Patterson's office. However, shortly thereafter, the Governor passed away. The petition has taken a back burner with the transition to the new administration of Governor Norblad."

"Really? Who's prowling into this case? How has Henry been able to manipulate allies from inside the State Pen?"

"I assume he still has a lot of connections and pull with important businessmen. Maybe Miss Weatherson has pleaded with these men or revealed some new evidence."

"Miss Weatherson? Isn't she still serving her time at the Women's Prison in Salem? I thought she was given six years!"

"Somehow, she must have been a good girl inside prison, and she was paroled earlier this year. She served her minimum of two years, which was required before being eligible for parole."

"Perhaps she has some damning evidence against these businessmen that she is using as blackmail to help get Henry out earlier. Didn't Ramona say that Henry had buried some money for her to assuage his guilty departure and help with their children?"

"Yes. But....."

"Think about it, Mother. If Henry was thinking ahead to take care of those loose ends, maybe this Miss Weatherson did something similar to protect both of them, if their plans went south. Oh, wait, they did literally go south, didn't they?"

"Don't be funny, Alex. This is serious business."

"I couldn't resist. Anyway, I bet they were caught before she could unveil her evidence and expose any accomplices. Now that she's out, I wouldn't put it past her to have dug things up and sent these businessmen photographic copies of what she has that implicates them. That would certainly be enough motivation for them to petition the Governor, don't you think?"

"Perhaps. The new development reported in this case appeal states:

"The Lane County State and Savings Bank in Florence, admits to the condition of the bank to not be at all as it appeared at the time of the sentencing of the 'Florence Pair'. The savings and the commercial departments were at fault, and will reimburse the depositors up to 92%. According to this new evidence, Bergman apparently just took enough money to flee with Miss Weatherson and get out from under the failing bank."

"So they are saying he took the fall for the men in those departments? And this information didn't surface until Miss Weatherson was paroled? Hmm, that's rather a strong coincidence, isn't it?"

"It sounds so. But, since the new Governor is the one to commute Henry's sentence, it might take a while," I hoped.

"Well, I hope this Miss Weatherson is smart enough to protect herself and her evidence. Do you think she told someone if she goes missing, where to locate her original evidence?"

"I don't really care. I don't think she's that smart. It was her idea to write a letter to her mother with a postmark leading investigators right to them. But maybe she learned a thing or two from the women criminals with whom she spent the last two years."

"Oh, Mother," Alex sighed. "Don't mention any of this to Ramona. She will be more upset to find out how much and how long Henry was romantically connected with this Miss Weatherson and possibly involved in her blackmail scheme, than to think of Henry as an inept and destitute banker who had a helper."

"I suppose you're right. Let's keep this to ourselves. I'll let you know if there is any action on this with the new Governor. Thank you Alex, for listening, and your advice. It has been wonderful to be back near you and feel at home."

Soon after Keith's high school graduation in June of 1930, we all celebrated with a trip to Yosemite. It was a four hour drive, in one of the borrowed used vehicles Ramona procured from her employer's auto sales lot. Grateful for the large back seat, Ramona and I put her two small children between us. Keith and June rode up front with their father. We chose early in the summer season for our road trip to celebrate my granddaughter June's sweet sixteenth and my upcoming seventieth birthday, together with honoring my grandson Keith's graduation.

There had been a lengthy discussion about the choice of accommodation for our stay in Yosemite. Ramona was definitely opposed to camping in the dirt, her memory of scorpions having never faded. I was watching our finances since the recent event of the past year's Stock Market crash and voted against staying at the newly built luxury Ahwahnee Hotel. We compromised on the Curry Tent Camp bungalows and having one special dinner in the Ahwahnee Grand Dining Room that overlooked Yosemite Falls.

Camp Curry advertised *"a good bed and clean napkin with every meal, for $2 a day."* Our big splurge was for two wood-framed bungalows set on stone foundations, each with adjoining baths. We took the scenic route, driving through a giant sequoia tree that had a tunnel cut through the base of it in 1881. They said it was almost 300 feet tall and over 2300 years old! It was a delightful trip for all, even four year old baby Ray loved the outdoor hikes, especially with the view from his uncle's back.

"May we stay up for the Fire Fall show at 9:00 o'clock tonight?" June asked her father.

"What's the Fire Fall show?" eight year old Patricia questioned, before Alex could answer.

"I read about it before we came," June stated. "It is done every night in the summer from Glacier Point up there," she pointed to the cliff way above the campground. "Each day, hotel employees stack red fir tree bark to be lit that night and burn it for a couple hours to produce a bed of coals. They place the coals on the valley side of the Point and gradually push the glowing embers off the cliff with long-handled metal pushers, when the Stentor, the title given to the really loud announcer, hollers that *'all's ready down below!'* It creates the illusion of a waterfall of fire."

"Sounds like the highlight of our trip. Of course," Ramona answered for Alex. "I think we should all stay up and watch."

Shortly after we returned from our road trip, I received more mail from Mary. I made sure to go out in the backyard by the oak tree, and sit on the bench facing the house, so I could see if Ramona came outside. The article was titled in bold with *"Release Will Be In July 1930"* - **Sentence Commutation Granted by Governor Norblad Thursday.** *Bank creditors join in asking lightening of sentence for Henry L. Bergman, former President of the defunct Lane County State and Savings Bank of Florence.*

I had to read on. I wanted to know what finally urged the Governor to make this decision.

"Judge Skipworth, and the DA prosecuting the case, both joined with a committee of 75% of bank depositors, who were the heaviest creditors of the bank, in urging Bergman's release. In the three years and four months he has been in prison he has been instrumental in saving the state thousands of dollars through installation of a new accounting system at the institution. His conduct since his entrance into prison has been exemplary."

So that's how he manipulated the new Governor, I thought. The Judge's petition continued:

"It now has developed that the bank failed a short time before the indictments were returned. At that time, it was believed that Mr. Bergman had completely looted the bank and that was why I imposed such heavy sentences. It is now

believed the bank robbery was "faked" to cover up funds which were short. Subsequent events have developed that the bank will, under the circumstances, pay the depositors quite well."

Maybe Alex was correct in his assumption of Miss Weatherson's hold over those men. I wonder what the 'events' were that developed all of a sudden? My head was spinning, reflecting on all these theories. I read on to the end of the Judge's petition:

"*Although Mr. Bergman did plead guilty to embezzlement of bank owned traveler's checks and fleeing an ongoing investigation. Although he confessed to knowledge of bank problems but didn't fix them while employed there, we believe that the sentence served should be enough for those crimes.*"

Another newspaper article, still in the envelope from Mary, had a similar July 3rd headline: **"Florence Bank President Will Regain Liberty**" - *Henry L. Bergman was today granted a commutation of sentence by Governor Norblad, reducing his prison term from thirteen years to time served, and will be released the latter part of this month.*"

This was all too much for my heart. I couldn't possibly pass this heartache on to my daughter. Henry had ruined her marriage, abandoned his children, scandalized her life in the town in which they made a home together, and left her almost financially destitute as a result of his choices.

I wanted Ramona to believe he was still locked up and that she was a "widow" starting a new life. I would never show these clippings to her. Alex could know, and protect her from finding out, if any relatives were to call or visit. I for one, would otherwise keep this news to myself.

Our lives were content for most of the next year of 1931, in Oakland. The stock market crash had brought on the Great Depression, but I was still determined and able to laugh and celebrate with children who were now growing up in a loving family.

Nevertheless, my heart did take a toll from all the indiscretions that followed me and my family from the time I had become the Station Master's wife so long ago.

One evening in November, after our family meal together, when we had retired to the living room to gather around the radiating warmth from the fireplace hearth, Alex asked, "Mother? Are you alright?"

He looked into my heavy, half-closed eyes and then turned to look at Ramona. With his head tilted towards me, he raised eyebrows and opened his eyes wide glancing in my direction, hinting at how worried he was that I had not responded.

Ramona walked over and sat down next to me. "Mother?" Ramona repeated the call to stir me awake. As I slumped over sideways on the couch, she placed her hand on my shoulder. "You look rather tired. Perhaps we should get you to bed." With her helping hand, I sat up, feeling taller.

With my final burst of energy, I managed to speak. "Be strong and always take care of the family with love in your hearts...... I love you both. I always have," I whispered with my last breath.

~ ~ ~

 **Epilogue: 1932-1955**

A lice Berry Kane, age 71, passed away on November 10, 1931 in the presence of both of her loving children. They decided to bring their mother back home to Jacksonville, Oregon to be buried with her parents and siblings in their Masonic family plot. Alice took her last train ride in style, on the *Shasta Limited*, from Oakland to Medford and then on the local rail line to Jacksonville Cemetery. The ground was quite soggy from the late fall Oregon rains, when the funeral coach brought Alice to her final resting place.

1931 - Alice's son, *Alex*, moves in with his sister Ramona.
1932 - Alice's brother, *Isaac*, dies at age 81, in Portland, Oregon. Alice's ex-husband's third son, *Ellsworth Peyton Kane*, age 35, is employed by a travel touring company. Alice's ex-husband's fourth son, *Jack Peyton Kane*, age 30, is a commercial artist for Safeway in Alameda, California.
1934 - Alice's friends from Ashland: *Miss Blanche Hicks* has a stroke and finally turns over the reins of the Ashland Library after 31 years. *Mrs. Anna (EV) Carter*, resigned in 1927 from the Ashland Library Board of Directors, after 36 years of service.
1935 - Alice's son, *Alex*, dies at age 50, in San Francisco, leaving two grown children, Keith, age 23, and June, age 21, who move in with their Aunt Ramona, taking their father's place, and help immensely with the raising of their cousins.
1937 - Alice's daughter's sister-in-law, *Mary Hollister*, dies at age 48, the same year her son Fred, Jr., age 27, gets appointed as Postmaster in Marshfield, Oregon.

1939 - Alice's daughter's father-in-law, *Captain Bergman*, dies at age 93. Alice's daughter's brother-in-law, Carl Bergman, is appointed as Chief of Police in Eugene, Oregon.

1941 - Alice's daughter, *Ramona,* dies of breast cancer at age 53, leaving her children, Patricia, age 19, and Ray, age 14, in the care of their cousins, ages 29 and 27.

1942 - Alice's son-in-law, *Henry L. Bergman*, at age 54, marries *Harriet Weatherson,* age 42, twelve years after being paroled from prison and just a few months after Ramona died. They finally move to the south and start their lives over in Florida.

1942 - Alice's daughter-in-law, *Irma Kane*, dies in Oakland at age 59.

1943 - Alice's ex-husband's second son, *Clarence Peyton Kane*, age 53, becomes a World War II Air Force Brigadier General.

1944 - Alice's Oregon coast hometown changes its name from Marshfield to Coos Bay, Oregon.

1948 - Alice's sister and sole surviving sibling, *Mary DeLatamer* dies age 90, in Portland, Oregon.

1949 - Alice's friend, *Louis Simpson*, dies at age 72, after his timberlands were sold and the palatial family estate called Shore Acres had gone to the state for back taxes. Shore Acres becomes a public State Park.

1949 - Alice's son-in-law's criminal friend, *Roy DeAutremont* has a frontal lobotomy for an agitated personality in prison, and being combative and a danger to others.

1955 - Alice's hometown of *Ashland:* Southern Pacific Ashland Train Depot, where Alice was the first Station Master's wife, ended passenger rail service to Ashland and the trains stopped their runs to the Rogue Valley of Oregon after 68 years.

NEVER AGAIN WILL THERE BE ANOTHER STATION MASTER'S WIFE in Ashland.

Acknowledgements

Thanks go out to all my friends who encouraged me to write my second novel. With my love of history and knack for storytelling, this tale easily came to life. Thanks to my teenage daughter, Lili, for her patience and making dinners, allowing me the time to write this book.

Opportunities for digging into historical events, places and people were opened up for me in this computer age with access to archived references online through Newspapers.com, US Census records, and Ancestry.com. I am grateful to not have had to sit squinting through reels of microfilm in dark corners of libraries anymore.

Southern Oregon Historical Society was particularly helpful in uncovering details about the Berry and Kane families, especially for locating Alice Kane's original wedding dress in their storage, and providing the 1888 book cover photo of the Ashland Depot Hotel. Special kudos to Chris M. at Book Savvy Studio for bringing the soul of Alice to life on this book's cover.

I would like to honor Alice Berry Kane for all her perseverance throughout the scandals that burdened her life. Her creative choices for survival, with love as the underlying theme that carried her through, should prove a valuable lesson for women of any age.

About the Author

S.K. DeMarinis, a native New Yorker, who has lived in Ashland, Oregon for the past 35 years, has always been intrigued by the events of history and hidden stories.

In 1985, the author painstakingly backtracked through records of local handwritten deeds and titles, comparing them with historic events surrounding her original Victorian Ashland home. In particular, she uncovered the fact that S.P. Railroad's Ashland Golden Spike Ceremony was documented in this home in 1887, which culminated with this house's inclusion on the National Register of Historic Places.

The author's husband at the time commented that the Historic Register wouldn't believe how she connected the facts uncovered by her, intertwined with her suspicions and assumptions to fill in the gaps. Not only did they accept the nomination, but a sequel was requested. It took a long time coming.

Not until 2019, when the author's interest was renewed in this family and historic home, did she utilize the expanded access to available historical data, and expose the previously unknown details of 'the sequel'. The author took great liberty in weaving known events with her fictional prose. Her daughter loves to hear the tales.

Made in the USA
Monee, IL
27 June 2023